Music of the Clown

ATLAS

Words Matter Publishing
P.O. Box 1190
Decatur, IL 62525
www.wordsmatterpublishing.com

ISBN: 978-1-958000-70-0

Library of Congress Catalog Card Number: 2023941929

Prologue

It was the spring of 2005, eleven years after the execution of "Killer Clown" John Wayne Gacy. When Gacy was executed, a young boy was there with his mother to say his goodbyes. Of course, his mother being close friends with John and hearing about what he did put her through a shock, but this little five-year-old boy knew no better; he just knew they were "putting a bad man to sleep," as his mother had referred to it. The boy wouldn't need to know this information, as he would be running from a terrible fate with a past he couldn't control.

Table of Contents

Chapter One

Christopher awoke at 10:13 a.m. per the ignorance of his sleep schedule and the thrill and love he had for playing music. He had slept in his dark blue jeans and an *Arctic Monkeys* t-shirt. Christopher sat up and opened the drawer of his bedside table. Pulling out his *Nokia 1110*, he saw he had a message from Nick. However, on Christopher's phone, he had him labeled as Nicholas because he knew Nick hated his full first name. Opening the message, he found, "Last nites reehursul wus rokin!"

Christopher chuckled to himself, Nick had never been a great speller, even when they first met. He replied with a simple, "Yeah, it was." Putting his phone in his back pocket, he stood with a yawn and a light stretch of his back. Seeing the window was still open from last night when he snuck out, he shut it quietly, drawing the curtains back over it in a normal yet haphazard way to match the mess that was in his room. He walked out of his room, and he could hear his father mowing the lawn out front of their trailer.

Since the death of Christopher's mother in 1995, he and his father had moved into a trailer park, *Breazeale Trailer Park,* to be exact. Mark, Christopher's father, said this trailer park was founded in 1984, eleven years before Christopher's mother died. Christopher looked at a framed picture of his mother, his father's wife, Maria, or Marinara. He was told his mother's sister called her that since she was little, but he brushed it off. He would never get to hear it anyway; why think of it? Maria was a beautiful woman in Mark's eyes; she had the best auburn-colored hair with her fade-to-orange hair dye. The last thing Mark remembered of his wife was the beautiful smile she had as she died while trying to shield six-year-old Christopher from the heartbreak of watching his mother die.

Christopher heard the mower stop as he looked away from the photo of his mother. He went to the kitchen. Some would say the kitchen was too small, but he found it perfect. It had all the things needed: a stove, microwave, fridge, and cabinets of food. What more could you need? Christopher listened as his dad pushed the mower up to the front porch; he heard the boards creak from under the weight of his father's body and heavy work boots.

The door opened, and Christopher was greeted with his father's warm smile and soft heart. "Morning Chip, sleep well when you got home last night?"

Christopher laughed and tried to play off his father's wording.

"C'mon, I know you snuck out; you're not exactly subtle, Son." Mark laughed and patted his son on the back. "It's okay, just let me know when you're leaving next time; I'll even give you a ride!"

Christopher looked at his father and smiled, "Sure, Dad, I'll do that next time. Do you have to work today?"

Mark nodded and sighed briefly, "Today is gonna be one hell of an evening; two of my guys quit my last shift. I might be stuck up there for the rest of the week, think you'll be fine? I can see if maybe you'd want to stay with a friend for the week?"

Christopher looked at his dad with surprise, "Sure, I'll see if Nick wants to have me over, if not, I can ask Nate, Tim, or Jenny."

Mark let out a soft laugh and smiled, "Well, just let me know, Chip, I'm gonna make lunch soon. I'll let you know when it's done. For now, you have two hours to do whatever you want."

Christopher nodded, getting ready to sprint out the front door, as he had slept in his shoes as well.

"Before you go, make sure after you eat lunch, shower, and try to pick up your room. I won't make you clean your room but pick up some in there. Thank God, that's not where I sleep. But you've worn the same thing for three days; take a shower after lunch, Chip."

Christopher nodded, embarrassed that he hadn't realized his own sanitary neglect. He promised he'd shower after lunch. Until then, he went back to his room and opened the second drawer on his bedside table, the one that contained a few magazines, such as *UNCUT Music Magazine* and the stereotypical teenage nude magazines. He kept a pocketknife hidden in the far back of the drawer. None of that was what he was looking for. What he sought was his *iPod nano*, the once popular music device of the time.

Grabbing the *iPod*, he put the headphones in his ears, turning on the playlist of his favorite songs. The first song was the top rock song of the time, *Best of You,* by Foo Fighters. He walked out the door humming with the tune. He grabbed his recently released *Yeti 575* bike from next to his dad's lawn mower.

Throwing one leg over his bike, Christopher performed his normal bike "ritual," as his father called it. The "ritual" consisted of popping his fingers, then his neck, and finally swaying side to side before riding at a slow start, then picking up speed quickly after he left his destination. One thing about Christopher that people overlooked or didn't notice was he was fast, on foot or bike. Pretty much if it moved, he could go fast. The only people who knew he was fast were his bandmates, Nicholas Thomson, Jennifer 'Jenny' Thomson, Nick's cousin, Nathan Campbell, Timothy Stewart, and himself, Christopher Robertson. They were an unofficial band of sorts, they had songs, sure, but they had no audience. They referred to themselves as "The Flunkies." They thought this was clever as they were all high school dropouts.

Chapter Two

Christopher arrived at Nick's garage at nearly 10:30 in the morning. Nick lived not far from Christopher and had also rushed himself out the door this morning. Nick lived on the corner of *Trask Street and Indian Avenue.* The rest of the band had stayed the night in Nick's garage. None of them were awake when Christopher went into the now-opened garage. He banged on his drums to wake them all up. Christopher wasn't concerned about Nick's parents getting him in trouble as they were hardly ever home for reasons unknown to him, as it wasn't his concern.

Nate was the first to wake up with a startled squeal. Christopher laughed as he continued to bang on his drums to the drumline of the current song playing on his iPod, *Feel Good Inc.* by *Gorillaz.*

Jenny woke up next, throwing her jacket she had used as a makeshift blanket at Christopher.

Nick came out with his bass and plugged it in, joining Christopher in the song.

Tim simply sat up, stretched, and yawned before he started to sing with his pitch-perfect voice.

Nate laughed with a tired huff and grabbed his guitar, strumming along to the song.

Jenny smiled, sat back, and watched. She had no reason to join in on this song, but she could play every instrument they could, maybe better. She was considered the writer and producer of their music. She was also used for backup singing, and if an extra guitar or replacement was needed, she was there. Some may view this as unfair, but she's the one who suggested all of it. Jenny had been the one to suggest the band in the first place.

Now that they were all awake and warmed up, Christopher decided to announce that his father would be out of town for the week and needed a place to stay. Nick offered first, as Christopher assumed he would. No one else seemed to offer, mainly because they knew Nick would let any of them stay over anytime they needed.

Christopher thanked Nick and said he'd be back after his father went to bed at around two pm.

Nick went back inside briefly to grab food for them. He tossed a veggie sub to Nate. For Jenny, he tossed hot roast beef and hot sauce with provolone. Tim got the salami, tomato, and mayonnaise. Leaving Nick with the loaded half sub of peppers, onions, and turkey with mustard. He looked at Christopher before throwing him a sandwich.

Christopher shook his head. "No thanks. I'm gonna be eating when I leave, thanks though."

Nick nodded, setting the sandwich aside.

Christopher checked the clock in the garage, it was five minutes behind, which bugged Tim, but the rest liked it. They all agreed it reminded them of themselves, always behind but never late. The clock read 12:55, meaning it was one o'clock. He said his goodbyes saying he'd be back. He left the garage and grabbed his faithful *Yeti*.

Chapter Three

Christopher was biking his way down *North Ohio Street* when he felt something that would haunt him until he died. He went faster, feeling a sudden unease as if he was being watched. Christopher sharply stopped his bike and looked around; he shook his head after seeing nothing.

Just spooks, calm down, he thought as he started to slowly pedal again.

Then when he heard it, a happy-go-lucky middle-aged voice call out to him, "Wanna see a magic trick, kid?"

Dumbly, Christopher turned around. There was a man; at least, he thought it was a man in his mid-forties. He wore heavy caked-on clown makeup with vibrant bright red makeup for the lips and nose and green diamonds on the eyes with indigo outlining every color. The clown's eyes were calm, yet that's what unsettled Christopher; the longer he looked, the more scared he got.

"Well?" the clown said, holding up handcuffs.

Christopher looked at the handcuffs, then the clown's eyes one last time. "No thanks, I've gotta get home!" Christopher's voice weakened as he talked. He clenched the handlebar of his bike as he turned away from the clown, getting ready to pedal once more.

The clown squeezed Christopher's shoulder before leaning his creepy clown lips towards Christopher's ear. His voice dropped to a deeper whisper, making his voice fit all that hideous makeup. "What if I walked you home? *Christopher*, to keep you safe from any creeps." The clown let out a low bellow of a laugh.

Christopher wriggled out of the man's grip and dropped his bike behind him as he faced the clown with raised fists.

The clown's face took on a creepier look as his grin became an open-mouthed shocked face. Putting up his hands and returning to that shrill clown voice, he said, "You wouldn't hurt an ino…."

Christopher kicked the clown in the groin with his ankle-high, red-laced black boots.

The clown groaned and pulled a switchblade from the back of his clown costume— hideous bright pink pom poms, unevenly stitched neon green, light pink, and bright red baggy costume– with a black puffy collar. The greasy hair was flipped from the clown's face, jostling an ugly party hat sitting atop his head.

Christopher saw the knife and backed up a small bit, still standing his ground.

"I tried to be nice, and now…now you're gonna die, kid!" The clown swung the knife wildly at Christopher, landing a few good cuts on Christopher— one on his right ring finger, left cheek up to his right nostril, and a gash down the front of his right forearm.

Christopher didn't make a sound. He took the slashings he received, and once the clown had tired, Christopher shoved the clown onto the seat of his pants. He kicked the clown in the nose with the heel of his boot; a crunch could be heard from the clown, the sound of his nose breaking.

The clown fell onto his back, clutching his nose, howling in pain; surely Christopher thought he'd be the bad guy here. He already had a bad run with the police because of his father. Christopher knelt next to the clown and spat in his face, "Fuck. You." Christopher stood and picked up his bike, riding away quickly.

Christopher rode his bike all the way back to his father's trailer, looking back from time to time to make sure he wasn't followed. He hopped off his bike, letting it fall onto the fresh-cut yard, and he ran inside, looking for his father. He found him in the recliner; the angle it was from the kitchen had the back of the chair and the back of his father's head facing Christopher. Christopher ran to his father; when he got face to face with him, he gasped and nearly screamed as he fell onto his butt, hitting the back of his head on the coffee table. He winced and grabbed the back of his head, all while staring into his father's lifeless eyes. His father held a gun in one hand and, presumably, a bullet in his brain, as Christopher saw no exit point.

Christopher sat dazed. He started to cry; his last parent was gone, taken from him. But not from suicide. That wasn't something his father would have done! No, to Christopher, this was a staged murder, and he had an idea of who did it. Christopher stood up and slowly walked to the kitchen sink, grabbing dishwasher gloves and old clothes that would cover his body, a few trash bags, and sunglasses with a mask to cover himself fully. After doing all of this, he grabbed a butcher knife from the kitchen, set the trash bags and knife on the floor next to the coffee table, and then pulled his father off of the recliner onto the coffee table.

Chapter Four

Christopher had finished the dismembering of his father's body. He had thrown the trash bags into the trash can outside his house, knowing trash pickup would dispose of his body within a few hours. Christopher deep-cleaned and disinfected every surface of blood in the trailer, as well as the gun that he now kept on top of his bedside table. Christopher then called Nick, asking him if he could extend his stay. Nick had told him it'd be fine, as Christopher figured. He told Nick he'd discuss further details once it was just him and Nick. Christopher began to cry again.

Christopher left the house after the trash had been picked up, still in need of a shower. It was dark once Christopher left the trailer. He figured he'd need to use his bike's flashlight that he had attached to the part holding the seat up. He rode to Nick's rather slowly, thinking of what he might say to him about his father, how he'd explain he just somehow knew the random clown had killed his father, but how?

Christopher sighed and slowed to a halt on the sidewalk of *North Ohio Street,* he stopped to think, unaware of where he actually was. Christopher heard a door shut, *probably someone enjoying the air,* he thought. Christopher heard steps behind him. He quickly hopped off his bike and spun to face the steps. As the figure got closer, Christopher tensed. He clenched his fists at his sides and waited. The figure came into view, it was just some girl walking her dog.

Christopher let out a sigh of relief and loosened up. The girl shot him an odd glance, and the dog barked playfully at him. Christopher ignored them and went back to his bike. He cursed when he realized he had broken the flashlight in the panic of turning around. Getting on his bike, he rode down the street, slowly picking up pace. He passed the dog he had seen earlier, but the girl was no longer with it.

Normally Christopher would've passed on by, but he stopped for a reason he's still unsure of. Once again, getting off his bike, he went to the dog. Without a word, the dog pointed its nose toward the tree line where the street supposedly had a dead end. Christopher grabbed the dog's leash and went to the trees. The dog nudged Christopher forward, urging him to go further into the woods. Christopher obliged and went, but once he got a short way in, the dog stopped moving. Looking back towards it, he saw it was whimpering. *If a dog like this was scared, then I should probably be cautious,* he told himself. Taking into consideration that the dog would no longer follow, he tied the dog to a tree. He petted it before walking further into the woods…alone.

Eventually, after walking for fifteen minutes, Christopher came across a shed in the middle of a clearing surrounded by deep woods. The trees were almost too thick to walk through. He couldn't help thinking that one could be lost and potentially stumble here. Christopher shivered, not just from the cold. The shed gave off an aura that shook him to the core. Not much scared Christopher, just this, his father's dead body *and fuckin' clowns*. He shook his head and walked forward. He had barely moved when he heard a scream come from the shed.

Christopher shot into a state of alert and looked around for some kind of defense. He found nothing. Running at the shed door, he crashed against it with his shoulder. The door creaked but didn't give. *There must be something latching the door, but why would it be on the inside?* He kicked at the door a few times, and eventually, the door swung open with a loud crack against the inside of the shed. Quickly looking around the room, he saw the girl was chained up, alone.

Christopher slid down onto his knees in front of the chained-up girl, "Who did this?"

The girl looked at Christopher with tears cascading down her face. "S…some…k…kuh…kind…of…c…c…cuh…clown."

Christopher gritted his teeth and looked around the shed once more. It was empty except for a toolbox just out of reach of the girl. *He toys with them, daring them to escape,* he thought. Opening the toolbox, he found teeth, human teeth. Christopher kicked the toolbox away with a disgusted sound. He looked back at the girl and told her he'd find a way to get her out.

The girl nodded, but fear suddenly took hold of her as she shouted, "He's back!"

Christopher turned around quickly, and there stood the clown with a broken nose and a gun in hand.

The chilling high-pitched laugh came from the clown. "It's you again! Isn't this just swell?"

Christopher swung at the clown with an annoyed grunt.

The clown shot at Christopher's feet, causing Christopher to stop and back up.

The clown spoke in a deep dark voice, "Don't fucking try anything. I might just shoot you."

Christopher spat at the clown's shoes and asked him, "Why are you doing this? What kind of sick fuck are you?"

The clown laughed, "I'm not sick; you're the sick one. You watched one of the greatest men that paved the way for serial killers die."

Christopher laughed quietly at the clown. "You're crazy! If I watched a serial killer die, which I haven't, how would you even know?"

A grin spread across the clown's face, showing his yellow crooked teeth, "I was there. I watched the man I idolized be killed. All because he was caught. I know you were there, Christopher, you and that bitch of a mother. How do you remember her dying, Chip?" The clown let out a shrieking laugh.

Christopher's mind raced, trying to understand the confusion even as anger flooded him hearing the name his father had called him. "What are you talking about? My mother's death was an accident!"

The clown doubled over, nearly falling as he laughed harder. "Do I have to spell it out for you? Are you that stupid? Or could it be you were never told?" The clown put on that fake open-mouthed shocked face again. "That's it! Your father kept a secret from you! Well…" Christopher was shoved down by the clown. "…sit, and I'll tell you the story."

Christopher was about to stand up, but the clown shot the girl behind him, her blood splattering on Christopher's back.

Then the clown put the gun to Christopher's head. "I said, *sit.* Or do you want to end up like the little girl behind you?"

Christopher's eyes were wild with hate and confusion. He wanted answers. But what he really wanted was to kill that demented clown!

Chapter Five

Christopher stayed still as the clown started to unfold the event in his life that had been hidden from him, not daring to move or interrupt with a gun to his head.

"Let me begin by telling you how this started. You see, your mother was close friends with the killer known as *John Wayne Gacy*. I knew John well. I worked with him when he managed the KFC's down in Iowa. I'm sure you know who John is, he was quite a popular topic once."

Christopher nodded, "Yeah, I know who he is, I know what he did too. Is that what this is? Some kind of twisted copycat killer?"

The clown grimaced, "I am no copycat to John! I can never reach the greatness he did. I'm just carrying on his legacy in my own way. I'm going to find and kill everyone who watched that great man die! Now, can I continue, or do I have to kill you without you knowing why you're here?"

Christopher responded in a state of deep thought, yet his eyes showed no fear, they were calm, brave even. He pushed his head against the barrel of the gun, "Continue, freak."

The clown laughed and smirked, "I will, but first, you'll call me Bolo the Clown. Got it?"

Christopher simply nodded, annoyed. "Just get on with it, Bozo."

The clown laughed. "Fiery kid, where was I?"

"Somewhere along the part where you stop fantasizing over that psycho, and you get to the point of why you're telling me this story."

The clown simply grumbled, "All right, kid, you wanna know why you're here? It's because your father interfered with your death. I was able to kill that mother of yours, but your father shot me in the leg as I held her dying body. You should've seen how funny his face was!" The clown started laughing again. The gun slipped off of Christopher's head while he laughed.

Christopher was filled with rage and sorrow. He sprung up and punched the clown, grabbing the gun from his hand. The clown fell, and Christopher held the gun to the clown's head. "You killed my father, didn't you? You killed them both. My parents are dead because of some sick idolization. I'm gonna fucking kill you."

The clown laughed as he shook his head. "Oh no, no, no, you won't kill me…not yet." The clown kicked Christopher back away from him, causing him to accidentally fire the gun, putting a bullet-sized hole in the roof of the shed.

Christopher regained his balance and looked around. The clown had disappeared. "Shit!" He ran out of the shed towards the woods. As he ran past the dog, he saw it was now on its side, twitching and whining from the bullet holes on his side. Christopher made it out of the woods and found his bike. It looked as if it was torn apart after being run over.

Christopher kicked the bike and wiped the tears from his eyes. *I have to get to Nick. Now,* he thought. He started running, pushing his body to go faster. He thought of it as racing against time, and that clown, rushing to make sure he could stop the clown from killing anyone else close to him. *He wants to torture me; once everyone close to me is dead, he'll kill me slowly. He's a sick man, and I'll be the one to put a bullet between his eyes,* he thought.

Christopher arrived at Nick's house and quickly ran in through the garage, shouting his name. No one else was home, but Nick and Christopher wanted to make sure he was safe. He kicked open the door that led from the garage into the kitchen.

Nick was standing in the living room with a perplexed look on his face. "What's up with you? You're all panicked."

Christopher explained what had happened. All of it—his first meeting with the clown, finding his dad dead, the girl and her dog, and what the clown had told him.

Nick listened, and he laughed; obviously, it was too much of a stretch to believe.

Christopher got heated at the moment and shoved Nick to the ground. "You asshole! My father is fucking dead because of that clown, and you laugh!"

Nick stayed silent on the floor, his facial expression changing to a mix of feeling sorry for his friend with a hint of fear behind his eyes.

Christopher took a step back and breathed in, helping Nick to his feet. "I'm sorry; I know it's a lot to believe."

Nick nodded and patted Christopher on the shoulder. "You're always welcome here, C."

Christopher nodded. "Thanks, but I'm afraid he knows I'd come here; that's why I had to tell you."

Nick went pale and shook his head to clear his nerves. "Okay, help me cover the windows and block the doors. My mom left some guns in her closet for me to defend myself with."

Christopher nodded and spent the next twenty minutes helping Nick barricade his home.

"All right, I'll grab the guns, sit on the couch, or something."

Christopher nodded as Nick went into his parents' room to grab the guns. He found it odd Nick's parents left more than one gun, but he just shrugged it off. After about three minutes, Nick hadn't come back. Christopher went to Nick's parents' room. "Nic…" Christopher froze.

On the bed was Nick's severed head, with a note next to it labeled—*Cristopr*. He swallowed the puke that was coming up his throat and wiped his burning eyes, trying not to cry as anger swelled within him. He snatched the note and opened it. Inside was a fake interpretation of Nick saying goodbye.

Christopher read the note slowly, looking at all the misspell-ings and shitty handwriting. He figured he could save this as evidence. *Just in case*, Christopher thought when he stuffed the note in his back pocket. Just as he was about to leave the room, he stopped, thinking, *where'd the rest of him go?* Christopher looked around the room and saw blood tracks leading to the window of the bedroom. He saw there was no broken glass on the floor; the window was opened. *He was already inside before I got here.* Christopher shut the window fiercely and let out a scream of anger. Shouting out, "I'm gonna fucking kill you!"

Chapter Six

Aweek after Nick's death, Christopher gave up looking for the clown. He checked the woods, but it was like the shed disappeared within hours. He went down *North Ohio Street* looking for the clown but stopped once the fatigue got to him. He was being tortured by the clown with letters in his mailbox with no return address, but they were all the same terrible handwriting with threats and sick jokes about how Christopher would never escape him.

Christopher knew he had enough evidence to go to the police, but he knew they'd turn him away, especially since his father was reported missing and the cops came by to interrogate Christopher. He lied and told the police he was just taking a long vacation somewhere in Nevada, and he had no contact with his father. Normally this would warrant someone having to come to take care of him, but he had told them he was just there to grab some stuff to stay at Nick's. The cops believed him and left him alone but said they'd be back in a month to see how his situation was, by law, of course, not because they wanted to.

The past week left Christopher feeling insane. He started to question if the clown was even real, but then how would he explain the deaths he'd seen? Christopher shook his head, thinking that this was what the clown wanted. He wanted to contact his other friends but was afraid the clown would find them if he talked to them, but when they went to Nick's, he'd have no choice. Christopher sighed and decided to meet them all one last time at Nick's before he decided he had to move away to protect them.

Christopher had gone door to door, wanting to personally meet his bandmates for one last time. He decided he'd start with the closest and work his way to the furthest. The closest one to his house was Nate. Nate didn't have the greatest house, but neither did Christopher. Nick lived down the street from Christopher, yet they had never actually met until their band.

Riding down the street on an old bike, his father had to go see Nate; Christopher was thinking about what to say. Should he be blunt and straightforward or try and explain later? He decided telling them all one on one would be best, forgetting about meeting them all at Nick's. When Christopher arrived at Nate's trailer, Nate was already outside, sitting in the grass. But something was off about Nate; when Christopher got closer, he saw that his throat was slit open; he had bled to death. Christopher tried not to puke, tears in his eyes again, even more anger swelling inside him. He knew who had done this, and he planned to make him pay. Christopher sped off, trying to reach his other bandmates before it was too late.

Chapter Seven

The next house Christopher sped by was Tim's, he lived on *North Ohio Street*. He didn't have high hopes of seeing Tim alive, yet when he got to Tim's house, he heard Tim's voice. He smiled and dropped the bike down, rushing to Tim's door, knocking crazily.

Tim opened the door, confused, and smiled once he saw Christopher. "Hey! What's up?" Tim asked in a surprised voice.

Yet Christopher felt there was more to it than that. "I need to talk to you," Christopher said in a low voice, almost too low for Tim to hear.

Tim offered to let him come inside, and the next thing Christopher knew, he was in Tim's room. Christopher sat down and looked at Tim. "Sit down. I have a lot to say."

Tim did sit right next to Christopher.

Christopher smiled awkwardly and took a breath in. "This is gonna sound crazy. I understand if you don't believe me."

Tim nodded, "I don't think you're crazy; I know what you're here for."

Christopher looked at Tim, shocked. "You do?"

Tim nodded again. "I do." Tim shifted his body to face Christopher as he put a hand on his thigh and leaned in to kiss Christopher.

Christopher realized what was happening and scooted away. "Hey, hey! No! I didn't mean anything like that!"

Tim stopped and got red. His face settled into a sad expression as he let out a small cough. "Right, sorry. I'll be right back, I'm gonna get us some water since you said it'll be long." Christopher nodded as Tim got up, leaving into the kitchen just out of Christopher's view.

Christopher never heard the water running, but he waited. After a while, he quickly got up and ran into the kitchen. Tim was dead on the floor. There was glass on the floor, stab wounds in his back, and the knife handle stuck out the back of Tim's head.

Christopher threw up before searching the house, wondering how the clown had managed to sneak in yet again. Finding nothing, Christopher sat and cried. He only had one person he could go see, and that was Jenny.

Christopher cleaned up his puke but left Tim on the kitchen floor. He left Tim's house and rode the old bike that he would call his steed starting now. If his father had been alive, he'd have noticed that Christopher, his Chip, wasn't doing his normal bike ritual. Christopher cried as he rode to Jenny's house, right across the street from Nick's.

Once Christopher arrived at Jenny's, he saw her staring him down. He got off his bike and approached her. "You, okay?"

Jenny furiously shook her head. "Someone killed Nick, Chris!"

Christopher nodded, "That's why I came over here, I know who did it."

Jenny looked stunned, "You do? Who? I'll get the police on them right now!"

Christopher hesitated. "I don't know who it is. All I know is it's some kind of man who dresses in clown attire. He looks up to John Gacy and wants to be like him."

Jenny looked suspiciously at Christopher. "How do you know all this?"

Christopher started to sweat. "He's after me. He almost had me. He's been writing me letters. Telling me he wants to torture me like some sick fuck by killing everyone I love."

Jenny paled. "That's terrible! I'll need evidence. Let's go to your trailer, you still have the letters, right?"

Christopher nodded and got onto his bike, waiting for Jenny to get hers. Once Jenny returned, they rode their bikes quickly but carefully to his trailer.

Christopher threw his bike down as he ran up to his trailer, flinging the door open and looking for the stack of letters from the clown. He found them; Jenny waited impatiently on Christopher's lawn.

Christopher grabbed all the letters and tossed them at Jenny, in a hurry now that he knew he had someone who believed him and could help him. Or so he thought, Jenny picked up each letter slowly, looking more and more confused as she picked them up.

Christopher was also confused, he asked Jenny, "What's wrong?"

Jenny looked at Christopher with concern. "Chris…these are hospital and medication letters for you. There are no letters about torture, just you and something about a medication called antipsychotics."

Christopher looked scared. He had no idea what Jenny was talking about. Why was she lying? Was she working with the clown? Was he the actual killer? All of these thoughts raced through Christopher's head. As he calmed down, he saw Jenny was dialing a number that she was reading off the letters. He panicked. The next thing he knew, he was running inside. His head was spinning. Running to his room, he locked the door. He pulled the gun his father killed himself with from the bedside table.

Jenny knocked. In a gentle tone, she spoke to Christopher, "People are waiting for you. They're gonna take you someplace and make you better."

Christopher didn't want to leave, he shouted to Jenny, "Leave! All of you leave!" He heard Jenny whispering to someone outside the door, and suddenly there was bashing against the door. Christopher panicked and realized they were gonna knock it down. He quickly scrambled to his window, trying to force it open. The door was kicked off the hinges, and in came two cops to arrest him and take him to some kind of prison. He fought back, shooting one of the cops in the leg soon after he was tased and knocked unconscious.

Chapter Eight

Christopher awoke in the back of a van, dazed and confused. He saw the shadow of a man in the back with him. Once he regained his vision, he saw it was a police officer, and next to him was that clown. He panicked, trying to move away, starting to go into hysterics. But the clown just stared at Christopher, laughing. The cop was shaking Christopher, yelling words he couldn't hear. The next thing Christopher knew, his vision was blurry and then black.

Christopher awoke once more, but now he was in a padded room in some kind of jacket. He was scared. Scared and angry. He wanted to get out of here, to find the clown, but Jenny had put him here. It was Jenny's fault, and he'd make sure to get back at her. She must've been working for the clown. This was an assumption he made and never let go of.

A doctor came in and talked to Christopher, but he wasn't listening, he was focused on how to kill Jenny. His pant leg was lifted, and he was injected with something. He winced and thrashed around, scared of what had just been put in him.

The doctor talked to him the same way Jenny did, calmly and as if he was a child. "All I did was give you medicine, it should calm you down and stop this clown you see from appearing."

Christopher froze. "He's not fake! He's real! He killed my father, my friends, my own mother."

The doctor shook his head. "No, the clown didn't. You did. You imagined this clown did all that, you blocked out the memory of you killing your friends."

Christopher shook his head. "No! No! I saw him kill a girl in a shed! He put holes in her damned dog! He admitted to killing my mother when I was younger!"

The doctor looked paler and more worried. "Your mother died of a terminal illness; your mind doesn't remember it. And that girl you talked about, there was no shed. She was reported missing. We found her body with a bullet hole in her head and the same bullets in the dog. We examined the bullets. They match the gun and bullet you shot the cop with before you came here."

Christopher sat still, unable to believe what he was hearing. "So, my father didn't kill himself? I did that...what about my friends? Why don't I remember any of it?"

"I can't say for sure, but if you keep taking your medication, you should be clear-minded and able to plead in court. If you can't, I can't say. You'll never see outside prison walls again, kid."

Christopher broke down and cried, "What if I don't go? Can't I just turn myself in immediately? I mean, I clearly did it, right?"

The doctor sat for a moment. "I'm not sure, I don't even think I should've said all of this." The doctor got up and left, leaving Christopher alone in the room.

Chapter Nine

A few months after Christopher was sent to the hospital, he was put on house arrest. He sat and ate or drank nothing. Refusing to take the medications he received, he knew he wasn't crazy, and he was going to prove it. He knew he could prove it wasn't him that killed all of them. Christopher heard a knock on the door and slowly got up to answer it. He was paler and weaker than normal; he answered the door, and at the door stood the clown; he screamed and was shot in the head by the clown.

Jenny arrived at Christopher's house on his court day, she knocked on his door, but there was no answer. She opened the door to find it unlocked. She quickly stepped inside, shouting his name. She stopped once she found him on the couch, a gun in his hand. She saw blood coming from his head. Christopher had killed himself a day before his court date. She broke down and cried as she stared at her friend's dead body.

Don't tempt me, chica. My hands started to shake. Liam knew my history—the horrific way I'd died in my previous life. How I felt about being locked in an enclosed space.

My gift raced beneath my skin as I tore at the bark with my nails until they broke and bled. Until I was no longer clawing at roots but a red door, surrounded by the scent of gasoline and screaming women and children choking on smoke.

My breath came in rapid little hiccups as walls and bodies pressed in around me. Sweat rolled down my face from the heat, and I refused to turn around, knowing what I'd see—my mother and sisters burning alive. But the heat wasn't coming from behind me. It radiated from my core and licked down my arms, scorching my palms as it pulsed into the door.

Wood cracked and popped like sap-soaked cedar in a fire, but the door in front of me didn't burn. It turned black and soft with rot. The rapidly decaying wood gave way, and I fell through the wall onto my hands and knees, still half inside Liam's cage. New thorn-covered roots grew up beneath me, slicing my stomach. I scrambled away from the wall as it knit itself back together.

Just breathe. I collapsed on my knees halfway down the beach and focused on each ragged breath in and out, attempting to slow my galloping heart.

This wasn't Liam. I pressed a hand to the bloody scrapes on my stomach. He would never hurt me. He'd pushed me with gentle breezes and attempted to discourage me with heavy rain, but he'd never used his gifts to confine me.

Until the lagoon. I'd let him restrain me with vines.

I studied the domed structure as it braided itself together like a protective shield over the roof of the bungalow. How many times had I watched Liam use the same technique to create a hammock? I'd recognized the pattern in the bramble wall surrounding the lagoon.

He did this. He'd set a trap to confine me after I'd warned him not to.

I squeezed my eyes shut and tipped my head skyward to hold back the tears.

This wasn't like him. This wasn't the man who understood that I needed to run, who'd sacrificed sleep to hold me as I'd screamed my way through the nightmares. The man I thought I could trust. I pounded the wet sand as I choked back a sob.

My stomach boiled as I picked myself up off the ground. I let my syphons unfurl as I stomped down the beach toward his studio as the storm settled to a drizzle. He'd gone too far this time. I yanked on the bond to get his attention. The controlling ass ignored the emotional projectiles I shot along the cord that connected us. The fire in my belly grew with each step and every passing minute he refused to acknowledge me and what he'd done.

"Now you choose to stay out of my head?" I clenched my fists as his studio came into sight. We were going to have a long overdue and *loud* conversation about boundaries and trust.

The structure was similar to the one that now enclosed the house. The domed roof was covered in lush green foliage that danced in the soft rain. The intertwined branches had grown and fused together, creating solid walls.

There was no obvious door to knock on. I didn't yell or call out to announce myself. The bond would alert him to my presence. My syphons twitched behind me as I circled the structure and let my fingers glide over the bark, leaving a trail of decay in my wake. My stunted healing gift wasn't completely useless after all. I couldn't create, grow, or mend things like Liam and the healers before me, but I could destroy them.

I slapped my palms and syphons against the living surface and began siphoning energy. All that was green turned yellow, then black, spreading like a blight beneath my touch. I continued to pull in energy until the section directly in front of me desiccated to ash. It mixed with the water running down the wall and turned to mud, leaving a hole large enough for me to step through.

What I saw inside took my breath away.

Dozens and dozens of glowing glass sculptures lit the cavernous space. Cool air caressed my wet skin, sending ripples of gooseflesh cascading over my bare shoulders and down my arms as I stared at a hundred versions of my face. Some were exquisitely detailed, others had been left unfinished. Each life-size figure glimmered like ice, casting ripples of light over the dark walls and ceiling. The one closest to me was sitting on the edge of a sink, completely naked, her head thrown back in ecstasy, one hand gripping the edge of the counter, the other between her splayed legs.

I studied each frozen version of myself as I moved through the room. One stood holding a motorcycle helmet as she shook out her matted hair. Another smiled gleefully atop a surfboard on her belly as she paddled to get ahead of a glass wave. The most detailed was the one inside the cab of a partially sculpted truck, hands tucked tightly under her armpits, taking up as little space as possible as she slept curled against the passenger door. I reached out to trace the curve of her jaw, and my fingers froze in midair at the sound of soft snores. I leaned forward, turning my ear toward her pursed lips.

The soft rumble came again, but not from the sculpture. I circled around it, and the bones in my chest twisted at the sight of Liam on the floor leaning against a large red tool chest. Sound asleep. A lighter and a tin of mints sat next to him, along with a needle. Even though I knew he was using, I'd tried not to imagine what that looked like. I wasn't prepared for this—for the anger I felt toward him for giving up.

I shoved that feeling deep down and locked it in the tomb at my core, along with all the other things I had no desire to confront. They were my problems to deal with, not his. The void had already taken enough from him. I refused to let it poison our bond.

Liam's sun-leathered chest rose and fell with shallow breaths as I picked up his things and placed them on the cabinet. I crouched next to him and brushed an amber curl away from his face, revealing the scar that cut a valley from his temple to the bridge of his nose. Vulnerable and broken, he was still my home.

"I like your glass menagerie."

"Renae?" His eyes fluttered open halfway. He tried to right himself and reached for the empty spot where he'd left his things.

I stilled his wrist. "I moved them."

He dropped his head back against the cabinet. "What are you doing here? I told you to stay in the house." He pulled his long legs up and rested his arms on his knees.

"We need to have a little chat about that." I swallowed hard as the fire rekindled in my gut.

He glanced at me through half-lidded eyes. "Does it have to be right now? I'm not in a good place."

That made two of us. I was wrong. I couldn't do this. Not when he was like this. It still felt too much like a betrayal. The drugs. The cage he tried to erect around me.

I stood and sucked in a sharp breath as the stinging cuts across my belly pulled taut. "Come find me when your head is in the right place. I'll be at the lagoon."

"Stop. Renae, wait."

I heard him struggle to his feet as I stepped through the hole I'd made in his sanctuary. The rain had cleared, but the sun was still nowhere in sight as I stalked down the beach.

CHAPTER ELEVEN

A LOW TONE VIBRATED through the temple, announcing the commencement of the rite. All eyes were on Brex as he reached around to unbuckle his leathers.

"Let me," I said, stepping closer.

"I'm perfectly capable of undressing myself."

"Everyone's watching, Commander. It's rude to deny me the honor of disrobing my mate."

He lowered his arms to his sides, and I took my time sliding my palms over his chest plate before tugging the buckles free at his back.

"I think you intend to torture me." His eyes darkened with desire as he stared down at my veiled face.

"I'm so glad we understand each other. Get on your knees."

Inanna gave an incredulous grunt. Brex shot her a dark look. The mind mage raised her hands in apology and offered him a somber smile as he dropped to the tile at the side of the pool. I lifted the armor over his head and tossed it aside.

I traced the puckered scar that arced across his torso from shoulder to hip. Brex's body was incredible, all hard planes and sensuous dips. Honed and battle damaged, just like his leathers.

"May I touch you?" His husky voice settled heavy in my core. No male had ever asked for permission. I nodded, and his brow furrowed as he brought his hands to my waist.

"I won't restrain you," he said, sliding his thumbs over my bare midriff. The gentle sensation sent a bead of frenzy down my spine.

"When was the last time you took the tonic?" I asked as his hands traveled up my torso.

"I've never taken targul venom." My skin pebbled as his knuckles grazed the underside of my breast. "It interferes with my scent receptors."

"So you're just naturally immune to my frenzy?"

"I'm far from immune." He leaned in and brushed his lips over my veiled ear. "Your scent has enslaved me. I have to block it with my shield when I'm in your presence to keep from making a fool of myself. If you only knew the things I've imagined doing to you."

He nipped at the sensitive skin between my throat and collarbone, his short beard and fangs a scraping promise against my skin.

"Why didn't you tell me Zwara had chosen you to be her martyr?"

"Everything hinged on your consent. You've shown nothing but contempt for me since the day we met. Would you have agreed to help us if you knew?"

"You didn't leave me much of a choice."

"You will always have a choice with me, Vaza." His muddy green gaze flicked to mine, and for a moment, I thought I saw a flash of gold. "We need to put on a show. It doesn't have to be real."

"This may be a ruse to you, zealot, but it's my life you're toying with. You manipulated me to further the Order's agenda. I'm not letting you escape this unscathed." I shoved away from him. "Either claim me properly, or I blow up the deal."

Brex shot to his feet and ripped off my veil. His mouth crashed into mine with bruising urgency. He slid his hands under the back panel of my skirt and grabbed my ass, spreading my cheeks wide as he lifted me from the floor.

I wrapped my legs around him and clung to his neck as he carried me into the mating pool. His tongue swept through my mouth, and it was all I could do not to whimper as an aching need throbbed at my core. Water lapped at my hips as he dropped my legs and backed me against the far wall.

"Fuck. I can smell how ready you are." Brex pressed his knee between my thighs, and my body instinctively ground against him. "I want you to come on my tongue before I claim you."

"My pleasure isn't necessary to complete the rite," I said, even as I rocked my hips in an attempt to bring him closer to where I needed him.

"Vaza, your pleasure is an absolute *necessity* to me." I sucked in a breath as he gripped my hips and dragged my body up his muscular thigh. "You're my queen. Let me kneel before you and worship you the way you deserve."

Goddess save me. This male and his pretty words were going to be the end of me. The truth was, I wanted it. Him, his touch, his mouth on my cunt. I shouldn't want any of those things. He was my enemy. The face I cursed when I closed my eyes and the first thought in my head when I woke.

"Yes." The word came out as a rasped plea.

He tugged the triangle of black fabric covering my breast to the side as his mouth traveled down my neck. Brex explored my flesh with the focus of a hunter in search of every erogenous zone, learning what I liked and what left me wanting more.

So. Much. More.

He met my gaze as he traced my seam and pushed two fingers inside me. I rode his hand, allowing myself to chase my own pleasure for the first time with a mate. I didn't need to fake anything with him, and I wasn't sure who was torturing who anymore.

I braced my arms along the pool's edge as he lowered himself beneath the surface. My body became weightless as he slid a calloused hand behind my knee and hooked my leg over his broad shoulder. Was I truly going to let this zealot claim me? Bubbles tickled my belly as he expelled the air from his lungs and laved at my entrance.

Fuck yes.

My chest lit, sending sparkles dancing across the surface of the water.

I threw my head back, and my eyes landed on Inanna. It wasn't until that moment that I noticed the silence. The missing cloud of pheromones and the clamor of spectators who'd taken to the long pools to celebrate the rite. Brex had blocked it all with his shield, and I knew it was his way of maintaining the intimacy of the act between us.

To anyone watching, he was a fallen faithful and I was his virgin queen. Expendable pieces played in a game between Zwara and the Order. Alone, under his shield, we were two desperate souls in need of release.

A buzz grew under my skin as he sucked at my clit. I closed my eyes, blocking out everything that wasn't him as he fucked me with his fingers. When my body bucked with the first wave of release, Brex gripped my hips, holding me in place as he growled against me. I fisted the thick braid that ran down the center of his scalp, holding him in place as the climax ripped through me in rolling quakes. He kept his fingers inside me, letting me ride out my pleasure until my body went boneless.

Brex eased my wobbling legs down slowly and rose from the water. He scowled as he cut his eyes to Inanna and back to me.

"The others are finished," he said, smoothing his disheveled beard. "They're all watching us now."

"Then we better give them a show." I shoved his wet pants down around his hips and freed both of his heavy cocks, stroking them one at a time from base to broad tip.

"If we had more time, I'd make you take them both." The erratic light of a mating frenzy pulsed from his chest as he lifted me to the edge of the wall and notched the larger head at my entrance. The other jutted up between us and grazed my clit.

I was no novice, but he was big, and I had to remind myself to breathe as he pushed inside me. The delicious stretch almost sent me over the edge. The thought of taking both of his cocks at once made my spine gush.

"I love it when you weep for me." He pumped slowly, letting me get used to the way he filled me completely. I braced against the floor behind me and fisted his other cock with my free hand. He groaned as I used my thumb to spread the silky bead over the tip.

"Hang on tight, little wraith. This is going to go embarrassingly quick." He lifted me off the wall and thrust deep. His fingers dug into my ass, pulling me tight against him as he pumped into me. My pleasure built as his second shaft slid over my clit between our pressed bodies.

"You need to leave a mark." I tipped my head to the side, offering him my neck.

"Does that feel real enough for you?"

"Yes." My claws pricked his back as I tilted my hips, pulling him in deeper.

"Good. Now come for me again and show everyone that you're mine."

I clenched around him instantly at the command. His breathing hitched as he thrust into me. Once. Twice. A guttural growl vibrated through his chest as he sank his fangs into the soft flesh between my collarbone and neck. Warmth flooded my stomach and spilled between our pressed bodies and inside me at the same time, clouding the water around us.

Brex retracted his fangs and smoothed his tongue over the dual drops of blood that welled at the wound.

"Thank you." His voice was a ragged whisper.

"For what?"

He slid out of me in a long, decadent pull as I dropped my feet. "For allowing me to be the first to claim your pleasure."

"How do you know about that?"

"It came up during negotiations. Zwara was very specific with her demands." I was so going to gut my sister the next time I saw her. Of course she told him. She couldn't resist digging her claws in and taking her pound of flesh from me one last time.

Brex trailed a finger along my jaw, tipping my face to his. "I meant what I said in the ruined city. I owe you a debt I can't ever repay for the sacrifices you've made to protect the *ki'sikilta*."

"Is that how you see me? As a burden you'll never be rid of?" I blinked back the hot tears threatening to streak down my cheeks for no good reason.

"That's not what I meant. When this is over… when the prophecy—"

"Stop." I jerked away from him, and he let me go. "I'm not one of your brainwashed disciples. I don't need to hear any more platitudes about duty or useless, dead gods. This was a business transaction and nothing more. You got to play martyr, and I finally have my freedom. I'll never allow anyone to use my body to advance their own agenda again."

Brex released his shield, dropping the barrier of silence he'd held over us. The roar of the crowd slammed into me like a wave as he tugged up his pants. I'd never had a male possess me so completely that I'd forgotten where I was.

Niva approached the steps as I climbed out on jellied legs. "We need to silver the scar before it heals."

I looked over my shoulder at Brex. The carved muscles along his back flexed as he lifted himself from the pool on the opposite side without giving me a second glance.

"Stay out of my head, Inanna." He kept his voice low as he snapped at the mind mage, but the alcove was designed to amplify even the faintest whisper. "It's irrelevant. We got what we needed and she didn't rip out my throat. Let's go."

The strange tightness in my chest returned as I watched him leave. I was a fool to think for even a moment that this was anything other than a game. His desperate declarations and lavish attention had been contrived to keep me compliant until the deed was complete.

I sucked a sharp breath through clenched teeth at the antiseptic sting as Niva rubbed liquid silver into the wound left by the zealot's fangs. A constant reminder that he'd broken the last sacred part of me.

I rinsed the stickiness from my stomach and between my thighs in Zwara's private bath.

"Why did the commander rush out of the temple before the closing tone and without paying his respects to Zwara? It's a serious snub." Tesk scrunched her nose as she fastened my soiled skirt around her waist.

"I don't care why he left. He's a zealot who'd see you imprisoned in the Rift for the rest of your life if it meant preserving the ridiculous prophecy."

Tesk's brow rose with amusement. "How is that any different from the queen's Keep?"

"The enemy you know is better than one you don't."

"He violated his sacred vow in front of the entire temple," Zwara said as she strolled into her chambers, followed by all three of Kor's forms. "I'm sure he didn't want to stick around to be congratulated for it."

"I didn't think it possible for a member of the Order to break so completely, but you had the commander on his knees. Well done, Vaza," Kor's softer male form said as they moved closer to Tesk.

"I take no pleasure in being the zealot's greatest regret." His inability to even look at me afterward spoke more than any of his pretty lies. I stepped out of the tub and put on Tesk's clean skirt.

"He seemed to be enjoying it well enough from where we were seated," Kor's willowy female form said.

Zwara smirked. "Yes, I daresay you went above and beyond what we agreed upon."

"Why did it have to be *him*?" I asked.

"My first choice was the prince. As a member of the Order and heir to his clan's throne, his participation in the rite would have made a powerful statement. Commander zurNaga rejected the idea and offered himself as tribute. It was one of his nonnegotiables. It had to be him."

"He volunteered?" My body froze. "Why would he do that?"

"I wondered the same thing," Zwara said. "The Order clearly has a vested interest in Tesk, but why you?"

"I can't speak to the Order's motivations, but after his performance in the rite, I'd think the commander's interest in Vaza would be obvious," Tesk said.

"It was an act. He despises me and didn't want to be there any more than I did. It must be something else. Something to do with the prophecy."

"I agree," Zwara said. "I've been studying the early translations looking for anything that mentions the sacrifice or the virgin queen that may shed light on what we're missing."

"Why did you tell him about the orgasm thing?" I asked.

"Since you failed to seduce him the first time, I added a little extra temptation. Males like Brex zurNaga like a challenge. He's a hunter. I gave him an elusive trophy to chase."

"My pleasure is mine to bargain with. Not yours. You had no right to offer it to him as a fucking prize."

"I did what needed to be done to guarantee a successful rite. You have no idea what it's like to rule when everyone is working against you and their own best interests. Keeping this city alive until the end of the wasting is all that matters." Zwara motioned to Kor's more menacing male form. "Tesk needs a mark identical to the one the commander gave Vaza."

"With pleasure," Kor said, approaching my sister with a dark smile.

"No." *It's mine.* My face flushed at the intrusive thought. I hated the scars on my body. Why did this one feel different? "I'm sorry. I just... It's going to hurt."

Tesk rested a gentle hand on my arm. "It's all right, Vee. Everyone in the temple witnessed the commander sink his fangs into you. I need to bear the same scar. I want everyone who sees it to know I've been claimed."

I stepped out of the way, and Kor didn't waste any time sandwiching my sister between their male forms.

"Hello, Tesk darling," the one with tousled hair said as they folded their arms around her from behind and tilted her head back to kiss her slow and deep.

Tesk's chest lit as the one with the shaved head licked the soft spot between her neck and collarbone.

"Such a wanton queen. We love it when your blood heats for us." Tesk moaned with pleasure as the male in front buried their fangs in her flesh.

I brought my hand to my neck, where the sensation of Brex's bite still throbbed.

Zwara stepped forward and popped the lid off the vial of silver solution. She coated her blackened fingertips in the shimmering fluid.

"This is going to sting," she said and ran them over the puncture marks on Tesk's neck, instantly sealing and silvering the scar.

Tesk inspected the mark with a proud smile. There was an instant lightness in her spirit now that she was no longer the subject of an ancient prophecy, thanks to Kor. But she was far from safe.

My stomach twisted at the memory of Brex's face after he exited the pool. If the zealots found out Tesk wasn't their mythical virgin, there would be blood to pay. The last trio of sisters who'd challenged the zealots disappeared without a trace.

Chapter Twelve

VAZA

"I think you scared him," Tesk said as I pulled the bone brush through her crimped hair, combing out what was left of the braids.

"Which one?" I asked, glancing through the jeweled window at the growing crowd of prominent males who'd lined up inside the temple immediately after the rite. All hoping to gain an audience with the high priestess to make an offer on the queen whose cunt had brought a member of the Order to his knees.

It had caused such raucousness that Tesk had to be moved for her own safety. I'd snapped my teeth at more than one handsy suitor who'd tried to touch her as Kor and the guards ushered us from the waiting room to Zwara's personal chamber while she dealt with the crowd.

"Not them, the commander. I know something went down between you besides the claiming. What happened?"

Tesk hissed as the brush caught on a knot in her hair.

"Nothing. I did my duty, and he fulfilled his end of the Order's agreement with Zwara. That's it."

She took the brush from my hands and set it on the windowsill. "You can close yourself off and lie to everyone else, but not to me, Vaza. I know all your moods. What did he say that upset you?"

"Things he shouldn't," I said. "Things that made me imagine living for something other than duty and silver scars."

"And you don't think he was sincere?"

I crossed to the crystal cabinet containing Zwara's collection of vials, running my hand along the tray on top that held extra bits of cork and her set of sea glass scalpels.

"I think he said what he believed I needed to hear to keep me from ripping out his throat." I picked up one of the thin blades and slid my thumb over the sharp edge.

"I'm sorry." Tesk sighed and shoved away from the window as the frosted double doors to Zwara's chambers flung open. Hazi strolled in with Inanna in his wake.

"My queen." He dipped his head to Tesk, ignoring me altogether. "I need you to come with us."

Tesk backed toward me. "What's going on? Where are our guards?"

Hazi jerked his head toward the jeweled-glass windows overlooking the temple. "Crowd control. It's not safe for you here anymore. I'm taking you to the Rift where the Order can protect you."

"We're not going anywhere with you until we speak to Zwara." The neat rows of vials inside the crystal cabinet toppled as I shoved her behind me.

Hazi nodded to Inanna, who circled toward us slowly.

"You're welcome to go down and get in line if you'd like to have a chat with the high priestess. But we're leaving with the *ki'sikilta*. You weren't part of the deal."

"What deal?" I growled.

"The one where we sacrifice one of our own in exchange for her. Let's go."

"She's done nothing wrong. You can't just barge in here and take her like you did me."

"I think you'll find that we can." He held up a scroll with the temple's seal. "Let's go."

My sister's eyes went wide as Hazi slammed his shield down around her and forced her feet to move toward the open door.

"Wait." I held up a vial of clear liquid I'd swiped from Zwara's stash and flashed a submissive pattern across my chest. "She'll need this. It will help dull the pain of her swollen spine. If you're going to imprison her, the least you can do is see that her suffering is minimized. Her scent glands will need to be drained every other day."

Hazi stalked toward me and held out his hand. "The Order will ensure she doesn't suffer. Tell Zwara to send a priestess tomorrow."

"Thank you," I said, making my voice small as I stepped closer. "How... how is the commander?"

Hazi's lips curled back over his fangs as he stepped to me. His face was inches from mine. "How do you think? You *ruined* him with your vicious cunt."

"That's a shame." I sighed as I placed the vial in his upturned palm and lifted the sea glass scalpel with the other. "Because my *vicious cunt* thoroughly enjoyed being worshiped by his tongue."

Hazi's growl shook the room, shattering the windows as I jabbed the brittle blade deep into the prince's gills.

Hazi released his hold over my sister as he slumped to the floor, coughing up blood.

"Run." I grabbed Tesk as Inanna dropped to help him. We just needed to make it to the crowd of hungry males in the temple below. Tesk's future mates wouldn't let the Order abscond with their new prize.

"Forget about me. Get them," Hazi yelled as Tesk and I flew down the spiral staircase inside the god of tides' long legs.

"Did you have to stab him?" Tesk asked through labored breaths that matched my own. Neither of us was built for speed, apparently.

"When you get to the bottom, start screaming and make a run for the dais."

She nodded as we rounded the last enclosed turn.

Tesk sucked in a breath, ready to scream as she stepped out of the stairwell. Kor snatched her from the doorway with a gust of air.

I threw my body through the opening and took out a temple guard. Her spear went clattering away as we sprawled across the floor.

My eyes found Tesk, who looked a little too pleased to be floating high in the rafters in Kor's arms among the ropes that worked the temple's bells. Kor's other two forms created a protective wind wall around them.

"I swear to all that is holy, Vaza, where you tread, chaos never ceases to follow." Zwara's features hardened. "Would you like to explain *why* Hazi zur'Aza is bleeding out all over my bedroom floor?"

I glanced at the shards of glass behind her and shuttered my eyes. Inanna. She hadn't even attempted to chase us, projecting the situation directly into Zwara's mind instead.

"He tried to take Tesk." It came out as a hiss.

"You better pray he doesn't die." Zwara nodded to Kor. "Get her out of here."

Kor's more menacing male form dropped to the floor and carried my sister to the exit. "I think it's time for another lesson in ancient linguistics, my queen. Did you know the words for rope and knot are the same in the old language? The meaning changed depending on context and the inflection used when spoken."

Tesk's eyes cut to mine with a questioning look.

"Go," I mouthed.

"Seize the barren queen and bring her to my chambers," Zwara said to one of the guards. "Vaza needs to learn how to fix what she's broken."

Inanna's hands were slick with blood where they pressed against Hazi's side. The unconscious male's already pallid hide had gone deathly pale.

Zwara grabbed a vial of clear fluid from the crystal cabinet and gulped it down in one shot. She dropped to Hazi's side, the hem of her crimson waist cloth slowly soaking a darker red as she tilted her ear to his mouth, listening to his rattled breathing.

"It's not good. I think the knife punctured both sets of lungs." Her eyes lifted to Inanna's tear-streaked face. "I'll do my best to save him, but I need you to do exactly as I say."

The mind mage gave an affirmative blink as she nodded.

"Vaza, bring me two vials of liquid silver."

I did as instructed and dropped to my knees on the floor next to Inanna.

"Inanna, on my mark, you're going to carefully pull the knife out at the same angle it went in. When it's free, I'm going to unleash my gift. You'll need to keep your hands clear. The magic has a mind of its own and will seek to replace the energy consumed by my attempt to heal him. If you're touching him. It will drain you." Zwara coated her hands in silver and placed her palms on the prince. One on his chest near the shoulder, the other between his stomach and ribs on his uninjured side.

"Are you ready?"

Inanna nodded.

"Remember, go slow. If any of it breaks off inside him, I won't be able to seal the wound."

Inanna wrapped her fingers around the glass hilt and exhaled as she began to slide the knife from her friend's gills.

Hazi's chest vibrated with a low growl as his eyes popped open. The arm at his side snapped up, knocking Inanna's hand away as he gripped her throat with his claws, his chest flashing with a blood frenzy. The mind mage's body went preternaturally still as his shield clamped down around her.

"Bloody ice," Zwara cursed, and I followed her gaze to the broken blade gripped in Inanna's fist and the fresh blood oozing from Hazi's gaping wound. The high priestess closed her eyes and unleashed her gift. The male groaned as the bioluminescent stripes beneath Zwara's hands flickered and went out. His skin beneath her hands turned black.

"Vaza, rub the silver all over your hands. It will block my gift from attacking you long enough to fish the other half of the knife out of his lung."

"You want me to stick my fingers inside his gills?"

"Would you rather witness before the Order's tribunal for murder?"

I poured the vials of silver into my palm and slathered my hands. In the moment I'd stabbed him, my only thought had been to protect Tesk. I had no wish for the male to die. I clenched my teeth and pressed two fingers into the hole left by the scalpel, ignoring the wet sucking sound it caused. A buzzing sensation kissed my skin as I sank my fingers all the way to the joint at my fist.

Hazi growled, and Inanna's labored breaths told me I needed to hurry. Whatever the mind mage was doing to keep him from ripping out her throat, I couldn't guess, but it was keeping his focus on her.

"I'm almost finished healing his air lung," Zwara said. "The tip of the blade is only in his water lung. I can see it with my gift. You're close."

Hazi's lips curled back, revealing his fangs as I pushed in as far as I could. I sucked in a breath as the tip of my finger sliced over glass. "I can't reach it."

"Use your claws if you have to. Just get it out."

"I'm so sorry," I said and protracted my claws. Hazi's body arched off the floor with an ear-numbing roar as I hooked them around the glass and ripped it out of his body, along with a stringy chunk of his flesh. "I'm clear."

Blood vessels popped in the whites of Zwara's eyes as she released the full extent of her gift into Hazi's chest.

Inanna gasped as Hazi released her throat. She immediately inspected the wound that had sealed shut, leaving a sloppy silvered scar along the length of his gills. Hot tears spilled down her cheeks as she curled forward to cup the male's face in her bloody palms.

A comforting rumble hummed through his chest as he slid a hand up her arm, his unwavering eyes searching hers. The skin around them crinkled with a smile as he tucked a loose strand of golden hair behind Inanna's ear and pressed his palm to her cheek, swiping at her tears with his thumb. Inanna leaned into his touch, brushing her lips across his wrist.

The hair rising on the back of my neck told me I should look away, that this intimacy between them was something deeply private, but I couldn't peel my eyes from the pair.

Intimate relationships were forbidden in the Order. This felt like something different. Something more.

Chapter Thirteen

Forty-five, forty-six, forty-seven, forty-eight, forty-nine...

I could feel the buzz wearing off as I counted out fifty jumping jacks that were helping to get the blood flowing to my brain before I took off after Renae.

My gifts didn't work great when I was high. The hazy glimpse I'd gotten of Renae's thoughts before she took off wasn't pretty. She'd had another one of her past life trauma episodes, and I wasn't there to help her. It must have been bad considering the hole she'd blown in the side of my studio wall.

She didn't even acknowledge me when I jogged up beside her and slowed to match her pace on the hard sand.

"Talk to me, chica."

She slowed to a walk. "You went too far this time."

"I know. I'm sorry. I keep the studio sealed when I'm inside because I don't want you to see me like that. I didn't even consider that it might trigger you if you came looking for me and couldn't get to me."

She stopped to face me. "You're an asshole."

"I'm trying to apologize for that. What more do you want from me?"

"Are you seriously going to stand here and act like you didn't erect a stockade around the bungalow to keep me from wandering off while you got high?"

"What are you talking about? I would never—" My body went rigid as I read the memory of roots jutting up from the ground that replayed in her mind. I dropped my eyes to the angry scratches on her stomach.

I'd caused a storm in my sleep that shut down a city once and nearly dropped a plane from the sky before I was in control of my gifts. The incoming tide washed around my calves as I ran a hand through my hair.

"Sending a storm to keep me in the house is one thing. What you did today is on a whole different level. I know you're struggling, but I don't understand how you could do this to me."

"It's this island. It has a mind of its own. You know I would never hurt you like that." She flinched when I reached for her, and that's when I knew I'd lost something I would never get back. Her trust.

I'd seen that look too many times to count from all the people I'd let down. From my brother. My unforgiving father. Logan, my NA sponsor. Even Monika. But never Renae.

I crouched in the sand to ease the pain that ripped through my chest. I was so fucking tired. Tired of lying to her. Tired of this cursed island. Tired of pretending I didn't hate what I'd allowed myself to become. I scrubbed my hands over my face. She deserved to know the truth about the monster I'd become.

"I need to tell you something, but I'm afraid it's going to change the way you see me."

"Is it something else about the drugs?"

"No." It was so much worse than that. I stood to avoid getting swamped by an incoming wave.

A fraction of the ache in my chest eased when she reached for my hand and dragged me past the high tide line.

I pulled her close, resting my hands on her hips. "Sticking the needle in my veins isn't the worst of what I've done to myself here. You asked about the marks on the table and why so many of them were horizontal."

"You said those were the days you looked for a way out. I still don't understand why you gave up."

"Because there's no way off this island. Not even in death."

Her face went paler than it already was as she put it together. Tears streamed down her cheeks. "Liam, there are hundreds of horizontal lines on that table."

"I started with the things I could pretend were accidents, paddling out to the storm and letting it pound me until I drowned. Diving to the bottom of a lagoon and getting stuck in an underwater cave. As my gifts evolved, I gave up the pretense and got creative with lightning and water, then there were the vines."

Renae's lips quivered as she gripped my face in her palms. "Why would you do that to yourself?"

"I was desperate to get back to you. I was so sure this was just some fucked-up dream. I thought I could wake myself up, and you'd be there next to me. But I didn't." Thunder rumbled in the distance as I pulled away from her. "Each time I died, I woke up alone in my bed the next day like nothing had happened. It's like this place has some kind of auto reset. Eat all the food. The fridge resets. Flush the heroin down the toilet. It fucking reappears. Every time I die, it's CTRL+ALT+DELETE."

She grabbed my shoulders as lightning lit the dark cloud over the ocean. "Liam, listen to me. None of this is real. Everything here is a manifestation of your subconscious enhanced by the properties of whatever dark energy space fluid the Void is made from. We need to find a way out before it contaminates your soul beyond repair."

"Haven't you been listening? There isn't a way out. Not for me." I threaded my fingers through her hair and swiped the wet tears from her face with my thumbs. "If you die, you won't come back. You're not part of the reset, Renae. That's why I begged you to stay inside and why my subconscious tried to put a cage around you. I'm terrified that you're going to disappear. Do you know what it's like to live in a constant state of fear?"

"I spent a lifetime running from fear. When I met you, I realized I was running toward something instead of away from it. Don't you see? If I hadn't run, if I hadn't kept moving, I wouldn't have found you. We have to keep moving forward, Liam. If we stop, if we let the fear catch us, if we let it twist our minds and control us, that's when we truly die. Don't let fear decide your fate. Help me find a way home."

A silent sob seized my chest. I wrapped my arms around her as my eyes leaked down my damn face. She was right. I'd given up and let the fear win. There was only one problem. I had no idea how to break out of this mind-fuck of a prison. But something told me Renae might. The heroin haze wasn't fully out of my system, but it had cleared enough to be able to read her thoughts. They flitted through her head faster than I could track.

I exhaled a ragged breath. "Wherever you run, I'll follow. Now tell me why you're contemplating ways to drain the lagoon."

She pressed a hurried kiss to my lips and pulled away to pace the sand. Her face bore the same focused expression she had when she wove her baskets. "You said your gift built a wall around the lagoon to protect you from drowning yourself again. But it didn't do that with any of the other ways you died. There has to be another reason your subconscious doesn't want you exploring down there."

I had to admit she had a point. Her brain suddenly switched gears to thoughts about her father.

"Did I miss something? What does fishing with your father have to do with this?"

"Nothing."

"Okay." I arched a brow and pulled my gift back as she continued.

"I've been mapping the island and using my syphons to taste my way around, looking for something that wasn't contaminated with sulfur. But I think I had it all wrong. At the lagoon, you said the energy lines all flow from there. It's also the only thing on the island where the rotten egg flavor is as strong as yours. No offense. Your projections cover it completely when I feed on your energy."

"Don't dance around my feelings, chica. What's your theory?"

"I think whatever's down there is connected to you. What did you see when you dove into the cave?"

"Not much. There are veins of some kind of rock or crystal that glow faintly in the dark."

"And you've never seen anything like it in real life that would have made your subconscious conjure it here?"

"I've never been in a lagoon or a cave until I came here."

Renae smiled for the first time in days. "You said it was the ass crack of the island. I think it might be its heart."

I was skeptical as hell, but Renae had always excelled at proving me wrong, so I let a little bit of the hope oozing along the bond seep into me.

"We can go explore on one condition. You will not, under any circumstance, do anything that could put your life at risk. I won't lose you again."

⁂

Renae worked at gathering her reed rope in a neat circle on the bungalow's deck in the dwindling light as I used my gift to force the island's living cage back into the ground.

Wherever she went, I would follow, but she was out of her fucking mind if she thought I'd let her free dive into the underwater cave in the dark. The hole at the bottom of the lagoon had to be fifty feet deep, and that was just the part you could see.

"We should wait until morning. You have no idea what we'll find at the bottom of that hole, and I sure as hell don't want to meet it in the dark."

"I'm hoping it's an Astral."

"What the hell is an Astral?"

"An astral projection portal."

"You think there's a portal down there?"

"It's just a hunch." She handed me the coiled rope. "Here, sling this over your shoulder. Your mother wouldn't have risked everything to send me here if she didn't think there was a way out. She told me you were the only one who could break us out of here."

I'd never met the woman who'd helped my father and his human genetics research partner create me as part of some superhuman science project. When things went sideways, she'd altered her identity and infiltrated the Corps—the clandestine organization Renae worked for created by the Nūkiri.

"Did she mention how I'm supposed to do that?"

"The same way she broke me in. By cracking the Astral open like an egg."

I leaned against the deck railing. "Can we just slow down a second and think this through? We don't even know if there's a portal down there."

"Don't worry, I have a plan."

I probed her thoughts. The memory of her father teaching her how to weave reed into rope played over and over on a loop whenever she worked with that damn rope.

"Please stay out of my head."

I raised my hands in defeat and yanked my gift back across the bond, giving her the space she needed.

"I suspected there was an Astral here somewhere. I had no idea where to start looking until you took me to the lagoon." Her eyes flicked to mine as she stuffed glowing glass balls filled with trapped lightning into one of the basket traps she'd woven. "The sooner we find a way out of here, the better."

There was so much hope in her pale gold eyes, I couldn't say no. Mostly because I didn't want to see the fucking disappointment in her face every time she looked at me.

"Fine."

She grinned and bounded down the deck toward the beach.

"It'll be faster if we go through the woods. Follow me."

I didn't need a lantern to find my way to the lagoon. The underground veins of energy lit up like a freeway when I switched to my enhanced forecaster sight. The underbrush thickened as we trudged through the jungle in silence. There was no moon or stars. No night birds or buzzing insects. Just the sound of sticks cracking like old bones beneath our feet.

Renae's silver blond hair shimmered in the light. Her stamina had improved over the last few days, but she still wasn't 100 percent. Her breathing was labored, and she sweated like an ice-cold beer left in the sun.

I pulled a gust of cooler air down from the tree canopy and curled it around Renae. "We should stop and rest here for a few minutes."

She swiped at the sweat slipping down her forehead and guzzled from the water bottle I'd made her bring.

"Say there is a portal down there, and by some miracle, I'm able to open it. What happens next?"

"We go back to the city of the dead and find Cyrena, your mother, and my sister."

Her last memory of the three women who'd helped her crash my personal purgatory flashed through her mind. She'd left them in the middle of an arena full of the dead to fight off the Nūkiri's thugs. The odds that they'd survived weren't good.

I knew the guilt was eating away at her, but if this worked, we needed a realistic plan. "It's been over a month, Renae. You need to prepare yourself for the possibility that—"

"No." She tossed me the water bottle. "Time moves exponentially slower in the city of the dead. The years for you here were only a few days for me in Almega and a few weeks on Earth. The month that I've been here with you isn't more than the blink of an eye for them. I have to believe they still have time." Their fate was a gnawing paradox in her mind, gone and not gone all at the same time.

"Okay." I gripped her clammy hand and wound her delicate fingers through mine. I'd spent years having my hope of ever seeing her again sucked away one failed escape attempt after another. I knew all too well how a soul devoid of hope twisted and warped into something unrecognizable until you convinced yourself that one kind of escape was as good as another. She didn't want me to shield her from the truth. So I played along and let us both cling to her hope a little longer.

The sulfuric stench thickened as we approached the walled-off lagoon. I lifted my hand to peel back the vines, but Renae stopped me.

"I got it." She unfurled her syphons and attached them to the wall. Leaves and vines shriveled beneath her touch. The vines creaked as they went bone brittle under her touch. The reaper gene was one I didn't get in the slurry of abilities my old man injected into me. Watching her suck the life out of something until it turned to ash made the hair rise on the back of my neck. It was the same thrill I got when she used her syphons on me, knowing the restraint it took for her to stop before she went too far.

"You're really good at that." I adjusted my junk as we stepped through the wall.

She'd stopped just inside the wall, her eyes fixed on the lagoon's faint glow.

"This doesn't mean there's a portal down there. It could just be a cave of glowy crystals."

"Or an Astral. They give off the same blue-green light." She started unraveling the rope. "You get rid of the water, and I'll secure the rope."

"How do you suggest I do that?"

"Try lifting it up like you did the first time you used your gift on the sea cliffs of Kilauea and drop it somewhere in the rainforest." Renae gestured to the lagoon.

"The lagoon is the lowest point on the island. All the rain runs here during a storm. If I dump it in the woods, it will just rush back in."

"Then dump it in the ocean."

"Your confidence in my gift is heartwarming, chica, but the beach is miles away. I can't carry it that far. There are millions of gallons of water down there. I can't carry that much weight. Even if I did it in smaller chunks, it would take weeks."

"Can you force it up into the atmosphere and turn it into clouds?"

I'd never vaporized that much water before, but there was a better than good chance that it could work. "There's only one way to find out."

I closed my eyes and gathered electrical static from the air. This wasn't as simple as melting a bit of sand into glass. I'd need a massive charge. Tendrils of electricity crackled over my skin, wrapping around my shoulders and chest. It shot down my arms and into the lagoon in a steady stream.

"Stop."

My chest seized as Renae screamed. I reined in my gift and glanced down at the black veins creeping out from the burn mark above my sternum.

She ran to the water's edge as the steam cleared. "Thank the gods. It's still glowing. For now. Astrals are living entities. If you electrocute it, we'll never get out of here."

"The only way to get water to rise into the atmosphere is by turning it into water vapor. I need to zap it to get rid of it."

Renae's eyes dropped to the black spot on my chest.

"Has that ever happened before?"

It hadn't, but I wasn't going to give her another reason to worry about me. The mark was already starting to fade. "It's fine. I just pulled in too much of a charge. I think we need to go back to plan A. If I lift out smaller chunks of water and drop them out as far as I can, it will take a long time to drain back into the lagoon. We should be able to explore the empty cave before it starts to refill."

"Are you sure you're okay?"

"Let's just get this over with." I gave her a reassuring hug and kissed the top of her head.

I widened my stance and stretched my shoulders before lifting a bubble of water that could easily fill a swimming pool. I floated it over the trees and let it rain down as I spread it out as far as I could in the rainforest around us.

My back and shoulders ached as I repeated the process over and over until Renae declared that she could see the bottom of the hole.

Renae secured the rope to a sturdy banyan root and strapped her lantern to her back like a backpack.

"Will this hold both of us?" I gave the rope a skeptical tug.

"Yes?"

"Why does that sound like a question?"

"I haven't tested it yet. We should go down one at a time."

I ran my hands down her arms as I used my gift to draw several sturdy vines from the rainforest. They slithered toward us like snakes between the small streams of water already trying to return to the lagoon.

"I love how industrious you are, and I respect your need to contribute," I said, recalling the story she told me about her father letting her figure shit out on her own. The vines curled around me as I scooped her up in my arms. "But I'm still an overprotective ass, and there's no way in hell I'm letting you lower yourself down."

To my surprise, Renae didn't argue. I brushed a kiss over her ear as she wrapped her arms around my neck. "Don't let go, chica."

My feet made sucking footsteps in the mud as I carried her toward the gaping hole. The vines creaked as I used them to lift us over the edge and lower us down.

She trailed her finger through the hair-like algae as we passed. The veins of fluorescent blue-green crystals widened as we dropped. Water rushed down the walls faster than I was comfortable with and sloshed around our ankles when our feet met the bottom.

Renae pulled her homemade lantern from her back and shone it around. The cave branched off in three different directions. Two were pitch-black and too narrow to navigate without slithering on our stomachs. The third was just tall enough for us to walk through if we bent at the waist and ducked our heads.

"Stay close." I tucked her behind me. The short tunnel opened to a chamber with a rounded ceiling and another wide hole in the floor.

Whatever was down there lit the opening like a beacon.

I toed up to the edge. The bottom was another hundred-foot drop to a bed of sharp crystals. "It's just more glowing rocks," I said, surprised by the relief in my own voice. Hope was a fickle ally when you'd grown comfortable in your own misery.

"Let me see." Renae dropped to her belly in the muddy water and peered over the edge. Her syphons exploded from her back and shot into the hole.

"I'm running out of steam. We should head back. We can start exploring the rest of the island tomorrow."

"Wrap your vines around me and lower me down." Her voice pitched up with excitement.

"What do you see?" I swallowed hard against the unease building in my throat.

"It's not what I can see. It's what I can taste." She shoved to her feet and reached for the vines that had followed us into the cavern. "I need to get closer."

"Renae, stop. What if it's not an Astral? What if it's just another disappointment? What if there's no way out because I don't deserve to go back? Is there even a tiny part of you that could learn to be happy here, with me?"

Her eyes cut to mine, and I didn't have to read her thoughts for the answer. She crossed her arms over her chest and stepped backward over the ledge.

I leapt over the edge after her without a second thought.

Like I had so many times before.

Just like she knew I would.

I sent the vines ahead of me and coiled them around her as I whipped up a violent updraft to slow our fall.

The rocks below flared with blinding light as I yanked her cocooned body back toward mine. My heart threatened to explode out of my chest as I wrapped my arms around her.

Renae tucked her face into my neck and pressed an apologetic kiss against my skin as we landed on the floor.

"What in the actual fuck?" I backed away from her and retracted the vines. "We agreed you wouldn't do anything to endanger your life."

"I knew you wouldn't let me fall." She closed the distance between us and smoothed her palms over my heaving chest.

"And if I'd been a second slower, your brain would be splattered all over the goddamned rocks." I grabbed the back of her neck and pulled her in. "As soon as we climb out of this fucking hole, I'm gonna teach you a lesson on following orders."

She melted against me as I claimed her mouth with a punishing kiss. Her syphons roved over my back, licking the sharp edges of my anger as I backed her against a glowing crystal pillar.

"Promise me you'll never do that again, or this little quest ends now."

She brought her hands to my face. "We can stop searching."

Relief drained from my body as I leaned into her touch. "Thank you. Can we go back to the bungalow now? I'm exhausted."

"No, you misunderstood. We're never going back up to that miserable illusion of life. Look."

She turned me toward the center, where light pulsed like a heartbeat from something in the middle of the floor. It wasn't big enough to be one of the jellied balls I'd seen in her memories that sent the soul of the dead back and forth between Earth and Almega.

"That's not an Astral." It was a man. Made of oil-black crystal. Curled in the fetal position and attached to a network of faceted veins that spread through the floor of the cave and climbed the walls.

The unease in my chest grew as we got closer. Like when you're a kid and you're sure there's a ghost watching you from the darkest corner of your room, but you pretend to not notice because as soon as you see it, it'll become real.

Renae touched the back of her hand to her mouth like she was holding back a gag as her syphons traveled over its body. "It's the source of the rot infecting the island. The thing holding us hostage here that you refuse to confront because you don't believe you deserve to leave."

"You learned all that from licking it?" I asked, backing away.

"No, Liam. I know all of that because I know you." She circled around and crouched by his face, letting her fingertips trace the crack that bisected his forehead in the same place as my scar. "And I'd recognize your soul no matter what form it takes."

Chapter Fourteen

VAZA

"They're definitely overcompensating for something," Kor's female form said.

The Rift sat like a heavy crown atop a lone pillar of basalt in the middle of the ocean. Eight octagonal sentry towers sat at each corner of the fortress's steep walls. The swinging rope bridge that stretched between guard stations on either side was the only way in or out.

"Come to finish me off, vow breaker?" Hazi asked, blocking access to the bridge.

"I'm here to see to my sister's needs."

"We agreed to a priestess, which neither of you are. I'm not obligated to let you pass."

I handed him a scroll with Zwara's seal. "The high priestess can't spare any blood mages right now. She sent me instead. I'm perfectly capable of expressing my sister's scent glands. It's all in the note."

Hazi popped the seal and scanned the scroll. "There's nothing here about the spirit mage."

"As a queen, I require an escort when I travel outside the Keep, and since Kor is Tesk's personal tutor, they came to ensure her studies are not being neglected."

"A tutor? Do you think I'm naive?" Hazi huffed.

"I've been a tutor to many of the noble houses, as I'm sure Inanna could tell you, had the Order not removed her lovely tongue. It's a shame, really." Kor sighed. "She had a true talent for linguistics."

An aggressive warning flashed across the male's chest as he took a step toward Kor.

"Kor has been tutoring Tesk in the ancient language," I said quickly. "As my sister is the subject of the prophecy, she has expressed a desire to read the texts for herself. Denying her the few basic rights she enjoyed in the Keep will do little to win her over."

Hazi stepped through the obsidian gate and motioned for us to follow. The bridge dipped and bounced beneath us. I held tight to the ropes on either side as the wind whipped at my veil, and I only made the mistake of looking down once. The red tide crashed against the rocks below like a raging sea of blood.

Kor settled the screaming wind with a flick of their wrist.

"You and Inanna seem very close," I said aloud, more to distract myself from the nauseating drop than anything else.

"We went through our ordeals at the same time. She took her vows alongside Brex and me."

"How wonderful it is to hear that you were able to set aside the rivalry to become *friends*. It was quite the shock when you both gave up your titles and took vows to the Order."

"My vow is to the god of tides." Every muscle in his body tightened as we passed through the gate on the other side.

"Inanna zur'Sidah is niece to the House of Spirit's high lord," Kor whispered behind me. "The House of Salt and House of Spirit have been fierce rivals since the beginning of tides, or near to it."

"Welcome to the Rift. The queen's private chambers are on the third floor. The library, should she need anything for her *lesson,* is on level four. Tesk and her guests are free to explore the grounds. Stay clear of the cliff's edge. The updrafts have swept more than one poor soul to their death.

Levels five and up are reserved for Order members only. If you're caught anywhere above level four, you'll be tossed over the cliff. When you're ready to leave, one of the sentries at the gate will escort you back across the bridge. Any questions? No? Great. Enjoy your visit." Hazi didn't give either of us a chance to respond before disappearing into the fortress.

"Do you think he was being serious about throwing us off a cliff?"

Kor's full lips curled in a sultry smile. "Why? Are you planning on hunting down your favorite zealot?"

"No." I grunted unconvincingly.

Kor hooked their slender arm through mine. "I wouldn't test the Order's patience on your first visit. Tesk will be devastated if they threw her beloved sister off a cliff."

"Zwara sent us here on a mission to find out what the Order is up to. We're not going to uncover any clues by walking around a barren rock or wandering the library."

"I disagree, darling. Every great library is a treasure trove of knowledge. All you need to do is look."

The Rift's interior was more crumbling castle than fortress once you passed through the obsidian doors. Coral chandeliers with crystal globes of bioluminescent algae hung from the vaulted ceilings. The refracted light gave everything the rippled appearance of being underwater, hiding cracks in the mineral-plastered walls. Dark stone peeked from beneath the peeling blue and green walls. Incense burned in small shrines to the god of tides in every room. It was more opulent than the temple or Zwara's chambers, even if the oversized furnishings were a bit threadbare.

Unlike Hazi, the few Order members we passed on the staircase inside one of the towers greeted us with kind smiles. They all dipped their heads in reverence to me—the queen who'd helped them protect the *ki'sikilta*. My skin prickled with unease as a gaunt elderly female stopped to anoint me with a blessing, hovering her palms over my eyes as she prayed. Was this what it was like for Tesk? To be revered by strangers, knowing their devotion was based on a lie.

We met fewer than twenty Order members as we made our way to the third floor.

"Shouldn't there be more of them in a fortress this size?" I asked Kor. "I thought the Rift housed thousands of members. Where did they all go?"

"The wasting doesn't spare the faithful. The Rift may have been hit harder due to their closer proximity to the sea and their charity work in the lower city."

We found Tesk sprawled ungracefully across a worn leather daybed, mouth agape and snoring. The book she'd been reading sat open on the floor where it had fallen from her dangling hand.

"Your sister is a treasure." Kor's usual smirk broke into a wide grin as they crossed the room plastered and furnished in soft blues. Kor kneeled at Tesk's side, gently pushing the hair away from her face and pressing a kiss to the corner of her mouth. "Hello, Tesk darling."

Tesk's eyes fluttered open, and her face lit as they landed on the spirit mage. She sat up and cupped their cheeks, pulling them in for a slow, sensuous kiss that made my chest ache, knowing what was to come. When the wasting was over and Zwara reinstated the rites, Tesk would become untouchable as a breeding queen, and Kor would be removed from her life.

"Should I leave?" I asked.

"Yes," Kor said, their sultry voice thick with heat as they slid my sister's black tunic up her thighs.

"Vaza." Tesk pushed Kor aside and threw her arms around me.

"How are you feeling? Are they treating you well? Do you have enough to eat?"

"Yes, yes, yes. I'm fine. Bored out of my mind, but fine. The few members that stayed behind have been kind. I don't know. It's strange."

"Stayed behind? What does that mean? Were there more?" I asked.

"There were hundreds in the great hall on level two when they brought me in to receive some kind of blessing prayer thingy. It was awkward. I just stood there while they all dropped to a knee and pounded their fists against their chests, chanting in the old language."

"Were you able to understand any of it?" Kor reclined on the lounge Tesk had vacated.

"Something about the *ki'sikilta* entering an eye or maybe opening one. It didn't really make sense."

"*Kisikilta* is one of many words in the old language that had different meanings depending on inflection when spoken. It was used to refer to a queen's status in contract for the mating rite. Ki*'sikilta* for virgin, Kisi*'kilta* for ripe or actively breeding, and Kisikil*'ta* for barren."

"Is it possible the Order got the translations wrong?" I asked, dropping onto a highbacked chair.

"Not likely," Kor said with the confidence of someone used to being the smartest person in the room. "The ancient scribes were meticulous. They noted the inflection in every copy of the prophecy we've ever seen."

"Have you seen the original version? The one written by Wu'uru himself?"

"Are you jesting?"

"Vaza's never made a joke in her life," Tesk said as she plopped down next to Kor.

"The original scrolls were eaten by moisture and mold long ago, like everything else in the ancient city. All that remains are the Order's translations."

"It's true," Tesk said. "When Brex gave me a tour of the library upstairs, there was a display case with three moldy relics. He said they were all that was left of the prophet's personal writings."

"Brex is here?" My pulse skittered to a momentary halt.

"Not anymore. They made him move out until he completes another ordeal. He left last night with a few of the new recruits who haven't taken their vows. I think they're making the pilgrimage to the prophet's tomb."

"Such a martyr," Kor said. "So eager to sacrifice his body to the cause. He gets stabbed by the wraith, volunteers as tribute to be ravaged by the killer queen, and still feels the need to prove his loyalty by taking the silent vow like Inanna."

"At least we won't be subjected to any more of his propaganda when he comes back without a tongue." I shoved to my feet and moved to the window overlooking the center courtyard. The incense-infused air made it difficult to breathe.

"Seems to me you rather enjoyed his tongue," Kor said. "You may have broken the poor zealot, but I'm not entirely sure he hasn't broken you as well."

"He held me hostage for an entire tide, and now he's got Tesk locked in a tower. The wraith should have done us all a favor and ended him when she had the chance."

"Where are you going?" Tesk asked as I stomped toward the door.

"To the library."

I didn't see another soul as I made my way upstairs. The Keep's modest collection paled in comparison to what I found on the fourth floor of the Rift. Bone dry and not a hint of mildew or rot. No cracked walls or peeling plaster. It was the only part of the castle that had been meticulously maintained.

Bright glowing balls of trapped lightning lit room after room. Shelves stretched to the ceiling twice as high as I was tall. There were sections on history and medicine and every mage ability. Three of the eight rooms were dedicated to the prophecy alone.

I ran my fingers along the spines as I explored the history section, searching for the display case Tesk had described. I stopped short in front of a section containing hundreds of tomes on the goddesses of death and fertility. A slow smile crept up my cheeks as I tugged out what looked like a leather-bound journal. I untied the cord and flipped through the pages of explicit illustrations depicting how the Nūkiri claimed *their* mates during the rite instead of the other way around. My fingers drifted to the bite mark at the base of my neck.

"Oh, you are definitely coming home with me." I glanced over my shoulder as I tucked the book between my stomach and the waistband of my leggings under my tunic. I hadn't seen another soul since entering the library, but one couldn't be too careful. If they threw nosy guests off the cliff, I didn't want to imagine what they did to thieves.

I combed the remaining rows quickly, scanning for the display case. The last room in the octagonal loop didn't contain any books at all. Rows of long tables with small algae lights stretched toward a set of jeweled-glass doors that led to a terrace overlooking the open sea.

A niche in the sidewall held a small crystal box. I pressed a hand to the front of my tunic to keep the book from slipping out of my waistband as I darted across the room. I wasn't naive enough to think I'd find an original copy of the prophecy written in Wu'uru's hand. But if I could find something that showed he didn't use inflections in his writing, I might be able to convince the Order that their translation of the prophecy could be wrong. It was a desperate reach, but it was all I had.

I slid the crystal box from the glowing niche in the wall. Inside were three flat scrolls no larger than a personal note like Zwara had sent with me to gain access to the Rift. All three were blackened and brittle with mold. I set the box on the nearest table and lifted the lid.

Black dust clung to my fingertips as I tested the structural integrity of the first artifact. It flaked apart at the lightest touch, too brittle to even lift.

The second piece of paper was sturdier, but there was no way it would survive a trip back to the Keep. I pulled the book out of my pants and laid it open on the table next to the box. As I lifted the second scroll from the case, the blue silk bottom lifted with it. It started to tear as I tried to peel it away from the fabric.

My spine stiffened as a deep voice floated toward me from the adjacent room. I held my breath as I picked up the third moldy artifact. It lifted away without damage, and I placed it over an illustration of a female riding astride a male. I closed the book and tucked it back in my pants as the voice crawled closer. Too close. I hurried across the room and returned the box to its resting place, slipping out one of the doors to the terrace just as Hazi and Inanna emerged from the stacks.

I pressed my back to the stone wall, heart thumping in my chest as I scanned for an escape route. The sentry towers on either end of the terrace had narrow doorways leading to a set of stone steps. I closed my eyes and offered my thanks to the Nūkiri for my good fortune when I heard Hazi spit my name.

"Vaza's a distraction we can't afford."

I rolled my body toward the door and peeked through the colored glass. Inanna sat on the edge of a long table facing the doors as Hazi paced in front of her, fisting a scroll. Her markings pulsed slowly, dimming and lighting like a heartbeat in unison with Hazi's heartbeat—an unconscious pattern expressed between fused souls. If one believed the stories about the bond, one of them had given up a piece of their soul to save the other from death. I pressed my face closer to the glass.

"You need to stay out of his head. Let Brex work through it on his own like he always does. We leave with the *ki'sikilta* in two days. I need his mind clear."

Hazi stalked to the table and spread out the scroll. Inanna twisted and jabbed her finger against the paper.

"You're right," Hazi said, planting a quick kiss on her cheek. "We're going to need another gorzin skin."

When he drew away, Inanna slid her hand over his chest and drew him back until Hazi was standing between her spread knees. She rested her head on his shoulder as he wrapped his arms around her.

"Remind me, my Gi'dari," he said.

The mind mage's eyes fluttered shut, and they remained like that, entwined and unmoving, for a long while until Inanna threw her head back and arched against him. My own skin heated at her groan of pleasure. Hazi curled around her and dropped his mouth to her neck.

I gasped as his body jerked with a release.

"Did they... did they just mind-fuck? In a library?" I whispered to myself.

"Did Hazi forget to mention what we do with spies?" Brex's voice poured over me like cool water over hot stone. I pressed my forehead to the glass, delaying the moment I'd need to look up and see the shadows of regret painted across his face.

"What are you doing here?" I asked.

"Watching you spy on Inanna and Hazi while they mind-fuck. In the library."

The book slipped from my waistband to my crotch as I spun toward him, full of questions. Did the Order know? Did vows not apply to mind mage projections? Hazi said the three of them were close. Was he on his way to join them?

Brex's arms were crossed, a shoulder pressed casually into the wall like it wasn't a big deal. As if it happened all the time.

"Did you know?" I asked.

"That you're a spy?" The corners of his mouth curled as he nodded up at the watchtower. "I scented you as soon as you stepped outside."

He was smiling. Not brooding in shame or disgust. Smiling. I'd never seen the male smile. It changed his entire face. The skin around his eyes crinkled, and goddess help me, I couldn't stop staring at the tips of his fangs. A drop of frenzy slid down my spine at the memory of them scraping across my throat.

I clenched my fists at my sides to keep my fingers from reaching up and tracing the silver scar where he'd claimed me. A jolt of terror shot through me. Fear that Kor might be right.

Brex cocked a brow as his eyes dropped to my chest. To my *glowing* chest. The traitorous markings pulsed, mimicking my erratic heartbeat. I banked my light and glanced over my shoulder at Hazi and Inanna as they walked away, hand in hand. This thing between them, it was intense and forbidden and everything I wanted for myself but could never hope to have.

"They're... lovers."

"Former lovers." Brex pushed off the wall.

"It looked pretty current to me."

"Hazi and Inanna." Brex paused like he was selecting his words carefully. "They have a special bond. She uses her gift to replay old memories with him from time to time."

"Is that allowed? What about their vows?"

"What Hazi and Inanna do isn't anyone's business but their own. As long as they keep taking the tonic and don't cross that line, the Order turns a blind eye."

He moved to the door and held it open.

"What I just witnessed definitely crossed some kind of line." I grunted and gave him my back to keep the stolen book under my tunic from brushing him as I squeezed past.

Brex's arm snaked around me, and he flattened his palm against my abdomen just beneath my breasts as he tugged me to him. "Did you enjoy watching, little spy?"

"No. I'm not a spy."

He took a deep breath, and his chest vibrated with a satisfied hum as he exhaled.

"Liar."

My muscles tightened as his hand drifted toward the rope of scar tissue on my belly.

"I wanted to kill Zwara when I found out what she did to you. It was all I could do to not rip her head from her shoulders right there in her chambers."

I put my hand over his to keep it from going any lower. I should have pushed him away and returned to Tesk and Kor before he discovered the stolen book, but I leaned into him instead.

"Why did you volunteer for the rite?"

"In the Order, we revere loyalty above all. And you, *my queen*, have the strongest, most fiercely loyal spirit I've ever seen." He traced the fingertips of his free hand down my arm, sending a cascade of pebbled skin over my flesh.

I closed my eyes and tipped my head against his shoulder. "You're wrong. What you see as strength is a shell of sharp, shattered pieces held together by scar tissue and spite." He had no idea how truly broken I was on the inside.

His lips brushed my temple. "I would worship at the altar of your scars and spite if you'd allow it."

"You'd worship a killer queen who sells her own scent for coin and consumes souls entrusted to her care?"

I gasped as his grip tightened around me. "I would worship you." His voice was a low rumble. "The selfless queen willing to sacrifice everything to save her sister."

"Who also happens to be your precious *ki'sikilta*." In that moment, I understood this thing about me. It wasn't even about Tesk. "Please, Brex. Let me go."

He spun me so my back was against the cool glass of the open door. I flinched, worried he would feel the bulge in my pants if he got any closer.

He registered my reaction and stepped back, putting space between us. Shadows of regret and shame flashed across his expression.

"I'm sorry. I wasn't trying to restrain you. Forgive me."

"How long are you planning to hold my sister against her will? You promised me she'd have a choice."

"She will. The prophecy is clear. The *ki'sikilta* must fulfill her duty willingly."

"Then let her leave with me."

"She's safe with us. If we let her leave with you, Zwara will sell her to the highest bidder, and she'll be subjected to the brutalities of the next rite. Is that what you want for your sister?"

"You don't need to remind me of the brutalities enacted upon a queen during the rite."

Brex took a step closer. "That's over for you now. You'll never have to submit to another mate against your will again. When the Order is in control of the rites, queens will be free to choose their mates."

"No queen will ever be free while the Order or the high priestess or anyone else seeks to control us."

I forced my gaze over his shoulder, blinking back tears of rage. Not at Brex. I couldn't fault him for his steadfast loyalty to his beliefs just because I didn't share them. I reserved the rage for myself. For wishing things could be different. That *he* was different.

"Zwara promised me a false freedom as well. She'll force me to assume Tesk's identity again in the next rite to collect on her contracts if you insist on holding my sister hostage."

His lips curled back in a snarl. "That will *never* happen."

My eyes landed on the scroll Hazi and Inanna had been studying. I stepped around Brex and went to the table, smoothing the text open with my palms. Except it wasn't a text. It was an architectural drawing.

"Vaza." He breathed my name like a sigh.

"Don't do that," I said, letting the scroll curl shut.

"What?" He was behind me, close enough that I could feel his heat at my back.

"Say my name like it means anything to you."

"It means everything. I meant what I said during the rite. If things were different—"

"Well, they're not different and they never will be." I turned to face him. "I don't want pretty words and promises you can't keep, zealot. I want the truth."

He pressed his fist to his heart. "Ask your questions, my queen, and I'll tell you anything you wish to know."

"Do you regret claiming me in the rite?"

His gaze dropped from my veiled face to the bite mark he'd left on my neck. "Yes." The word came out like a low growl. "Now ask me why."

I'd heard enough. Even though I'd already known the answer, hearing it from his lips was the closure I needed. A corner of the stolen book poked my hip as I shifted on my feet, reminding me of why I was there. Rescuing Tesk from whatever they had planned was the only thing that mattered. "I don't care why. I'd like to be alone now."

He dipped his head. "As you wish, my queen."

CHAPTER FIFTEEN
VAZA

"It's called trona ash," Zwara said as she sprinkled white powder over the blackened piece of parchment I'd stolen from the Rift's library.

"Are you sure this will work?" I asked.

Her icy blue eyes cut to mine. "My priestesses maintain thousands of titles in the temple library. I know how to remove a little mold."

"That's more than a little mold," Kor's softer male form said as they studied the artifact we were about to either save or destroy. "Looks like a targul ink stain."

Zwara opened a vial of clear liquid and dripped it over the white powder. The concoction foamed, and my eyes watered as the noxious fumes crawled up my nose. How the others could stand there and breathe it, I had no idea.

"Bloody ice, that's caustic." I retreated to the still broken window and took a clear breath.

"And effective," Kor's other two forms said in unison from where they leaned over Zwara's stone exam table.

The one with the shaved head winked at me as a brush of cool air kissed my cheek and steered the noxious fumes away from me. "Better?"

"Thanks." Even though I knew Kor was a single entity, it was easy to forget they were simultaneously aware no matter the distance between them. The two who'd stayed behind when we went to the Rift had already reported everything from our visit by the time we returned. Zwara had the restoration supplies waiting.

Black foam and stringy bits of sludge sluiced off the paper as my sister lifted it carefully with a pair of tweezers. A tight, jagged script was visible beneath the thin layer of slime that remained. She floated the scroll in a shallow basin. The clear water grayed as she wiggled the paper and the remaining mold lifted away.

"There's nothing to be done about the stains, I'm afraid," Zwara said, frowning at the dark splotches covering the ancient symbols before turning to Kor's softer male form. "Can you read it?"

A smile tugged at their mouth after a moment. "This may be the last thing the prophet ever wrote. It's dated three days before he overthrew the Nūkiri."

"What does it say?" My lungs tightened as I moved to get a closer look at the pictograph.

"It appears to be a hastily written supply list." Kor read off the items.

"Those numbers can't be right," Zwara said.

Kor read them again. "What would Wu'uru need with that much incense and liquid silver?"

"Did he use inflections?" I scanned the relic, unable to decipher any of the slanted symbols. "If he didn't use them for this, he may not have included them in the prophecy. This proves the Order could have translated it wrong."

"I don't think the prophet wrote this list. Look at this." Kor held up the ancient piece of parchment with a pair of tongs. A triangle with a slit eye in the center had been embossed on the back.

"The Nūkiri's mark," I said.

Zwara scowled at the paper. "That makes more sense. They silvered the marks they left on their mates. But these amounts would have been enough to fill an entire mating pool."

I scrubbed my hands over my face. "I risked my life to steal an ancient artifact that turns out to be completely useless."

"The mission was hardly a failure." Zwara motioned for Kor to clear away the mess and walked to the opposite end of the stone slab. She smoothed her hands over the map I'd stuffed under my tunic before leaving the Rift's library. "At least we know where they're going. What does the Order want with the gorzin-infested ruins of the Nūkiri's ancient palace?"

"I overheard Hazi tell Inanna that they're leaving in two days and they're taking Tesk with them. Whatever they have planned for her is happening soon."

Kor's fluid grace evaporated as they flashed three sets of fangs and spoke as one. "We need to retrieve Tesk from the Rift. Now."

Zwara arched a brow at the vehemence in their voice.

"We counted four guards in addition to Brex, Hazi, and Inanna, plus two dozen elder scholars. If you send Vaza to the bridge as a decoy, we can fly in from behind and rescue Tesk." Kor's lip curled back in a possessive snarl that had me wondering which of my sisters held their loyalty.

"I can't go back there. They'll have discovered the missing artifact and map by now. The Order throws trespassers off the cliff. What do you think they'll do to a thief?"

"After the price the commander paid to claim *all* your future matings, I doubt he'd let them harm you. It was the highest amount ever paid for a queen."

"What?" The word came out with a dry rasp.

"Did you not read the contract, darling? It was for you. Not Tesk. Brex zurNaga purchased you outright from the House of Blood."

My lungs stopped working. *That's over for you now. You'll never have to submit to another mate against your will again.* I braced my palm against the windowsill.

"Why would he do that?" I needed to sit down.

"It doesn't matter." Zwara glared at Kor and helped me to a chair. "Whatever they're up to is bigger than Tesk or the commander's obsession with you. The Order has been aggressively recruiting new members and moving supplies into the old city. I need to know if they're building an army to overthrow me, which is why you, dear sister, are going to use your newfound freedom to follow them. Two of Kor's forms will accompany you and ensure you remain hidden. The other will stay behind to convey everything you see and hear back to me."

"Brex can scent me at two thousand paces. We can't afford to get caught trailing them."

The corner of Kor's mouth hitched up. "Don't worry, darling. We know how to stay upwind of the commander's nose." Their confidence did little to ease the hard ball in my stomach.

⁊

Niva spent the next two days milking my spine dry and soothing the tender flesh with targul venom to reduce the swelling and neutralize my lingering scent. If we were caught, I'd have to face him. I hated everything about him. His muddy green eyes that saw too much. The cocky smirk that made my chest ache. The way his deep voice made my pulse race and my blood heat. *Come for me and show everyone you're mine.*

My core throbbed at the memory of his words as I pressed my back to the cool tunnel wall across from Kor. Their ability to mimic any color or surface allowed them to disappear in the shadows of the ruined city. The only thing that gave them away were the whites of their eyes as they blinked back at me in the dark.

Their female form nodded to the open archway. I followed as they dropped to their knees and bellied out onto the ledge overlooking the underground city. Across the cavern, Tesk marched ahead of Brex. Her stiff posture and the way her bioluminescent markings flashed angrily told me she wasn't moving of her own free will. Brex placed a hand on her shoulder, and she halted without blinking.

"They have her under a shield," Kor's male form bit out. "He doesn't need to touch her. If he—"

"He won't." I didn't let them finish the thought. Aside from myself, and possibly Kor, Brex was the only other soul I trusted with my sister's life. He'd lied and manipulated and devoted his life to keeping her safe. He wouldn't hurt her. It was a truth I knew in my bones. Protecting her was the cord that connected us. The one thing we had in common.

I watched as he and Hazi secured a rope around a triangular boulder wedged into the crack that paralleled the waterfall all the way down. Inanna kept watch on the path behind them. They knew I'd stolen the map and expected me to follow as they repelled into the bowels of ancient Eden.

Brex searched the levels above, scowling when he didn't find what he was looking for. He said something to Inanna, and she pulled a set of lightweight climbing leathers from her pack that matched the form-fitting suits they all wore to protect their hides from rope burns and rock rash. She shook it out before folding it neatly and placing it in the middle of the path.

"Looks like the commander is hoping for company," Kor's female form said where they pressed against my side.

"Or setting a trap."

Hazi tested the lines hanging from the tether and descended first, with Inanna close behind. Tesk followed, copying their movements under compulsion. Brex crossed the ropes behind his back and fed them between his thighs, tightening the slack and cinching the harness around his body. He glanced over his shoulder at the path behind him one last time before stepping off the ledge.

They repeated the process several times until they reached the level below where I'd passed behind the waterfall to escape the gorzin. The crack widened from there down, and I could make out two sets of ropes already attached to anchors embedded in the stone. The foursome moved faster, repelling two at a time. Tesk winced with every forced movement, and I wished I could yell out that I was here. That I was coming for her. Zwara made it clear that this was strictly a reconnaissance mission, and we were not to engage. But she didn't own me anymore, and there was no way I was leaving this dank hell without my sister.

Brex kept a constant eye on their surroundings. I told myself he was scanning the cavern walls for hungry gorzin. Unlike Tesk, his movements were smooth and practiced. His muscular back bunched and flexed beneath the body-hugging armor as he eased himself down. Whenever he found a foothold, he thrust his hips up and pressed his body against the wall in a way that made my scent glands begin to swell. He was the most ruggedly beautiful thing I'd ever seen.

"Stop simpering over your zealot." Kor stood without making a sound. "It's time to fly."

"He's not *my* zealot." I yanked my fingers away from where they brushed the silver scar on my neck.

"The same way Tesk isn't *our* queen?" Kor's female form asked as their brooding male counterpart grabbed me around the waist and clasped a palm over my mouth.

"Don't scream," they whispered against my ear as we leapt over the edge.

My stomach climbed into my throat as wind rushed past my face and whipped the hair from my braid. Kor's chest vibrated with a low chuckle against my back as we slowed, landing softly on our feet four levels below.

I shoved away from them and gripped the wall for support. "A little warning next time."

Kor smirked as their female form landed silently beside them. We continued like that, quietly jumping and waiting, keeping eight to ten levels behind Tesk and her captors. I couldn't blend into the environment like Kor, but they kept my scent upwind, and we only moved when the others had their backs to us. I'd lost count of how far we'd descended when the mist from the thundering waterfall thickened, forcing us to follow at a much closer gap to keep Tesk and the others in sight.

The architecture grew more elaborate as we approached the heart of the ruined city. A web of crumbling stone bridges stretched from one side of the cavern to the other. I tried to imagine what ancient Eden looked like with its white marble arches and glowing algae lanterns intact. In the dark, it resembled the skeletal remains of a great beast.

We slipped into what must have been an apothecary once upon a time, given the broken vials strewn across the dusty floor. I watched from the shadows as Tesk let go of the ropes and immediately fell to her hands and knees. The way she flopped onto her back and unleashed a verbal tirade on Brex told me he'd released her from his shield. He went through a series of stretches and motioned for her to get up and do the same. She vehemently declined with a rude hand gesture.

"That's our feisty girl," Kor's male voice whispered from the stone wall they'd camouflaged themselves against. "Don't worry, love, we'll give you a full-body massage when we get you home."

I smiled against the cool dark. "So this is a rescue mission after all."

"We need to find another way in," they said in unison as the mist parted to reveal an ornate triple archway flanked by a dozen guards.

A possessive growl vibrated from Kor's chest as Inanna helped Tesk stand on wobbly legs. The mind mage had to support most of my sister's weight as they made their way to the Order's new stronghold.

Hazi greeted the sentries as Brex scanned the ruined city. I held my breath as his unseeing gaze darted past our hiding spot the same way it had a dozen other times during the descent. Apparently, I was invisible to him without my scent. Hazi gave him a sympathetic look as they disappeared inside the ancient palace.

Kor's female form retreated into the abandoned shop and stared at the floor.

"We're consulting the map in Zwara's office," their male counterpart offered as they leaned against the doorway.

"When this is over, you'll need to give Tesk up," I said, pressing my frenzy-swollen spine against the cold stone wall next to the door. "Zwara won't let you keep her to yourself."

They dropped their head back against the marble. "What other choice do we have? We can't afford to buy her from the House of Blood."

"Does she know how you feel about her?" I asked.

Kor rolled their face toward mine. "Does the zealot know how you feel about him?"

"That I hate everything he stands for? Yes. I've made my feelings quite clear."

"Good. That means we can still be friends after I kill him. He won't give up the *ki'sikilta* without a fight."

I shoved off the wall and wrapped my claws around Kor's soft throat. "No one touches Brex but me. Your job is to protect Tesk. I'll take care of the commander."

"Retract your fangs, darling," Kor's female form said behind me. "We're all on the same side. Let's go retrieve your sister."

We used the mist as cover and flew to a balcony five stories above the palace entrance. One of the doors was missing, and the other hung at an odd angle from broken hinges. I pulsed a soft glow from my chest as we entered the pitch-black room. It had clearly been ransacked after the fall of the Nūkiri. The once gilt furnishings were tarnished and pitted with holes where precious gems had been dug out by thieves long ago.

My fingers trembled as I ran them over the back of a broken couch that had once belonged to the vicious queens. I imagined their slippered feet dangling off the end as their consorts fed them delicacies off golden platters.

"Through here," Kor said in unison.

I followed them down a wide corridor to another set of pillaged chambers. The furnishings were bigger, as if built for a large male. Empty bookshelves were strewn among the debris. I let my light flare to get a better look. Chunks of mineral plaster painted to look like the sky hung from the ceiling. A cracked marble tub big enough to hold multiple bodies occupied the far end of the room, but it was the mosaic wall behind it that struck me motionless.

Wu'uru had destroyed nearly every drawn, painted, or carved rendering of the Nūkiri after he ended their cruel reign. But here they were, depicted in an illicit scene with the god of tides. The two younger goddesses restrained him while the crone rode astride his hips.

I couldn't breathe as I stared at an all-too-familiar face. The only difference was the eyes. Instead of muddy green, they were gold.

They stripped him of his power and dignity when he refused them.

His hair was shorter, and he didn't have a beard, but there was no mistaking the cast of shame on his face.

You could at least pretend my entire life isn't a joke to you.

"It's him," I gasped. "It's all true. The prophecy and the god of tides are real."

"You see one ancient mural, and now you're a believer?" Kor gave an incredulous grunt.

"Brex tried to tell me... the story about the gorzin on the beach... it wasn't a fable about the god of tides. When the Nūkiri stole his power, he blamed himself. Without his gift, he couldn't protect Eden from the red tide. Brex thinks Tesk can resurrect his power. But she can't. We lied to him just like the Nūkiri lied to the god of tides. When he finds out Tesk isn't the *ki'sikilta* and the prophecy will never be fulfilled, the betrayal will destroy him."

Kor shook my shoulders. "Get yourself together. You can have an existential crisis after we rescue your sister."

"I need to be the one to tell him. Let him take his wrath out on me and not Tesk."

"This is our way in." Kor's male cranked a lever. The water lock in the wall above the pool opened. "It's an old aqueduct that supplied water to the bathing chambers and palace mating pool down below." They glanced at the empty bath. "The pool is likely dry as well. If the map is correct, it's a near vertical drop from here. We'll go first and use the air currents to slow our descent and cushion the fall."

I squeezed into the stone sluiceway behind Kor and elbowed up the gentle incline to the adjoining aqueduct. Kor lowered their female counterpart into the vertical shaft by their ankles and instructed me to hold on to theirs the same way as they bellied over the edge. A stiff wind hit me in the face as I slid into position behind them. All the blood rushed to my head as we descended at a snail's pace.

"Can we go any faster?" I asked. "I'm getting dizzy, and I can feel my pulse throbbing in my head."

The wind died, and we moved faster.

Too fast.

"Kor." I yanked on their legs, but their body had gone limp. They'd passed out from being upside down too long.

I let go and pressed my hands and feet against the walls to slow myself down. It was no use. The shaft was too wide. I was going to die.

The aqueduct made a gentle curve, and my fall became more of a slide. I tucked my chin and hugged my arms around my chest. A scream tore from my throat as my body shot out of the tube and plunged into a deep pool.

I sank to the bottom like a rock in my leathers, gulping water.

A strong arm cinched around my middle and yanked me to the surface.

"Let me go." I coughed and sputtered as he dragged me to the shallow end of the massive pool.

Brex turned me in his arms and pushed the wet hair away from my face. "Never."

The water in my stomach turned into a hard ball and pressed up into my throat. "Where's my sister?" I asked, unable to look the god of tides in the eye.

"Resting. The climb took a toll on her. She's in good hands with Inanna." He traced my lower lip with his thumb. "I'm glad you made good use of the map she left you."

I glanced at the edge of the pool. Kor stood dripping wet and preternaturally still under Hazi's control. Guards blocked every exit and lined the wall where the aqueduct emptied into the pool. They'd set a trap, and we'd fallen right into it.

"You've been waiting for us."

He bent forward and whispered into the shell of my ear. "I've been waiting for *you, little spy*."

Kor was locked under Hazi's shield and couldn't communicate with their counterpart or call Zwara for backup. Even if I could fight my way out alone, I had no idea where they were keeping Tesk. I needed a new tactic.

"I know what you are. Will you send the others away so we can talk privately?"

His muddy green gaze didn't stray from mine as he ordered everyone to leave us.

"I don't think that's a good idea," Hazi said as the other guards shuffled out. "She could have a weapon."

"He's right." I spread my arms wide as I backed away from him. "You're welcome to strip me down and find out, *Commander*."

"Don't tempt me with a good time, *wraith*."

"Brex—" The prince hissed his name.

"Get. Out."

Hazi dipped his head and left.

I climbed out of the pool and kicked off my waterlogged climbing slippers. Brex watched me intently as I removed my soggy chest plate and leggings. His eyes burned a trail over my wet tunic and the set of knives holstered under my arms as I plopped down and sat on the edge of the pool.

"Did you come for a fight or something else?" he asked.

"Does it have to be one or the other?"

The corner of his mouth twitched as he stalked toward me. "I'd be disappointed if it was anything less."

"Do the others know?"

"That I want to fuck you instead of locking you in a cell with the others?" He placed his hands on my knees and slowly pushed them apart.

"That's not what I—"

"I'd never ask anyone to follow me blindly, Vaza." Beads of water clung to his beard as he stepped between my thighs.

"Why didn't you tell me when we were in the catacombs?"

"Would you have believed me?" His fingers whispered over my flesh, drawing invisible lines between the scatter of bioluminescent marks, watching each flare in response to his touch. "You made your disdain for the god of tides and his devoted disciples abundantly clear. Would you have believed me if I told you I was a powerless deity, cursed to watch the people I was supposed to protect die over and over again for my sins?"

"What they did to you isn't your fault."

"You asked me if I regretted participating in the rite. The only thing I regret is that it was against your will. I did what I needed to do to create a situation where I got everything I wanted. You. The *ki'sikilta*. Enough food to keep this city alive for one more tide. I created a scenario where you couldn't say no and selfishly took what I wanted like all the others before me that you never chose." He dropped his eyes to the scar at the base of my throat. "The fact that you didn't fight it doesn't make it right. I will never forgive myself for that."

The way his shame played across his beautiful face made my chest ache. I knew what it was to carry the burden of regret. Hemeda hadn't died by my hand, but it didn't make me feel any less responsible. Brex had been alive longer than I could wrap my head around. He'd watched Eden wither away. I didn't want to imagine what that kind of burden felt like.

There were so many questions rushing through my mind. I blurted out the first thing that popped into my head.

"Why did you buy me from the House of Blood?"

"Because I couldn't stand the thought of another male touching what was mine." Light flared across his chest at the admission. "But Inanna kicked my ass after the rite and made me promise to give you your freedom. I went to the library at the Rift with the intention of telling you everything, but you made it clear you wanted nothing more to do with me, so I let you go."

"That was unwise." I pressed my hand to his chest. Above his beating heart. "I might try to kill you tomorrow."

Brex braced his palms on the edge of the pool, bracketing me in the space between his arms. "I trust you."

"You shouldn't." I was there to liberate Tesk, spy on the Order, and feed information back to my horrible sister.

"You won't hurt me."

"What makes you so sure, zealot?"

He dropped his eyes to the steady glow pulsing from my chest like a heartbeat. His heartbeat. The same rhythm that thrummed beneath my palm.

"It doesn't mean anything," I said. The lie was an ache I felt deep in my bones. Brex was my enemy. He wanted to sacrifice my sister to regain his power.

He held his mouth above mine, waiting for me to claim it. "As you say, my queen."

"You're wrong about the rite." I let my lips brush against his. "You didn't need to lie or manipulate me into it. I wanted it to be you." I'd never stop wanting it to be him. Brex was the only male I'd ever truly given myself to—the only male I would choose over and over if I could. If things were different.

"And what do you want right now?" His deep voice rolled through me like a wave, threatening to sweep me under if I let it. A bead of frenzy rolled down my spine, and Brex's chest lit in response.

"I want you to kiss me."

He dropped his gaze to my lips, then his mouth was on mine. His hands tangled in my hair as I wrapped my legs around him, both of us trying to eliminate the space between us.

I sucked his bottom lip, letting it drag through my teeth. A low growl vibrated in his chest as my fangs nicked his flesh. The sweet, metallic decadence of his blood would be my undoing.

"I'm sorry," I said, forcing myself to pull away before he did.

Brex brought his fingers to his swollen lip and smiled when they came away with a crimson smear. When his eyes lifted to mine, his pupils had blown wide open and were surrounded by a glowing ring of gold.

"Don't ever apologize for taking what you need from me. I would give you my life if it would please you."

There was a time when all I wanted was to end him. I traced the scar I'd given him the night we met in the alley. He didn't even flinch when I stabbed him, and he made light of my violent threats. Brex had survived being bitten by a gorzin, and the Nūkiri had failed to kill him.

"A trivial platitude from someone who's immortal."

"I still feel every wound. When you've lived as long as I have, you learn to crave pain. It's far better than the numbing monotony of a life that never changes."

"And what of pleasure? Do you crave that as well?"

"I crave you." He kissed the silver bite mark on my neck as he pushed the tunic up my thighs. "I crave your scent when you're not near me, and I can't stop thinking about the taste of your sweet cunt on my tongue. But I can't fuck you here." Brex pulled away abruptly and ran a hand over his beard. "This place holds too many phantoms."

My chest ached as I watched the shadows play across his face.

I stood and offered him my hand. He'd offered me the comfort of oblivion once. It was the least I could do to return the favor.

"Then take me someplace else and let me help you forget."

Brex didn't say a word as he climbed out of the pool and wound his fingers through mine. I let him lead me deep into the palace. I was too busy counting my steps and memorizing each turn to ask where he was taking me. The soft algae lights, crumbling plaster, and elaborate mosaics gave way to dirt floors and dark tunnels. I couldn't see anything past the steady glow from his chest.

We passed a series of unadorned doors that must have been servants' quarters. The passageway narrowed, and Brex had to duck his head as we entered the last room. Three alcoves large enough for a Kateri to lie down in were carved into the walls. Something had been carved into the red clay that had been smeared over every surface. I ran my fingers over the ancient symbols.

"What is this?"

"The prophecy. These were Wu'uru's chambers. The Nūkiri locked him down here when his visions became unfavorable to their reign."

"Can you read it?"

Brex wrapped his arms around me from behind. "Are you asking me to read you the prophecy as foreplay?"

"Does it include inflections?"

"Inflections?" He slid a hand down my abdomen.

"The symbols. Did Wu'uru note the speech inflections?" I groaned and leaned into him as his hand sank lower and cupped my mound.

"His visions were all-consuming." Brex dipped his head and ghosted his lips over my throat. "He'd go into a manic state for days and weeks on end trying to get them out of his head. His writing was repetitive and rarely adhered to formal conventions. I did my best to translate it after he disappeared with the Nūkiri."

I turned in his arms, my mind racing. "Has anyone else ever seen this?" I had to find a way to get Kor into this room.

"Only those who choose to become silent disciples during their ordeal, like Inanna."

"If you think I'm going to let you cut out my—"

Brex brought his finger to my lips. "I have other plans for your pretty mouth, my queen. I plan to spend all night worshiping at the altar of your body, if you think you can handle it."

"In here?" I asked, unable to hide the unease from my voice. Getting railed by a deity was one thing; doing it surrounded by ancient religious relics was where I drew the line.

Brex laughed. "Inanna would gut me if I desecrated this room. Come, there's something else I want to show you."

Brex led me to a hidden passage. The opening appeared to be a narrow crevice until he stepped around it and disappeared behind a false wall. It opened to a vast cavern and underground lake. The mirror-like surface reflected the glowing crystals that clung to the ceiling.

"It's beautiful," I whispered.

"It's the only place in Eden palace where the Nūkiri never set foot. The caves connect to a tunnel in the catacombs. It's how Wu'uru's disciples snuck in and overthrew the vicious goddess after they stripped me of my power."

A strange scent laced the air as we approached the lake.

"What's that smell?" I asked, scrunching my nose.

"Sulfur from the hot spring that feeds the lake." A soft buzzing sensation kissed my skin as he used his shield to block the scent. He untied his pants and let them fall to the floor. I couldn't take my eyes off his muscular ass as he waded into the lake, stirring up silt in his wake. Brex was all sinew and scars. He moved with preternatural grace for someone so absurdly large.

"You're beautiful," I said.

Water rippled around his hips as he turned to face me, a strip of dark hair visible above the surface.

"Come swim with me, my queen."

My hands trembled as I stripped off my knives and tunic. I was no stranger to being stripped naked in front of an audience. Disrobing in front of him felt different.

Clay squished between my toes as I joined him next to a flat rock the size of my bed just beneath the surface. The warm water sparked with flecks of gold.

Frenzy dripped down my spine as he fisted his cocks with one hand. The monster he'd fucked me with during the rite was nestled under his slightly less intimidating shaft.

"Would you like me to teach you how to take both of them?"

My heart raced in panic as I met his gaze. I honestly didn't know if I could take all of him at once, but I wasn't going to let that stop me from trying.

"Yes."

"Get on your hands and knees, *my queen*, and let me savor you."

I crawled onto the rock and caught my breath as Brex spread my legs apart from behind. He ran his calloused hands over my pebbled flesh, moving up my outer thighs to my hips.

"You're incredible, Vaza." He kneaded my ass, spreading my cheeks wide. "Being inside you is the greatest pleasure I've ever known."

My body tensed as his fangs and beard scraped over the curve of my ass. He pressed a kiss to my cunt, and I let my head drop as he did glorious things to me with his tongue. A tingling heat spread through my core as he brought me to the edge. The orgasm rolled through me like a gentle wave, washing away all the pent-up tension in my body.

I collapsed onto the rock, completely relaxed. Brex massaged my legs, working his way up to my back. His hands were firm and warm. I didn't want him to ever stop touching me.

"Your hands are like magic."

"They're at your service anytime, my queen." He slid his fingers down my spine, collecting a gush of frenzy and pulling it down to my ass.

"Can I touch you here?" he asked, spreading me open.

"Yes." I clenched as he made a circle with his thumb, coating me with the slippery aphrodisiac.

"Relax your muscles."

He kept a reassuring palm on my backside as he applied gentle pressure with his fingers. Brex took his time familiarizing me with the sensation of him at my untouched entrance.

I sucked in a breath as he pressed the tip of his finger into me.

"Squeeze and relax for me again."

If he had to do that much work for just a finger, there was no way he was getting his cock in there. But I did as he asked, and his finger slipped inside me with ease. I whimpered as Brex moved slowly, satisfying an itch I never knew I needed to scratch. The tightness around my outer rim eased, and he pressed down and then from side to side, stretching me open.

He added another finger and repeated the process. No one had ever touched me so intimately or with so much care. My chest suddenly felt too full. The intimacy was almost too much.

"Are you ready to take more?"

I cut a glance over my shoulder as I swallowed the lump in my throat. I wanted it all. His grumpy demands and stubborn devotion. The muddy green eyes that saw too much. The way he said my name like a sigh.

I didn't tell him any of that.

"Do your worst, *zealot*. This is the only chance you'll ever get to rearrange my insides."

"As you say, my queen." His mouth twitched as he rinsed his hands in the steaming water.

I squawked as he gripped my hips and dragged me off the rock. I planted my feet in the mud as he bent me over the edge. He stepped up behind me and notched his primary shaft at my pussy. It felt just as big as it had the first time. The new angle allowed him to go even deeper. My pleasure built with each excruciatingly slow thrust.

Brex swiped more frenzy from my spine and stroked his second shaft.

I exhaled as he pressed the tip into my tight entrance. "Oh, gods." The pressure was intense, and I instinctively squeezed against it.

"Relax, my Gi'dari. You can take it."

How was I supposed to relax when he threw out words like Gi'dari? The mythical bond was sacred. An irrevocable connection seared between two souls. At least, that's what I'd read. Maybe the meaning had gotten lost in translation and meant something entirely different thousands of years ago.

I forced my sphincter to unclench and felt a small sting as the god of tides sank his second cock inside me. The deep pressure was overwhelming. He held still, letting my body adjust to accommodate him.

Brex confirmed that I was all right before resuming his slow thrusts. I reached between my legs and rubbed my swollen clit that was still hypersensitive from his thorough attention.

He held my hips as he settled into a gentle rhythm. My need built to a sharp peak with each long, backward pull.

"You feel like silk and sin." He bent over me and snaked an arm around my chest, lifting me off the stone without disconnecting our bodies as he repositioned us so that I was sitting on his lap.

I leaned back against him as he reached down and stroked my clit. Light from my chest danced across the water as I rolled my hips, moaning at the incremental slide of his cocks inside me.

My entire body went molten as his lips brushed the shell of my ear. "You have possessed me with every heartbeat and every inhale of breath. Your power over me is as irresistible as the pull of the moon on the tides."

I angled my face toward his. He captured my mouth in a kiss that laid waste to the spiked walls I'd built around myself. His chest vibrated with the same steady hum I'd once awoken to in his arms, only now, I felt it in my core.

Release ripped through my body as Brex bucked his hips, driving up into me as we broke together. His growl echoed through the cavern as he filled every empty crevice inside me. The volume of his release was greater than my body could hold. It gushed out as he separated our bodies and cradled me in his lap.

Something primal flicked across his eyes as they shifted from green to gold. He'd shown me his true self once before—when I was a breath away from death on the stone slab in Zwara's office.

I let my fingers drift over his face and scrape through his beard. "You really are a god."

His chest flared as he pressed a kiss to my forehead. "When I get my powers back, I'll make you a goddess."

Chapter Sixteen

WATER LAPPED AT MY thighs as Brex shifted beneath me. We'd fallen asleep in an exhausted tangle at the edge of the lake.

"Are you hungry?" he asked, tracing a slow circle on my lower back with his thumb.

"That depends. Are you going to force me to eat rancid meat again?"

"It's an acquired taste."

I tipped my head back and let him kiss me in the same unhurried way we'd worshiped each other's bodies all night. Like we were the only two souls left in the world. Like we weren't treading along the edge of the razor-sharp lie that would gut him the moment he learned there was no more *ki'sikilta* and he'd never regain his power.

Someone cleared their throat, and Brex smiled against my mouth. I twisted to where Inanna stood at the entrance to the cavern.

"My presence is required for a meeting," he said. "We descend to the tomb today, and I'm needed to discuss strategies now that our number has grown by three. Inanna is here to take you to your sister."

The mind mage dipped her head in greeting. I wasn't sure how to respond, so I gave her an awkward wave as I pressed off Brex's chest and went in search of my discarded clothes.

Brex pulled on his pants and gave Inanna instructions on how to ration their remaining supply of food. "If everything goes according to plan, it won't matter."

Inanna's eyes stole a curious glance in my direction.

"Soon. Don't let her out of your sight, and tell the others to keep their thoughts to themselves if they value their tongues."

Brex hugged me from behind and brushed his lips across my temple. "I'll come find you when I'm done." He turned me in his arms and tipped my chin up to face him. His eyes faded from bright gold to muddy green. "There is much I need to tell you before we make the descent. Inanna runs the outpost. She'll take care of you until I return."

I rubbed the uncomfortable pull at my chest that came whenever he wasn't near me. Like there was a tether tightening between us.

Inanna eyed the movement with a sympathetic look.

"So you're to be my guard, then?"

She grinned in silent confirmation and gestured for me to follow her. I was surprised she hadn't come for my throat. It's what I would have done had our situation been reversed. The stinging sea nettle of guilt awoke in my stomach at the memory of her leaning over Hazi as he lay dying.

"I'm sorry," I said. "For what I did to Hazi. I know what he is to you."

Inanna halted in front of me.

"I don't expect your forgiveness, I just... I wanted you to know."

The mind mage faced me, her deep brown eyes bright with an emotion I couldn't read, and I felt a gentle brush at the back of my mind.

"There's nothing to forgive." Her lips didn't move as her liquid voice flowed through my head. "You were protecting the *ki'sikilta*. I cannot fault you for that."

My chest pinched. Would she be so forgiving if she knew the truth?

The corner of her mouth twitched as she continued walking. "I should actually be thanking you."

"For what?"

"For putting Brex out of his misery. He's been unbearable since the rite. I believe you wrung every last drop of sourness out of him last night."

I bit back a smile. Maybe it was the lingering euphoria buzzing through me or the knowledge that she harbored as many secrets as I did, but I felt a kinship to the female who had every reason to hate me but didn't. "The pleasure was all mine," I said.

"Yes. We're all very well aware. The stone echoes terribly down here." Inanna pulled a waxed cloth from the belted pouch at her waist. "You should eat something. It may be a weary day for you otherwise."

I felt my face redden as we approached a guarded chamber. The sentry gave me a knowing smile as he bowed low and allowed us passage. "My queen."

"Vaza." Tesk leapt from a narrow cot and threw her arms around me. "I heard the strangest noises. I was terrified someone was being tortured."

"That's one way to define it." My mouth curled into an involuntary smile. "Don't worry. I gave the commander as good as I got."

Tesk's vivid blue eyes went wide. "I need to know everything. Now. Please tell me you made him beg on his knees."

Inanna groaned and stepped into the hall with the guard, having no interest in hearing the details.

As soon as the mind mage was out of earshot, Tesk dropped her mask of sisterly excitement and grasped my hands. "Where's Kor? Are they all right? I overheard Hazi tell one of the guards they helped you sneak in."

"I'm not sure. This place is huge. They could be anywhere. There are rooms and secret tunnels that aren't on the map. I don't think I could find my way out if I tried."

"Zwara sent me to the Rift. Why would she send you and Kor in to rescue me?"

"You were a decoy. Zwara wants us to find out what the Order is up to. She thinks they're amassing an army to move against her. Has the Order said anything about why they're taking you to Wu'uru's tomb?"

Tesk shook her head. "The commander won't let anyone talk to me about the prophecy or what's happening, even when I ask. He keeps saying that wasn't part of the deal."

He'd kept his promise not to fill Tesk's head with propaganda. My chest prickled with unease. Brex had also promised that Tesk would have a choice, then dragged her into the bowels of the ruined city under compulsion and held her against her will.

She massaged her shoulder through the fitted gorzin-skin climbing leathers they'd given her.

"Did he say anything else?" I unwrapped the waxed cloth Inanna had given me and offered Tesk the salt-dried meat.

"Hazi and Brex argued over who would use their shield to help me make the climb and keep me from falling to my death," she said through a mouthful of meat. "Brex insisted it had to be him because of a vow he made to protect me. Hazi relented and asked him if that vow was going to be a problem when it was time to open the Eye."

"The Eye?" I asked.

"The Eye of Wu'uru," Hazi said, strutting into the chamber with a set of gorzin-skin leathers draped over his arm. "The final descent will be the most dangerous part of our journey. You're going to need this." He tossed me the surprisingly light bodysuit that matched the ones he and Tesk and Inanna were already wearing. "Inanna will help you put it on."

I didn't miss the way his eyes drank up the sight of the mind mage's ass as she crossed the room. Inanna's mouth quirked at whatever silent words passed between them before Hazi left.

I dropped my skirt and stepped into the scaled armor. It was snug at my hips and hung off me like a molting skin everywhere else.

"Why does mine look like a slug carcass?"

I felt Inanna's caress at the back of my mind before her voice filtered through my head. "This one was made for someone else. It should tighten to your body if you wet it in the pool."

"And if it doesn't?" I asked.

Her nose crinkled with amusement as she turned and motioned for us to follow. "Then you'll look like a *wet* slug."

Tesk locked her arm through mine as we followed the mind mage into the corridor. "Did she just mind-speak to you?"

"It's weird, right? Do you get the tickle at the back of your brain too?"

"No. I've been asking her questions and attempting to get her to talk to me for days, and she just ignores me. Brex said I shouldn't take it personally because Inanna only does it with him and Hazi. You break the commander's vow, attempt to murder the prince, and break into their secret compound, and you're instantly part of the inner circle?"

I hugged Tesk to my side as we approached a group of guards. They brought their fists to their chests and bowed their heads as we passed.

"See," Tesk said. "They don't do that for me, and I'm their *ki'sikilta*."

"I need to tell you something," I said, keeping my voice low. "But you have to promise to let me finish before you freak out."

Her grip tightened on my arm. "You telling me not to freak out is making me freak out. What's going on?"

"The god of tides isn't dead," I said, keeping my voice low as we approached the archway that led to the massive pool I'd dropped into with Kor.

Tesk laughed and loosened her grip. "Have the zealots brainwashed you into the fold?"

"I'm serious. He's very much alive." I glanced at Inanna ten paces ahead and dropped my voice to a whisper. "And I might be his Gi'dari. At least that's what he called me when he claimed me last night." It was the first time I'd allowed myself to acknowledge the very real possibility that I was bound, for better or worse, to a deity.

Tesk halted next to the pool. "I'm sorry, did you just... did you just say the commander is the god of tides?"

"And my Gi'dari... I think."

"You think?"

"I don't know." I rubbed the tight pulling sensation at the center of my chest. "I thought the mating bond was a myth, but I thought the god of tides was dead until I saw the proof with my own eyes."

Her eyes dropped to the soft light pulsing across my bioluminescent markings. "I'm not saying he's not your bonded mate, but there's no way Brex zurNaga is the god of tides. He'd have to be thousands of years old. That's not possible."

Inanna sent a gentle brush over the back of my mind. Tesk brought her hand to the back of her head, and I knew she'd felt it too. "He's immortal," Inanna said, "just like the Nūkiri. He can't die or be killed. That hasn't stopped some from trying."

Tesk scrambled away from the water's edge as the transparent form of a gorzin swam past. Three ghostly females I recognized as the Nūkiriappeared at the far end of the pool as Inanna's projection came to life around us. The youngest goddess led Brex to the edge by a chain attached to the spiked choke collar on his neck. They'd stripped him naked and bound his wrists and ankles.

My claws extended and my body went hot with rage as they shoved him over the side. Every instinct told me to dive in after him. Inanna placed a hand on my shoulder, reminding me that it wasn't real. The water bloomed red as Brex fought the Nūkiri's pets with his bare hands. He disemboweled three of them with only his claws. A fourth serpent slithered out of the pool and coiled itself into a pile.

The serpent lunged at Brex. Its frothy mouth slammed into his side, clamped down on his torso, and pulled him beneath the surface in a death roll. I watched as the crimson water stopped churning and the lifeless body of the last gorzin floated to the surface. Brex crawled up the shallow steps in front of us and collapsed at the edge of the pool. I watched as the Nūkiri ordered their guards to drag him out to the palace gates.

Inanna's projection shifted around us, and we were in front of a gleaming triple archway overlooking ancient Eden's underground city. Mist from the waterfall gave a halo-like glow to the algae lights shining at each door and balcony. Maybe it was the sound-deadening drone of the waterfall or the missing thud of body carts in the streets, but the ancient city's past life had an eerily quiet hum.

A sharp pain pulled at my ribs as I looked up at the body hanging from the palace's gate. Blood dripped from the crescent-shaped wound on Brex's torso and pooled beneath his suspended form.

"I've seen that scar," Tesk said as her face went pale at the realization. "He told me he got it during his Ordeal."

"This was his Ordeal," Inanna said grimly.

Tesk gasped as the ghost of a figure in dark robes with a graying beard passed through her and cut him down. More robed figures came out of the shadows. Together, they lifted the god of tides and carried him into the shadows.

"Was that Wu'uru?" I asked as the mind mage's projection faded from my perception.

Inanna nodded and gestured to the crystal-clear pool that had been teeming with gorzin moments before. "You should get the leathers wet. They won't be of much use if they don't fit like a second skin."

I sat on the edge and slipped into the water. The baggy material slowly shrank around me.

"Wait." Tesk tilted her head toward Inanna. "You said Brex is immortal like the Nūkiri. If they're still alive, where are they?"

Inanna scrunched her brow as her voice floated inside my head. "I've said too much already. He'll explain everything when we get to the tomb."

I squeezed the water from my hair and climbed out of the pool. We followed her through the halls and exited through the broken triple archway. I couldn't unsee the phantom of Brex's body dangling from the stone gate.

The only light in the dark city came from the algae lanterns carried by the Order and the soft glow that pulsed from the god of tides' chest as he gave instructions to those gathered around him. A rush of relief poured through me at the sight of him. Brex stopped talking and turned toward me, as if he'd sensed my approach.

The intensity of his gaze stalled in my lungs. It was the same way Hazi looked at Inanna—possessive and reverent all at once. The truth settled like a weight in my bones. I was irrevocably bound to the god of tides. The enemy I was determined to destroy. The only male who'd ever made my body quiver with pleasure.

A knowing smile twitched at the corner of his mouth as he stalked toward me. He slid his hands over my shoulders and down my arms.

"Are you... am I your Gi'dari?" I whispered.

"We don't need to talk about it until you're ready to accept the bond."

"What if I don't want to accept it?"

His fingers snaked into my hair as he cupped my face in his massive palms. "You're already halfway there. Your body craves mine the same way it craves air. I've waited an eternity for you, *my queen*. I can wait as long as it takes for you to accept that you're mine."

I shook my head. It was too much.

"Where are your leathers?" I asked, desperate to change the subject.

"They look better on you, my love."

"Please don't call me that."

"What terms of endearment am I allowed to express?"

"None."

He dipped his head and ghosted his lips over the shell of my ear. "Then I shall make do with *Vaza* when I ache to be inside you. *My queen* when

I want to get on my knees and worship at the altar of your pleasure." Heat licked through my body as he kissed the crook of my neck where he'd claimed me. "And when I want you to know that I would lay down my life for you because you have stolen my heart and my soul, I'll call you *wraith*. When you're ready to return the sentiment, you can call me *zealot*."

"I think you intend to torture me."

"Good. I'm so glad we understand each other, *Vaza*."

I shoved away from him before I lost my resolve and begged him to call me all of those things and more.

Tesk sauntered up to us and looped her arm through mine. "What's the plan? If you're not dead, why are we traveling to Wu'uru's tomb to resurrect you?"

Brex flashed her a fanged smile. "We're going to open it so I can resurrect my power. And you, little *ki'sikilta*, are the key." He gestured to the remains of an ancient bridge that jutted out like a broken limb across the center shaft of the ancient city.

Tesk tightened her grip on my arm as we approached the jagged stone edge. The half-submerged tomb of Wu'uru rose from the mist at the base of the waterfall. Dozens of gorzin swam around the stepped rectangular structure. A giant eye with spears for lashes had been carved into the flat top where it looked up at the city above. Always watching.

"How are we supposed to get down there without being eaten alive?" Tesk asked as she pulled me back from the edge.

"That's the fun part," Hazi said, approaching with Kor in tow under his shield. "There's a rope line suspended between the underside of the bridge and the top of the tomb."

I dug my claws into her arm in warning as her body twitched with the need to go to them.

"Hazi will fly down with you and Zwara's spies," Brex said to Tesk. "It's safer than scaling down the rope line. I'll descend with Vaza, and Inanna will follow with the others."

"He's blocking their auditory senses and ability to communicate with their counterpart. We can't have them reporting what they see inside back to Zwara."

"I'll descend with you and Inanna," he said, taking his time strapping a blade to my thigh.

"What could Zwara possibly be interested in inside a dusty old tomb?" Tesk asked.

"Wu'uru's eye isn't a tomb," he said, his gaze landing on me. "It's a door."

"To what?"

"Not what, but *where*," Brex said. "Wu'uru's real name was Issor zurNella. His unique set of gifts made him the Nūkiri's favorite form of entertainment."

"Gifts? As in more than one?" I asked. "How is that possible? No mortal form can contain more than one vein of magic."

"The Nūkiri liked to experiment. They were obsessed with divining a way to create gods. Like Kor, Issor's soul was split between multiple forms. One was a seer. The other was a shadow mage."

"What's a shadow mage?" Tesk asked.

"A soul with the ability to travel great distances from their physical body without dying," Brex explained. "Issor could send his consciousness to the bottom of the ocean, the surface of the moon, and other worlds. His favorite was one covered in blue water that was free of the wasting and teeming with life.

"The goddesses were enthralled by his stories and became obsessed with traveling to this new world to gorge themselves on its bounty and seeding a new civilization to rule over. They devised a way to use the power they stole from me to alter Issor's gift and turn it into a permanent gateway between the two worlds. Once they passed through, however, it locked behind them."

"I don't understand how fucking Tesk and relieving her of her virginity is going to help you unlock this door or get your powers back." The words were out of my mouth before I could pull them back.

"Do you still have so little faith in me?" Disgust and disappointment flashed across Brex's face in turn. "No one is going to defile your sister. How could you even think me capable of such a thing after all we've been through?"

"The prophecy, the vows of celibacy in honor of the virgin queen. The Order's sudden willingness to participate in the rite. The abductions and all the effort you've put into keeping her pure." I massaged my forehead to relieve the throbbing sensation pulsing through my skull. I was tired of lies and manipulation. Brex deserved to know the truth. "Tesk isn't your—"

She gripped my wrist. "Let's hear them out before we say something we can't take back, Vee." Her gaze darted to Kor, and that brief look of desperation told me she would do anything to protect the secret they shared.

"What kind of sacrifice is required to open the gateway?"

"We're not sure," Brex said. "But the Nūkiri scrawled an inscription on the stone altar beneath the portal. It says only the *ki'sikilta* can open Wu'uru's eye."

Tesk glanced over Brex's shoulder at Kor. "I'd like to read this inscription."

༄

I told myself none of this was real. That I was having a nightmare and *not* dangling above a lake of hungry gorzin between Brex and Inanna. The burn of rope against my blistered palms begged to differ.

My only consolation was that Tesk was already safe at the top of Wu'uru's tomb with Hazi, thanks to Kor.

Brex hadn't spoken a word since I'd refused the help of his compulsion to repel down from the bridge to the horizontal rope that stretched between the two structures. I kept my arms straight and my shoulders relaxed as I passed one hand over the other and let my legs do the work as we traversed backward at a snail's pace.

We paused so Inanna and I could rest and catch our breath. Brex's bare shoulders were raw from repelling down without the protection of his climbing leathers, but he wasn't even close to being winded. I let my head fall back and groaned. We were only halfway across.

A familiar caress brushed the back of my mind as Inanna projected her voice into my head. "The worst part is almost over."

"Until we have to go back."

"If you choose to go back."

I didn't have time to dissect the mind mage's comment. A juvenile gorzin lunged from the water to escape the snapping jaws of a larger predator. It slammed against my back, knocking me from the rope.

I heard Tesk scream before my body hit the surface. My skin buzzed as Brex wrapped his shield around me and dropped into the lake. The metallic scent of blood stuffed up my nose as he compelled me to swim faster than I ever thought I'd be capable of.

My chest tightened with panic as I propelled away from him. Something big swam beneath me toward the spot where I'd dropped into the water.

"I'm right behind you. We're almost there."

Something slimy brushed against my leg. "What was that?"

"Keep swimming. The snakes won't be able to scent you with all the blood in the water."

"Please tell me it isn't your blood."

"Your lack of faith is really starting to sting."

My feet found the submerged level of the stepped tomb. Brex shoved me toward the wall where Hazi leaned over the edge on his belly. He grabbed my wrists and pulled me up to the platform.

When I scrambled back to the edge to help Brex, he was gone. Hazi dove into the black water with a blade in each hand. Inanna dropped to the ground and wrenched an arm around my waist when I moved to follow.

Light flashed beneath the surface, and I caught glimpses of Hazi's pale hide. Brex's head popped up a moment later, followed by the prince. Three juvenile gorzin floated to the surface behind them.

Inanna let me go and threw down a rope. I ran to Brex as he shoved to his feet, checking him for injuries.

"Did it bite you? Are you hurt?"

He wrapped his arms around me with a smug smile. "Immortal. Remember?"

"I'm pretty sure you can still lose an appendage."

He brought his lips to my ear. "I know how fond you are of my various appendages. It would be a shame to disappoint you by losing one."

"We have a problem," Kor's female form said from where they stood with my deathly pale sister. "The high priestess is on her way with a small army to collect the queens. They left yesterday when they lost touch with us."

"You need to get Tesk and Vaza inside the tomb before Zwara gets here. I'll take care of the mind mage," Hazi said, moving toward Kor.

"Wait." Brex studied the protective wall Kor had made around Tesk. "You didn't fly off with the *ki'sikilta* the moment you were free. Why?"

"Because I wouldn't let them," Tesk said. "And if you want me to help you, they stay with me."

"Fine. We don't have time to argue." Brex dipped his head and pounded a quick rhythmic pattern on the tomb's stone door. He stood back as it pivoted open on a central axis. A dozen guards emerged. "The high priestess will be here soon. Put out the lights and pull in the mist to hide the entrance. No one gets past this threshold. Seal the tomb behind us."

They brought their fists to their chests and took up a defensive position. The echo of a low chant replaced the thundering rush of water as the stone slab pivoted shut.

The temperature dropped as Hazi led us down a ramped tunnel into the heart of the tomb. Globes of bioluminescent algae gilded the walls with an eerie green glow.

Brex intertwined his fingers with mine as the chanting grew louder. My skin pebbled with the vibration of so many voices speaking in unison.

Four more guards met us at the end of the ramp. The stench of unwashed bodies crammed up my nose as we stepped into a ledge overlooking a chamber twice as high and wide as the temple baths high above in the upper city.

"I believe we've solved the mystery of the missing Order members," Kor's female form said. "There must be thousands down here. How is the Order feeding everyone?"

"We're not," Hazi said, gesturing to the side. But I didn't turn in the direction he indicated. I couldn't. My attention was fixed on the dais rising above the sea of bowed heads at the center of the chamber.

An undulating pearl-like sphere as tall as two Kateri hovered above the stone. Iridescent light swirled over its surface like oil on water.

"Now you know all my secrets, little spy," Brex said beside me.

"The Nūkiri made this?" I said, reluctantly dragging my eyes away from the orb, unsure if I was asking a question or making a statement. "It's beautiful."

A somber smile pursed his lips. "Come, let me introduce you to Wu'uru."

My empty stomach knotted around itself as we followed the others down a final ramp to the chamber floor. If anyone noticed Brex's possessive arm around my shoulder, they didn't show it. I couldn't help but wonder if I had been the last to know.

All eyes were on Tesk.

Reverent hands reached up to touch her as we skirted around the edge of the crowd, and an entirely new fear jolted through me. The Order didn't worship Brex. They worshiped my sister—their saint and savior. The *ki'sikilta* who they believed could open a door to another world. A new beginning. A different life. One free of the wasting.

Except Tesk wasn't the *ki'sikilta*. Kor's female form shot me a wary look, having come to the same realization. What would a crowd of devout, desperate souls do when they found out my sister wasn't the precious virgin queen they'd been waiting for?

Chapter Seventeen

LIAM

Renae ran her hands over the thing's faceted surface. A faint light at its core pulsed softly like it recognized her.

"That thing isn't me." Static gathered and sputtered out in my palm. It was impossible to gather a charge in the damp cave.

"It's part of you. The part of you controlling this entire island. The one that won't let you leave." She swallowed hard as her syphons roved over it. "It tastes like you."

"The island tried to kill you, Renae. No part of me would ever hurt you."

"Not intentionally." She stood and placed her body in front of it like a shield, spreading her arms wide. "Your father planted all seven sacred gifts inside you in an attempt to create a living god. One of those gifts is the ability to split your soul between multiple forms. When you had the aneurysm, I think it triggered that gift to protect you."

"Is that what *it's* telling you?"

"It's what *you're* telling me. You're my Gi'dari. I'm bound to every piece of you. Even the broken bits you try to hide. That's why you walled this place off. Your subconscious knew what I'd find if I went poking around."

"Nice theory. Now I need you to step aside. I don't care if it's a part of me or not. It hurt you and needs to be destroyed before it tries again. We'll both be safer with it gone."

Renae lunged for me as I sidestepped around her and grabbed my crystal doppelganger's skull. She clawed at my arms, trying to pry them away from the thing that had almost killed her.

"Stop. You're going to destroy him."

"That's the point." I shoved her away from me, and she landed on her ass on the wet floor. "I need to cut out the rotten, useless part of me. Once it's gone, everything will be better. I'll be in control."

"Liam, please. If you destroy that part of yourself, it could sever our bond. Is that what you want?"

My palms went hot as I squeezed its head. Fire exploded in my head as the black crystal flashed red and the entire network of crystal veins strobed erratically. The cavern shook as I screamed.

Renae was right. I couldn't destroy it without hurting myself. I ripped my palms away and sat back on my heels, seething with rage.

I'm not sure how long we sat there in silence with Renae hugging her knees while I stared at the worst part of me.

"You don't understand," I said.

She heaved a sigh beside me. "You're right. I don't understand what it was like to be an addict. But I know what it's like to feel helpless and out of control—to be a hostage in my own body when the panic takes over and I spiral until all I want to do is cocoon myself in a dark hole and never climb out again."

Okay, maybe she did understand.

Renae rose to her knees and brushed the hair away from my face. "You asked me not to give up on you. I need you to not give up on yourself."

I hugged her to my chest. She'd always been my anchor in a goddamned storm. I wanted to be that for her too—the person who was willing to crawl down in that dark hole with her and help her drag her ass back into the light.

"Any brilliant ideas on how we can get back to Almega without an Astral?"

I felt her smile against me. "First, we need to figure out how to reconnect the two splintered parts of your gift."

"The thing is attached to the floor. We'd need pickaxes to get it out."

"We don't need the body. We need the energy inside it. I can connect you to it with my syphons, but you're going to have to take control of them through the bond to pull the power back inside you."

"You're confident this will work?" I stood and helped her up.

Her lips curled into a wicked smile as she tipped her head back, revealing the long column of her neck. "Do you need a refresher on how the claiming works?"

I'd relived taking full control of her body and gift in my head more times than I could count. I'd never forgotten the way it felt to pour myself into her. To fill her up completely until she overflowed.

I placed my palm over her thudding heart, then slid it up and wrapped my fingers around her throat. "Oh, I remember."

"Don't hold back. This only works if you take me completely."

I backed her against the glowing crystal column and could already feel the power rising inside me as I teased her mouth open. She'd trusted me with her gift once before. This woman who didn't trust anyone and who'd been a pawn in everyone else's agenda was giving me complete access again, and I'd done nothing to deserve it. I'd been prickly and controlling and an absolute ass, and she still offered me everything.

She brought her hand up to mine where it was braced against the wall above her head and wound her fingers through mine. The first time I'd claimed her had been fueled by an overwhelming need to possess. To take what was mine. This was different.

I swept her mouth with my tongue and let my energy seep into her, slow and languid. She arched against me as I poured my energy into her. Sulfur slicked my tongue for a brief moment before I blocked it with the projection of brandy and cream from her memory that she loved. Renae's groan of pleasure reverberated through my chest, and I wanted—*needed*—to give her more. To fill every crevice inside her.

She already had my heart and my bond, but it wasn't enough. I needed to give her all of me. Even the broken and rotten bits that left a foul taste in her mouth that I was doing my best to cover with a projection.

Stop trying to protect me and let go. Renae's thoughts echoed through my head as if she was miles away.

A prickling sensation crawled over the back of my head as I dropped the façade. Renae let out another deep, throaty groan as my power surged through her body and I took control of her syphons. I sent them behind me and speared my doppelganger with their hollow hooks, taking big, slurping gulps of his oily black core. The burn of cheap bourbon slid down my throat and exploded through my chest.

Sharp crystals jabbed my shoulder and hips. My entire body ached as I stretched out my stiff, heavy limbs.

"You did it." Renae jumped on top of me as I rolled onto my back.

She kissed my forehead, and I was immediately aware of three things. I was lying on the ground in the center of the cavern where my crystal doppelganger had been. I was covered in some kind of iridescent black dust, and the cavern was disintegrating around us.

The cave rumbled, and I didn't have time to process what had just happened. Renae yanked me up off the floor as part of the ceiling collapsed.

"What the hell is happening?"

"I think you broke the illusion that has been holding this place together when you reintegrated your conscious mind with your subconscious self."

"How do I unbreak it?"

Renae's eyes shot to what remained of the ceiling. "You need to travel us out of here. Now."

"I'd love to, chica, but that is the one gift that abandoned me when I arrived. I haven't been able to travel since."

"It didn't abandon you. It was here the whole time, sleeping in crystalline stasis. You're not fractured anymore." Renae gripped my shoulders. "Ziggy had to punch a hole in the Void to send me in. If we can repeat what she did, you might be able to jump us back to Almega. Take us to the spot I landed when I first got here. If I haven't healed yet, maybe the Void hasn't either. That's where we need to try to rip a new hole."

I had no idea if it would work, but Renae hadn't been wrong yet, so I wrapped my arms around her and let my memory drift to the day she crashed my personal purgatory. She'd hurtled across the sky like a meteor and crashed onto the beach right in front of me, leaving a huge impact crater. It was the second time she'd crashed into my life unexpectedly. The first was the day we met. She'd stepped right out in front of my motorcycle in that blue dress.

The scent of gasoline burned my nose as I opened my eyes and looked over Renae's shoulder at my wrecked bike in the middle of the empty street. The absence of any other signs of life and earth-shaking rumble beneath my feet meant we were still in the Void.

"Why are we in downtown Hilo? This isn't the right spot, Liam."

"This is where our story began. Where my traveler ability awoke." The pavement made a groaning sound as a narrow crack split down the center line.

"It will be where it ends if we don't get out of here. Take us back to the beach. The membrane between worlds will be thinner there and easier to break through."

The hair on the back of my neck rose as the memory of another beach crept into my head.

"Say that again."

"We need to find the spot where the membrane between worlds is thinner so we can go home."

Monika had said almost the exact same thing to me the night I broke her heart and chose Renae.

"We need to go to the sacred beach in Kona. Monika dragged me to a play there years ago. She said the membrane was thinner there because it was a door to the spirit realm. I thought it was just another one of her ghost stories, but there might be something to it." I grasped Renae's hand. "I need you to show me exactly what my mother did to send you here."

"Okay."

I closed my eyes and read what Renae had seen right before she was sucked into the Void.

"Can you replay it a little slower?"

"I can try."

Her memory replayed through my own filtered perception, revealing nuances only I could see. My mother drew energy from everything around her—the air and the ground beneath her feet—and shot it into the Astral in a single massive bolt.

Renae grabbed my arm as the ground opened up and swallowed my motorcycle whole.

"Liam, we need to go."

I closed my eyes as I pulled her against my chest and recalled the memory I needed from the night Monika dragged me to that damn play. I focused on the way the soft sand had still felt warm beneath my feet that night despite the icy breeze that rolled off the mountains. The way the jetty wall buffered the waves and made the beach eerily quiet.

A wave of chicken skin ran down my arms and legs. When I opened my eyes, Renae and I were at the Point just south of Kona, or my memory of it, anyway. The moon was high in the sky, and I wasn't sure if we'd moved or if the Void had transformed around us. Deep fissures had split the ground, and it felt like the island was coming apart at the seams.

"Come on." I grasped her hand and ran down the narrow jetty wall as I forced my vision to shift. There was a dark spot at the end, a void in the chaotic energy that surrounded it. "I found our exit."

Sand and water rose into the air. The jetty wall shook violently. We lost our footing and cracked down on our hands and knees.

"We're gonna need to jump. But I'm not sure that I can steer us to Almega on my own."

"Then use me as your anchor. Draw on my memories of the harvest fields."

"I'll need both my hands to wield my gift and rip a hole in the door. We've only got one shot at this, so I'm gonna need you to do exactly what I say. You're gonna cling to my back like a jet pack and think of the exact spot you want to land."

She climbed onto my back and locked her arms and legs around my body. I stood and took off in a dead run. Her memories of a blood-red field and the obsidian city behind it played through my mind. Ghostly figures flickered in and out of existence as the golden haze collected around them.

My bare feet pounded against the lava stone wall. I pulled in energy from the water and air around us and sent a bolt of electricity directly into what I hoped was an exit. I had no idea if it would work or what we'd do if it did, but we couldn't stay here any longer.

An ear-splitting crack pierced my skull. The end of the jetty cleaved from the rest of the wall and dropped away beneath my feet. I braced for the impact of cold water as we fell, but there was no splash.

We were falling in the dark.

The rock we'd been standing on was falling too, tumbling ass over end and coming straight for us. I shot it with another beam of plasma, trying to direct it away from us. It blew back toward the expanding hole I'd just ripped in the Void, and I could see the island disintegrating on the other side. More debris came flying toward us as we fell. I unleashed everything I had. The chunk of rock and rebar melted and sealed itself over the hole like a patch.

We exploded onto the field like a bomb, sending out a shockwave that was sure to draw attention. A blob of water and debris hit the field like a giant water balloon, sending insects hissing into the air.

I immediately rolled over to check Renae for injuries, but she was already on her feet.

"Fuck, that was close," I said as she yanked me up off the ground.

"It's not over yet."

I followed her gaze to the three cloaked figures moving toward us.

"That doesn't look like a welcoming party."

"When I asked the Nūkiri to send me into the Void, they refused because they knew I was determined to break you out. With all seven gifts sown inside you, you possess the power of a living god. They have a long history of destroying anything that could rise up against them. They must have sent a patrol to the field to intercept us."

"What's the plan?" I asked as I gathered a charge and forced my vision to shift.

Renae grabbed my wrist as I raised my arm, ready to strike. I wouldn't hesitate to fry these fuckers if they tried to take her.

"No. Keep your head and hands down and don't do anything that could be perceived as a threat unless you want to get sent right back into the Void."

"That sounds like a surrender."

"Exactly. The only way to return to Earth is through an Astral. The Nūkiri control every Astral in Almega. If we want to get back to our bodies, we need to beg them for forgiveness and do whatever they ask."

CHAPTER EIGHTEEN

V/AZA

THREE INKY-BLACK POOLS STRETCHED from the base of the dais. Up close, Wu'uru's eye looked less like a pearl and more like the body of a giant sea nettle. I could see almost all the way through its gelatinous flesh.

"Why are the pools filled with silver solution?" Tesk asked as she circled the dais, getting a look at the sphere from all sides.

"Wu'uru communicates through touch and will drain your energy if you don't coat your hands first." Brex nodded to me. "Go ahead, give it a try."

I dipped my hand in the pool and climbed onto the dais. The hair on the back of my neck rose as I got closer. I could swear I felt it looking at me. The iridescent swirls on its surface shifted toward me as if it could sense my presence.

A buzzing sensation bit at my palm when I touched the surface. It felt the same as when Zwara's gift had tried to attack me while I dug the glass from Hazi's lung. A body-shaped shadow appeared beneath my hand, as if someone pressed back from the inside.

"It's been so long since we've felt the touch of a queen." I yanked my hand away at the strange voice that echoed through my head.

Brex climbed up beside me and placed a dripping hand on the orb with a scowl. "I should have warned you. He hasn't eaten today. He may be in a mood."

"A mood?"

Brex stroked the glowing ball gently before pulling his hand away. "He wants to talk to you."

The buzzing sensation returned as I pressed my palm to the opaque surface.

"I can taste him on you." The voice had a mushy affect, like its tongue was too thick to form words properly. "You are exactly as I envisioned so long ago. Place your other hand on me so that I may get a better look at my master's Gi'dari."

Brex caught my wrist as I lifted my arm. "That will only tempt him to drain you."

The orb flashed, and the shadow shot over the surface to the other side. I raced around the dais and found Tesk with both of her bare palms pressed against it. The dark shadow crawled up her arms in snaking black lines. Kor's male form tugged at her body from behind, but Tesk's hands remained seared to Wu'uru's eye. The black shadows crept to her elbows. I made to pound my fist against the blubbery mass, and my hand shot through it as if it were made of water.

The entity released Tesk, and Kor tumbled off the dais with my sister in their arms. The crowd surged forward with a collective hum of concern. Hazi pushed them back as Inanna and Brex built a protective wall around her.

I pressed my oiled hand to the surface again—a singular thought in my mind. *Did you just try to consume my sister?*

"She asked to see how the *kisikilta* opened me once before. It's ravenous work, I'm afraid. There will be a heavy cost to unlock me."

"Let go." Brex's arms were around my middle, tugging me back from where I gripped someone else's hand.

When I forced my eyes open, my arm was buried past my elbow inside the gelatinous orb. There was no shadow. Just the sensation of someone gripping my hand from the other side.

"I look forward to meeting you soon, my queen." It released me, and I fell back against Brex.

"How did you do that?" he asked, turning me around and inspecting my arm.

"Where's my sister?"

"I'm fine," Tesk said as Kor helped her up. She didn't have enough energy to even stand on her own.

I shoved away from Brex. "You promised she'd be safe. That fucking thing just tried to eat her."

"She didn't silver her hands. How is it that you were able to breach the Eye's surface? No one's ever managed to do that before."

The weight of every gaze pressed in around me. The silent crowd. Tesk. Brex.

"I don't know. It just pulled me in."

"What did he say to you?" Brex asked.

"He called the Nūkiri *ki'sikilta*, but the inflection was all wrong. He said the goddesses used blood, fire, and ice to lock him. I think what he did to Tesk was a warning about the cost of attempting to open him again."

"Did he say anything to you?" Brex asked Tesk.

She shook her head, but I knew my sister. The innocent look she plastered on her face told me it was a lie.

"We'll make sure he's properly fed. Are you willing to try again, with the silver, after you've rested?"

Tesk gave him a reluctant nod, and Brex instructed someone to collect a donation of rations for the *ki'sikilta* while Inanna found a secluded alcove where Tesk could recover without everyone watching.

There was just enough space for the four of us to spread out on the floor. Kor's female form leaned against the wall next to me while their counterpart cradled Tesk's head in their lap. She'd fallen asleep as they stroked her shimmery blue-black hair.

"She loves you best," Kor's female form said, gently tracing the fading black veins on my sister's outstretched arm.

"I'm not so sure about that. You're the first face she'll look for when she wakes and the only soul I trust to put my sister's safety above whatever that thing is out there."

"A sentient portal to another world with a craving for Kateri flesh?"

"Do you think it's true? That there are other worlds out there?"

They shrugged. "Does it matter if Wu'uru's eye can't be opened?"

"What if it can? There has to be something we're missing. How close is Zwara?"

"They're almost at the ancient palace," Kor's male form said. "It won't take them long to realize no one's there and come looking for us."

I lowered my voice. "Can you send her a message?"

Kor cocked a curious brow.

"Brex showed me the original prophecy. It's etched into the walls of Wu'uru's chambers inside the palace."

"You're just now telling us this?"

"It was a little difficult to work it into conversation while we were surrounded by zealots. They cut out tongues to keep its location secret." I extend a claw. "But I can draw you a map."

I scratched out the path on the floor. "Take Zwara there and tell her everything except the part about Brex being the god of tides. I know my sister. When this is done, she'll find a way to use that information for her own benefit."

Kor's female form straightened. "As soon as the high priestess finds out about the giant eyeball out there, you know she'll do whatever it takes to control it."

"We don't have a choice. Like it or not, we need her. We won't be able to get out of here on our own when they find out Tesk can't unlock the Eye."

"You would betray your Gi'dari to see Zwara maintain her power?"

Tesk stirred in their lap.

"Brex knows where my loyalties lie." I dropped my gaze to my twin. I believed Brex when he said he wouldn't hurt her, but he had no control over Wu'uru. There was no way I'd allow Tesk to put her hands on it again.

"The entire Order is out there," Kor said. "It's us against thousands. Even with Zwara's help, we won't be able to take them if there's a fight."

"It won't come to that if you can decipher the original prophecy and find a way to open the prophet's eye."

"We have a more immediate problem," Tesk said as she sat up. "The Eye knows I'm not the *ki'sikilta*. He warned me not to come back without the real virgin queen."

"Did he mention where we might find this mythical creature?"

"We need to go back out there and read the inscription beneath the dais."

❧

Tesk stood next to Kor and studied the symbols chiseled into the stone.

"Is this intended to be a jest?" she asked, glancing between Kor's dual forms.

"It's an epitaph," Brex said. "A bit of poetic levity meant to be hurled back and forth between drunken mourners in honor of the dead. The tradition grew tiresome when the bodies piled up in the street began to outnumber the living."

"What does it say?" I asked.

Tesk cleared her throat and stumbled through the inscription and then read it a second time. "The great prophet Wu'uru worshiped the god of tides with his last breath. Too bad he failed to foresee his master's death. In blood the key doth lie, to unlock Wu'uru's all-seeing eye. When all are gathered, his eye will bloom, for only the *kisikilta* can open his tomb."

"That's it?" I asked.

"The word *kisikilta* is repeated multiple times without any inflections, but that's the basic translation."

"Actually," Kor said, circling around the dais, "*kisikilta* is repeated exactly three times, which would indicate a plural form of the word."

"As in more than one virgin queen?" Tesk asked with an incredulous grunt.

"It's also etched into the floor at the end of each pool." Kor's female form crouched and ran their fingers over the dusty markings. "When was the last time these floors were cleaned?"

"Never," Brex said.

Kor glared up at him. "These are ancient artifacts. You should take better care of them."

"You'll have to excuse our lack of hospitality. The Order's been a little busy fighting the wasting and taking care of the sick and dying."

"May I borrow your water skin, Commander?"

He handed it over, and Kor doused the floor. They used the tip of their claw to scrape out the millennia of grime that had settled into the chiseled word.

"Come look at this. It's worn down, but this one includes a mark indicating inflection."

Tesk and I squatted next to them.

"See this dot? It means the inflection comes after the first syllable. Ki'*sikilta*," Kor enunciated. "It means untouched."

"This one has two dots," Kor's male form said from behind the dais. "Kisi*'kilta*."

Tesk grabbed the water skin and darted to the final oil-filled pool. "This one has three." Her voice lilted up. "Kisikil*'ta*."

"Virgin, fertile, and barren," Kor said as they stood. "All used to describe a queen's mating status in old contracts for the rite."

"The Nūkiri referred to themselves the same way," Brex said. "Those designations were derived from their names."

"If I'm reading this correctly," Kor's female form said, "it requires the touch of three blood-related queens."

"Which means we can't open the Eye." Tesk exhaled with relief. "Vaza and I are the only queens who survived our spawn. That proves I'm not the *ki'sikilta*."

Every head swiveled to a commotion on the ramp where a patrol of shield and storm mages escorted Zwara and Kor's second male form into the tomb. No one would be able to touch her under their protection.

Brex pulled me behind him as Kor stepped in front of Tesk.

"Please excuse my late arrival, Commander zurNaga. I came as soon as I got the summons."

"What makes you think you were invited, blood mage?"

Zwara's gaze swept over Tesk and me. "I received a rather urgent one from my dear sisters that Kor was more than happy to relay."

"I told you we couldn't trust the spirit mage," Hazi said, flashing his fangs. "Seize them."

"Don't blame the messenger, Prince Hazi. Kor merely relayed Queen Vaza's request that I bring an army to come retrieve them."

Brex turned to face me. "Is it true?"

"The only thing I've ever tried to do is protect my sister."

"What about last night? Were you protecting the *ki'sikilta* then?"

"Last night was a temporary truce."

His face pinched as if he was in physical pain. "You betrayed me."

"I told you I was a spy."

"You're my Gi'dari." The tugging ache threatened to rip the ribs from my chest as he backed away from me. "I would have done anything to protect you and your sister."

"I made no promises to you beyond agreeing to take Tesk's place in the rite."

"I think we can all agree about what a beautiful performance it was." Zwara smirked as she moved toward the dais. "Vaza went above and beyond my expectations when I asked her to get close to you and learn all your secrets, Commander. My stubborn little wraith turned out to be my most valuable asset."

"You knew?" I asked through clenched teeth.

"Who do you think ordered Hemeda to follow you out to the cliff after your first rite? I couldn't allow you to embarrass me again by killing another mate, so I allowed you an outlet to work out all that pent-up rage. I paid Hemeda to keep you from doing anything foolish. Like stabbing a member of the Order."

Hot tears welled in my eyes. "Hemeda's dead."

"What?" Tesk choked back a sob.

"An unfortunate bit of fate that could have been prevented if you hadn't been so reckless and led the Order straight to her door."

"Enough," Brex growled as he drew his blade. "What do you want, Zwara?"

"I'm here to help you open the Eye of Wu'uru. Tesk isn't the *ki'sikilta*," Zwara said, dipping her hand in one of the silver pools. "She can't open the portal because she's not a virgin."

Whispers slithered through the crowd like the slow hiss of scales over stone. Every head swiveled to where two of Kor's bodies made a protective circle around Tesk, claws and fangs primed.

Brex's eyes flashed gold as he pointed his blade at my chest. "Did you know?"

The tears I'd been holding back for days spilled down my cheeks. "I'm sorry."

I was sorry that I'd lied to him. I was sorry that he was my enemy and that I'd wished him dead more times than I could count. That I hadn't been there for Hemeda and that I couldn't allow myself to love someone who'd held my sister and me hostage, no matter how he justified it. A cage was a cage.

"Did you really think I'd allow the Order to usurp my power without putting in a safeguard? I knew whatever you planned hinged on my sweet sister being a virgin, so I arranged for a private mating ceremony in my chambers between Tesk and Kor."

There was a palpable shift in energy from reverent devotion to confused panic as realization spread through the starving crowd. There was no more virgin queen. The prophecy wouldn't be fulfilled.

Zwara's guards forced the Order back as the high priestess climbed the dais, hand dripping with the black oil.

"Faith is such a fickle thing. It can turn in a moment, transforming a horde of worshipers into enemies with their teeth at your throat. That's why I only deal in death and desire. They're the only constants in this unforgiving world."

More of Zwara's soldiers pressed into the chamber as she circled the iridescent orb. The shadow within followed her. She trailed her fingers over the surface in a gentle caress. Light pulsed from the center of the orb like a beating heart beneath her touch.

Zwara's lips twitched as she threw a command at Kor's softer male form, who stood at the base of the dais. "Bring my sisters to me."

"So you can feed them to the Eye? We think not, darling."

Zwara flinched.

In all my life, I'd never seen her unflappable demeanor erode. The stunned look of betrayal that washed over her features only lasted a moment. "Seize the queens."

My skin buzzed as Brex wrapped his arms around me, dragging me away from the dais as the chamber erupted into chaos. The high priestess's storm mages carved a path through the crowd, most of whom were too weak to fight back. Those who did were cut down easily by the well-fed mages. Lightning shot from their hands and crackled over Brex's shield.

The first few attackers who crossed through the barrier dropped to the ground and didn't move. Kor sent out a violent gust of wind from the base of the dais, toppling the guards headed for Tesk.

Hazi and Inanna drew their blades as his shield disintegrated under a barrage of electrical strikes. The tickle at the back of my brain was the only warning I had before the growl of a giant gorzin shook the stone walls. The beast slithering through the entrance drew the soldiers' attention.

"The projection won't fool them for long," Brex said as he extended his shield over Inanna, Hazi, and Kor.

I scanned the gaunt faces of his followers—every single one of them had willingly sacrificed something to serve him. That kind of devotion couldn't be bought and sold, and I knew that Brex would do whatever it took to protect them. Zwara would do whatever it took to protect herself and her power.

And when I want you to know that I would lay down my life for you because you have stolen my breath and my heart and I am irrevocably possessed by you, I'll call you wraith.

I struggled against his grip. "Give me a blade, *zealot*. I can help."

"By stabbing us in the back again?" Hazi asked as Zwara's storm mages resumed their assault on Brex's shield.

"It won't hold much longer. Be ready," Brex warned. He brought his lips to my ear and pressed the hilt of his knife into my hands. "Let's give them a show, *wraith*."

He shoved me away from him and drew his remaining blade.

"What are you doing?" Hazi growled under his breath.

"*My queen* would like to see me on my knees with a knife at my throat." Everyone stilled as Inanna projected his deep voice through the chamber. "But she's still my mate, and I won't leave her without a weapon to defend herself." He raised his blade to me.

"I don't want to fight you, *zealot*."

"Don't threaten me with a good time, *Vaza*." His lip curled in a seductive smile. "Do your worst, *wraith*."

"Only a fool would pick a fight with an immortal." I flashed my fangs. "Release Tesk and let us be done with this."

"Take your sisters and get out of my tomb."

Kor's male and female forms went preternaturally still behind Brex as Hazi and Inanna stepped aside. Tesk scurried toward me. The way her feet shuffled awkwardly along the floor told me she was moving under his compulsion. I hugged her to my side and whispered for her to play along and run to Kor's male form at the base of the Eye.

Zwara laughed as I left the safety of my mate's shield and took an obedient position behind her. "Thank you for returning my sisters to me, Commander. Like my priestesses, they are loyal to the core. I harbor no hard feelings toward you or the Order. We want the same things after all."

I reached around from behind and held the blade to her throat. "I doubt that very much, your highness."

"Love and loyalty are fickle when forced," Brex said. "They must be earned. If you want someone to share their secrets or lay down their life for you, you must be willing to do the same for them in return." Every member of the Order got on their knees as his chest erupted with a blinding light that matched the flare shining through my gorzin-skin leathers. "It took a knife to the gut and the sharp tongue of a snarky, irreverent, scornful, and exquisitely perfect queen to remind me that a dead god makes a good martyr and a terrible leader for a dying world."

He let his eyes shift from green to a brilliant glowing gold.

"I'm tired of living in the shadows." One by one, Zwara's soldiers took a knee as Brex strolled toward the dais. "I will find a way to open the Eye. I will get my powers back, and I will take my revenge on the Nūkiri."

Zwara's face went pallid as she dropped her chin to her chest before the god of tides.

"Forgive me. As high priestess, I ask only to continue to serve at your mercy."

"Give me one reason why I should allow such a farce after the horrific things you've done to my Gi'dari to further your own power."

Zwara smiled as she lifted her eye to Brex. "Because I'm the *ki'sikilta*, and I've been saving myself for you."

I choked back a laugh. There was no end to the lengths Zwara would go to maintain her position as high priestess. "You're no more a virgin than I am. Everyone in Eden knows you pay Kor as your personal consort."

"I've paid them very well for their services as an adviser and spy. Nothing more."

"It's true," Kor's male form said, threading their fingers through Tesk's. "We've spent many nights in the high priestess's chambers, but we've never fucked her."

"If you were a queen, I would have scented it," Brex said. "I wouldn't have missed something like that."

"I was studying under Hemeda when I came into my first heat. I was the best apprentice in the House of Blood, and she'd already presented me to the previous high priestess as a potential successor. If anyone ever found out I'd been stealing souls from my clutch and faking my gift right under their noses, they would have cruciated me and thrown us both into the Rift's prison. So I convinced her to remove my scent glands."

"That's why there are so few healers left. You've consumed them all." Brex's arm shot out, and he wrapped his huge hand around Zwara's delicate throat. "Do you know how many lives could have been saved if we had enough blood mages to go around? I should fucking kill you right now."

I placed my hand on his forearm. "Zwara may be a manipulative cunt, but she's still my sister, and I'm not sure I could forgive you if you rip out her throat."

"Zwara is right," Tesk said, climbing the dais. "Wu'uru showed me what we need to do. It can only be opened by all three of us. A virgin, a fertile female, and a barren one. He showed me a memory of the Nūkiri bathing in the silver pools. It allowed them to hold his eye open for a short time before it sucked them in. If we do this, it's a one-way trip."

"To where?" Zwara asked.

"Earth," Brex said. "The realm of the Nūkiri and a thriving civilization of Kateri hybrids."

⁊

My butt went numb sitting on the floor, listening to Hazi explain the Order's extensive plans for what would happen after we open the Eye of Wu'uru. Brex wrapped his arms around me as I leaned back against him.

"The Nūkiri took Wu'uru's other form, Issor zurNella, with them when they went through the portal. Through him, we've learned many things about life on the fertile blue planet. The Order's scholars are well versed in the history, languages, and cultures of the human civilization. Issor has been hiding from the goddesses among the humans and preparing the way for us."

Tesk entwined her blackened fingers with one of Kor's male forms. The way her face softened as she watched the shadow move within the orb told me she didn't hold a grudge against the part of Wu'uru's soul that was trapped inside, even though he attempted to eat her.

"Why is he in hiding?" Tesk asked.

Zwara gave an incredulous grunt from where she sat off to the side a good distance away from the rest of the group. "I'm assuming he's no longer in the goddesses' favor."

"Humans thrive while we struggle to survive, but they're not without their problems," Hazi continued. "The planet was nearly destroyed when Issor led a rebellion against the Nūkiri in the All Souls War. In the time since, he's been evading their assassins and preparing the way for the god of tides and his followers to join him. A mind mage has been assigned to every scouting pod, and we've imbued them with the rudimentary knowledge of the language, culture, and instructions on how and where to find Issor zurNella. Once we open the portal and start sending pods through, Wu'uru will send us to hatchling nurseries all over the planet, where we'll find hybrid human-Kateri husks to inhabit."

"Wait, are you saying the ones that go can't take their bodies? They have to die?"

"The energy cost to send so many through will be high," Brex said. "That's why we're only taking volunteers. They'll have new, fully matured bodies waiting for them on the other side."

"Volunteers? Who specifically?"

"Hazi and Inanna and anyone who's proven their loyalty to me and the Order."

"And you."

"I would never ask them to make a sacrifice I also wasn't willing to make myself."

Goodbye, my queen. Those were the last words Brex said to me in the library at the Rift. I stood and stomped off to the alcove where Tesk and I had rested with Kor when we first arrived.

I pressed my forehead to the cold stone and bit my lip to hold back the tears as he snuck into the small space and leaned a shoulder against the wall next to me.

"Talk to me, Vaza. What's going on?"

"How long have you known that I'm your Gi'dari?"

His cheek twitched with a fleeting smile. "I suspected it in the alley when I couldn't control my reaction to your scent. The bond clicked into place for me when you almost died in my arms, just as Wu'uru said it would. The same way he predicted the fall of Eden. I've been trying to save this city from its fate for two thousand years. It's a fight I can't win without my powers."

"So you knew about the bond when you left me in the library at the Rift."

"You ordered me to go. The bond makes it nearly impossible to deny you when you issue a direct command."

"If I hadn't followed you down here, were you just going to leave me and vanish without a trace?"

"I went to the library to tell you the truth and beg you to come with me. But you made it abundantly clear you wanted nothing to do with me. I did the only thing I could after being rejected. I left a trail and hoped beyond hope that you would follow." Brex reached out and ran his knuckles down the length of my arm. "Come with me, Vaza. Let me make you my goddess queen. There's a new world waiting for us on the other side of the Eye. One we can reshape together with our own offspring. Once you reciprocate the bond, your body will slowly repair itself and you'll share my immortality as my Gi'dari."

My heart sputtered at the words.

"Are you saying I could spawn again, that you and I—"

"Yes." Brex's eyes flashed with a different kind of desire. "If that's what you want."

Immortality. Goddess. *Queen*.

I'd spent my entire life imagining what it would be like to have all those things, even just a fraction of the freedom and power the Nūkiri wielded. To be able to choose my own mate. To choose how, if, and when I wanted to breed. To have a purpose beyond Zwara's political agenda.

"Is there some kind of rite we need to perform?"

"It has to happen here." Brex placed his palm on my chest, above my light and heart that already pulsed in time with his. He bent forward and kissed my forehead. "And here, before we can be one. You must be willing to bond yourself to everything I am and all that comes with it. You can't harbor any doubts. I will always be the god of tides before anything else, and I will always put the lives of those who have devoted themselves to me first, above my own needs. Otherwise, I'm no better a leader than the Nūkiri."

He didn't have to explain. I already knew I would never come first because we were the same. Brex would never put me above his duty, the same way I would never put him above Tesk. It's who we were. That unbreakable devotion to his beliefs had gone from the reason I hated him to the thing I loved most. He would always do the right thing.

"Can you really not deny me if I give you a direct order?"

Brex closed his eyes and sighed like he hadn't meant to let that bit slip. "Not unless your life is in danger."

I was tired of being powerless and letting others decide my fate. If Brex wanted to make me his immortal equal, he needed to understand that I had no intention of being a silent partner.

"Offer everyone in Eden the same choice you've given your faithful followers. Tell them all about the Eye and let them choose for themselves whether they want to come with us."

"Us?"

I lifted my palm to his cheek. "Us."

His lips curled into a seductive smile. "As you say, *my queen*."

CHAPTER NINETEEN

LIAM

"Where are you taking us? This isn't the way to the Eye." Renae grasped my hand as we followed the cloaked guards through the city of the dead. Every building was made from the same dark material that shifted from blue to black depending on the way you tilted your head.

The strange mix of architecture changed as we climbed farther away from the fields, from flat roofs and simple stone arches covered in vines with blood-red leaves to a mashup of buildings that spanned the entire history of humanity. It was as if someone had shaken a bag of buildings from all over the world and dumped them in a pile. We passed pyramids, cathedrals, and skyscrapers all made from the same iridescent blue-black material as we climbed farther away from the fields.

"You've only been gone a few minutes, reaper. We have orders to escort him to the arena. The Nūkiri want to test his powers before they decide what to do with him."

Renae's eyes flicked nervously to mine, and I caught the worst-case scenario image that flashed through her head of her sister Lucy, my mother, and Cyrena lined up firing-squad style in front of me as I leapt from my hands and shot toward them while she watched.

I hugged Renae to my side reassuringly. "Let's not jump to any conclusions."

"You don't know the Nūkiri. They're vindictive and extremely creative when it comes to punishing those who've dared to defy them. They know seeing you kill the people I love would destroy me."

I didn't voice the worst-case scenario I'd already considered, or what I would be willing to do if they tried to hurt Renae or take her away from me.

The guards pushed through a horde of panicked faces running in the opposite direction as we approached a stepped temple. It was bigger than any arena I'd ever seen and looked like something ancient civilizations might have used to perform ritual sacrifices to the gods.

The same black vines and blood-red leaves that covered every building in the lower part of the city grew from the walls. They wove together to form arched balconies around the upper mezzanine, and I suspected the entire structure had been shaped from a massive tree. Trunks stretched up from the level we were on to support the domed roof. Their bark-less surface shone like it was made from metal instead of wood.

"Liam." Renae tightened her grip on my hand as the arena floor came into view.

Hundreds of giant bioluminescent spheres that had to be ten feet wide and just as tall hovered above raised platforms on the arena floor. The arena had been packed when I'd seen it in Renae's memories. Lines of souls feeding themselves to the portals.

The place had been evacuated, save for two women, a little girl, and about fifty guards.

My gaze locked on the familiar bone-thin form of a woman clad in green silk.

Cyrena—the mind-fuck assassin who'd tried to kill me twice and then helped Renae break into the Void for reasons I hadn't been able to sort out—stood at the base of what I assumed was the Astral they'd destroyed. Its glowing remnants swirled around with an oily black fluid that must have spewed out of the Void when they cracked it open. The dome grew inch by inch as it spread toward the other surrounding Astrals.

A woman I recognized as my mother backed away from the encroaching mass. Lightning wreathed her arms as she directed her energy into the body of a young girl with a floppy blue ribbon tied on the top of her head.

"Lucy." Renae breathed her sister's name in a desperate gasp as our escorts ushered us down to the arena floor. She sprang into a run, but her body froze before she'd made three strides. Her unnaturally rigid posture and the way her arms snapped to her sides meant one of our guards had taken control of her body with their will.

Sleep. My gift leapt away from my body on instinct before I'd even finished the thought. All seven of our escorts dropped to the ground.

Renae twitched as she regained control of her body and backed toward me. "I thought your compulsion didn't work."

"Looks like I was wrong."

Every head swiveled toward us as I pushed the elastic shield out farther and dropped the remaining guards in the room before they could turn and attack.

"I knew you'd be powerful, darling," Cyrena said as we approached. "But that was impressive. They really did implant you with the powers of a god."

"What's happening?"

"Turns out ripping a hole in the Void wasn't a great idea. If the brat drops her shield, it'll expand like a black hole and eat everything else in the arena before we can get out of its way.

"I don't know how much longer we can hold it." My mother's arms trembled with the effort of feeding energy into the girl. "Lucy and I are both nearly spent."

"There's gotta be a way to seal it," I said, scanning for something I could melt. The odd sheen of the arena's tree-like structures caught my attention.

"The same thing as everything else in the city," Cyrena said, reading my mind, "a grove of bio-metallic snakewood trees. Most of the metal is concentrated in their roots."

I shifted my sight and focused on the floor beneath the blob. Cyrena was right. The structure was a massive hollow tree.

"We need to bury it." I pushed my gift into the floor beneath my feet, following the humming energy through the web of roots that made up the foundation of the arena and forced them to grow.

Renae and Cyrena backed away as obsidian fingers pushed up through the floor, twisting and weaving around the growing black blister.

White-hot lightning wreathed my wrists as I raised my arms and locked eyes with the woman who'd given birth to me and then abandoned me to my mad-scientist of a father and ran for her life.

"I need your help to melt the roots and seal the surface while I open the ground and bury this thing in a tomb."

"As soon as I stop channeling energy into Renae's sister, she's going to collapse and drop her shield. She's standing too close. She could get sucked in before we get it sealed."

I cut my eyes to Renae. "I need you to grab your sister and run like hell."

"I'm not leaving you here to get sucked back into the Void."

I caressed her cheek with a gentle breeze and projected my voice into her head. "The Void can't hold me anymore. Save your sister. If shit goes sideways, go to the place we first met. I'll meet you there. You are my anchor, my heart, and my home, and I will rip the universe apart to get back to you. I won't let anything keep me from you ever again."

Renae shook her head defiantly. *I'm not leaving you.*

"Run." I released my gift and did the one thing I'd promised to never do again and compelled her away from me.

Renae lunged for her sister and ran for the exit as I nodded to my mother. "Now."

She sent a blinding, white-hot net of energy over the tight-woven snakewood cage, fusing the seams as Lucy's shield evaporated. I shot lightning into the ground. The black blister sank sideways as the floor went molten and swallowed it whole. I blasted the spot with cold air and ice, sealing the broken Astral's tomb.

I let go, and my gift sputtered out, temporarily spent. The compulsion I'd held over the sleeping guards and Renae broke.

"Someone's been practicing. Glad to see you made the best of your time during your vacation in the Void, darling." Cyrena gave me an approving once-over.

"A decade in purgatory being stalked by your demons is hardly a vacation," I said.

"Ten years?"

I turned and stared at the face that matched the photograph I'd carried in my wallet. It was like looking in a damn mirror. We had the same dirty blond mess of hair and blue eyes.

"Hello, Liam," she said, her face softening with a tentative smile.

My hand twitched, unsure of the etiquette for greeting someone who conceived me as part of a lab experiment, abandoned me, and then infiltrated the Corps under an assumed identity to keep tabs on me.

I clenched my fist. "Which name do you prefer, Amelia or Ziggy?"

"I prefer Ziggy. Amelia was a name assigned to me by the Corps. That's not who I am anymore. The same way I suspect you're no longer the same person you were before you were imprisoned in the Void. Our experiences change us, and I look forward to getting to know who you've become." She lifted her eyes to the mezzanine above us, where dozens of guards entered the arena and clamped their shields down around us.

"You just saved the Corps' entire fleet of portals from being sucked into the Void. That should buy us some grace with the Nūkiri. Your power is your greatest bargaining chip. They may see you as a novelty as much as a threat."

"You've been summoned to the Eye," a guard said behind me, where he stood with Renae isolated under his compulsion. Renae grasped her head and doubled over in pain as I reached for her thoughts. "We have eight isolators restraining you. Every time you attempt to wield your gifts, your Gi'dari will receive pain on your behalf."

"Release her," I demanded through clenched teeth.

"She knew there would be consequences when she chose to defy the Nūkiri. She must witness before them to receive punishment."

"Save your energy for the witness chamber, darling. You're going to need it," Cyrena said as one of the guards I'd dropped earlier marched her past me.

My feet moved under someone else's will as we were taken from the arena to the dark spire towering above the city. We climbed the polished steps in a line, Lucy, Renae, and Cyrena ahead of me, Ziggy behind. The walls of the tight stairwell were carved with the faces of children who watched us with hollow eyes as we ascended the tower.

I didn't miss the way Cyrena trailed her fingertips over their lifeless faces as we passed or the pained expression that flashed across her features.

"Who are they?" I asked the guard next to me.

"Abominations."

"The only abomination is what was done to them," Cyrena whispered. The ancient assassin had two moods—vicious and snarky. What I saw playing across her face cut deeper. Her usual smirk returned as she dropped her hand, but it felt different. Like something cold and calculated swam beneath the surface.

More guards greeted us at the top of the stairs.

"They want him first," one of them said, glaring at me and nodding to a set of smooth metal doors. "Alone," they added as Renae protested and her guard yanked her away from the group.

"Don't worry, reaper. You'll get your chance to beg for your life as well."

There was no mistaking the fear that flashed across Renae's face. If the Nūkiri were as vindictive as she claimed, I had no doubt they would choose a punishment that inflicted the maximum amount of pain on both of us. They would try to break our bond.

"If you want to convince them you're not a threat, you need to show them you're willing to play by their rules," Cyrena said, cold green eyes narrowing on the doors as they opened. "Before the accident that unlocked your powers, the Nūkiri were using you as bait to catch your father's missing research partner. Issor Nella is Almega's most wanted fugitive. If you offer to hunt him down, it might buy you some freedom."

Renae held my gaze as the guards shuffled me forward. I didn't care about my own freedom. The only thing that mattered was protecting Renae and our bond.

"No matter what happens to me, know that I have no regrets. I love you," I said as the doors slammed shut behind me.

A white-hot crystal the size of a bowling ball rested atop a pedestal made to look like three sets of metallic hands in the center of the room.

"Place your hands on the Eye." A reedy feminine voice floated down from above. I stepped forward and pressed my palms to the surface. Tendrils of razor-sharp electricity rose from the ball and snaked around my wrists, sealing me in place.

"You may drop your shields. He's under our control now."

The guards released me and moved back toward the walls of the circular room as three syphons erupted from the Eye and struck my chest. Pain pricked at the edges of my awareness as they began to feed.

I didn't fight it, letting them take what they wanted as I pushed my gift into the Eye and across the open connection the same way I did when reading Renae.

There were no discernible thoughts or emotions, just a strange familiarity. It flashed like the silver glint of sunlight on water. Impossible to grasp. There one second and gone the next.

"It's been a long time since anyone has attempted to read us." There was a hint of amusement in the childlike voice that spoke.

"You taste like him," a third, sultry voice said nostalgically. "He was a god too, until he betrayed us, and we killed him."

They drained my energy through the Eye, and I had no doubt they could consume me through it the same way Renae could reap a soul.

"Tell us, Anzillu, where do your loyalties lie?" the dry, reedy voice asked, and I didn't dare lie while they clutched my soul in their grip.

"With anyone who offers their protection to my Gi'dari."

"Are you making us an offer?" the childlike voice asked.

I pushed my power through the glowing ball, forcing it into the metallic pedestal and floor beneath my feet. The sculpted hands glowed orange and the metal spire groaned with instability as my gift spread through the floor and up the walls to the balcony where the Nūkiri hid in the shadows.

"I melted the floor of your arena. This tower is made of the same material. It would take very little for me to bring it down around us."

"You dare to threaten us?" They laughed in unison.

"Let's call it aggressive negotiating. Absolve Renae of her crimes and give her the freedom to choose her own fate, and I'll bring you the one thing no one's ever been able to deliver. I'll bring you Issor Nella's head on a stick."

A beat of silence passed as they considered my offer.

"Do you think you're the first desperate soul to sacrifice themselves for our mercy?"

I lifted my eyes to the three entities sitting on their elevated glass thrones. "None of them could offer you what I have. The power and allegiance of a living god."

Their golden eyes flared with hunger, and I knew I had them.

"We cannot set the girl free. She pledged her eternal service to the Corps, but we will extract no further punishment from her if you agree to do the same."

"If I pledge my eternal service to the Corps, you'll absolve Renae of her crimes and allow us to go back to Earth to hunt down Issor Nella?" I asked, making sure I'd heard correctly. It seemed too easy.

"No. If you accept our terms, you and the reaper will go back to hunt down Issor Nella and the army of ancient souls he's recruited to rise against us. War is coming, and you may be the only one who can stop it from endangering the lives of every human on Earth."

"A war?"

"Do you agree to our terms or not?" the sultry voice asked as their syphons drew another gulp of my energy through the Eye.

I had no idea how I was supposed to stop a fucking war between the living and the dead, but that didn't matter. The Nūkiri wouldn't punish Renae, and as long as we were together, I could protect her from everything else.

"Make me your weapon."

"From this day forward, you will kneel before us alone." Their power surged through the Eye and knocked me to my knees as they floated down from the balcony.

From a distance, their cloaked forms appeared human. Up close, they were anything but. Their snakelike eyes flared as they lunged for my throat with their fangs. Every nerve in my body came alive as they pumped their venom into my veins. It was better than heroin or any drug I'd ever known. When they pulled away, the eldest of the three gripped my chin and turned my head from side to side, inspecting the wounds.

"You now carry our mark. It will appear on every form you take and prevent you from raising your power against us. Your soul may belong to the reaper, but your power binds you to us. You will not able to refuse the call if we summon you. Return to the arena for immediate deployment to Earth. Your new handler will give you your orders."

An electrical jolt zapped against my palms as they released me from the Eye and I regained full control of my gifts.

"Send in the isolator, projectionist, and traveler to receive their sentences for acting against our orders."

My stomach dropped as my head snapped up to her calculated gaze. In my desperation to protect Renae, I hadn't even considered what would become of her sister, Cyrena, and my mother.

"I'd like to renegotiate," I said. "What else can I give for their freedom?"

"You have nothing left to bargain," the childlike voice said. "Unless you'd like to give us your Gi'dari bond."

"My bond to Renae is irrevocable."

"We are the goddesses of life and death. We control the worlds of the living and the dead," they said in unison. "Do you think us incapable of something as easy as severing a bond? As long as you are willing, it can be done, but it comes at a great price. If we remove the bond, it will rip out every memory you have of her."

"No." I didn't even hesitate. It was too great a price. As much as I wanted to help the others, they'd made their choice when they agreed to help Renae, and I was selfish. Renae was my anchor and the glue that had pieced the broken parts of my soul back together. I needed her, and I would never let her go.

"We wonder whether she would make the same choice. Leave us before we change our minds and feast on you instead."

The doors swung open behind me as they floated back up to their perch. I unleashed my gift as I stood and dropped the guard holding

Renae. She ran to me as I exited the chamber and stopped short when her eyes landed on my neck.

"What is that?" Renae asked.

"A contract," I said.

Cyrena smirked. "You're going to hunt down the man who created you."

"I offered them my eternal service in the Corps in exchange for clemency for Renae. She and I are to be sent back immediately."

"And what did you negotiate for the rest of them?" Renae asked.

"He didn't," Cyrena said as she read my thoughts and glanced at Renae. "He gave everything to save you."

The Nūkiri's last question played through my head. Would Renae have made the same choice or would she have given up the bond, and me, to save her sister and Ziggy?

Cyrena projected her voice into my head as she strolled into the witness chamber. "Don't worry, your secret is safe with me. She'll know you refused to save the rest of us when you had the chance."

Renae watched Ziggy disappear behind the doors before pivoting toward me. "Did you even try to save them?" She stepped away as I reached for her.

Cyrena was right. Renae could never know about the other option. Not because I'd fucked up and left money on the table. She could never find out that there was a way to break the bond between us.

"Be pissed at me if you like, chica, but I won't apologize for negotiating your freedom. You are the only thing I cannot live without. It was a fair exchange."

Ziggy placed her hand on Renae's shoulder. "He's right. The Nūkiri can see into your soul when you touch the Eye. They don't haggle or negotiate terms unless it is to their advantage. To push for more than the minimum he was willing to accept would have been a mistake. Cyrena has served them for centuries, and Lucy warned them of our plan. That should buy them some grace."

"We can hope," Lucy said.

"What will happen to you?" I asked my mother. I hadn't spoken more than five sentences to her my whole life, and that had all been in the last hour. I had so many questions about my father and Issor Nella. If I was going to find him, I'd need her help.

"Helping Renae is the least of the crimes I've committed against the Nūkiri." She grasped my hands and used her gift to project her thoughts into my awareness. "I stole everything Issor Nella needed from the Nūkiri to imbue you with the power of a living god. My only regret is leaving you with the man you knew as your father and not finding a way to get to know you sooner."

"There's still time," I said.

My mother gave me a wistful smile. "The Nūkiri will force you to do things that will make you hate yourself. Don't let them strip you of your humanity. You were created to pave the way to a better future for all of us. Keep sight of who the real monsters are."

I dug deeper into her thoughts as the doors swung open again. "What aren't you telling me?"

Issor Nella isn't the enemy the Nūkiri would have you believe. There are two sides to every story. When you find him, give him a chance to tell his side before you hand him over.

She squeezed my hands as I read the thought. "You are everything we hoped you would become."

"Why does it sound like you're saying goodbye?" I asked.

She reached for Renae's hand and placed it in mine, sandwiching them between hers. Her voice wavered as she continued. "Take care of each other."

Ziggy pursed her lips, unable to say more without breaking down.

I'm proud of you both. I projected my mother's thought into Renae's head as she gave our hands a final squeeze and turned to walk into the witness chamber with her head held high.

Renae turned to Lucy. "What will they do to her?"

"She destroyed an Astral. The Nūkiri will require a sacrifice of equal value from her to replace it. An eye for an eye, so to speak. Astrals can only be created when a traveler's ability to hold the gift inside a physical form finally cracks and their soul evolves into a being of pure sentient energy."

"Or when the Nūkiri force the transition," Cyrena said.

Static condensed around me as I pounded on the door. It was a solid two-foot slab of metal, and the only way through it was to melt it. I focused on the seam and raised my palm, ready to release a bolt of plasma into it, when Renae's sister stepped in front of me.

"Get out of my way, kid," I said in warning. "I don't want to hurt you."

She grasped my hands, hugging her shield around me like a warm blanket instead of shackles. "This choice is not yours to make."

I shook my head. "There has to be another way. I just found her."

"Her service as an Astral is a fair exchange for her continued life. Your mother isn't dying. She's evolving. You'll be able to visit and communicate with her whenever you find yourself in Almega."

I let Renae drag me away from the door as it opened, revealing an empty chamber. Ziggy didn't reappear. My mother was gone.

The air crackled around as lightning split the sky outside. "I'm going to kill them. I want to rip their heads from their bodies with my bare hands and watch the fucking light fade from their creepy snake eyes."

Renae's syphons erupted from her back and pierced my body. She didn't try to suck out my ice-cold rage to keep me from feeling it. This time, she dumped everything she felt for me into the storm building inside me. She flooded my system with love, compassion, and warmth as she cupped my cheeks.

"You can't kill the Nūkiri, darling. They're immortal."

I glared at the assassin, scanning her from head to toe. "What was your punishment?"

"Trust me, you don't want to know. We need to go back to the arena. The sooner we get you back to your body, the better. Marcella and your new handler have been keeping an eye on it in the hospital."

Chapter Twenty

My demands delayed the Order's plans to open the Eye by an entire tide. The uncomfortable tightness in my chest returned when Brex took Hazi, Inanna, and Zwara back to Eden to arrange public hearings about the Eye and the Order's invitation to join the exodus. Zwara, of course, used her position as *ki'sikilta* to take credit for delivering the Kateri to the salvation promised by the prophecy.

Tesk and I stayed behind with Kor to learn everything we could about Earth and the Nūkiri's engineered guards who lived secretly among humans.

I spent hours with the Eye, getting to know the eccentric soul trapped inside. He told me things I didn't share with the others. Things about Brex's past. His tireless devotion to victims of the wasting, to keeping the prophecy and hope alive. Leading by example and never giving up, no matter how dire it got. Things that opened my eyes to the truth that had already settled into my bones.

Hundreds of new volunteers joined us every day. The tomb buzzed with a frenetic energy that felt like hope. When Tesk and I weren't absorbing information, we spent hours undergoing the death rite. Zwara had maimed my womb and emptied the souls from my clutch, but she could never take away my ability to incubate the dead.

Priestesses fanned sickly sweet curls of smoke toward me from the pedestaled bowls that had been placed at the corners of the inky-black pools at the base of the dais. Smoke clung to the liquid silver surface as it crawled over me and down my throat, carrying the souls into the clutch at my core. No one would be left behind. Not even the dead.

I could feel Wu'uru watching me as I floated on my back—naked save for the veil covering my face. He knew the secret I carried. The thing I refused to show anyone but Brex and the reason I'd gone back to wearing my head covering.

The tightness in my chest loosened even before the clamor of the crowd dimmed and everyone inside the tomb dropped to their knees. My heart thudded against my ribs as the god of tides made his way toward me. The immortal male had waited for me for thousands of years. He'd bonded his soul to mine to save my life, knowing I despised him. He'd purchased my freedom and had been willing to let me choose my own fate, even if it meant I might reject the bond.

The heat of his gaze slid over me like a caress as I climbed out of the pool. I couldn't look away from his glowing golden eyes as he stalked toward me.

"You're going to ruin your leathers," I said as he wrapped his arms around my silver-slicked body and tugged me to his chest.

"I don't care. I need to touch you."

"You couldn't wait for me to clean myself off?"

"Not after what I just felt through the bond. Show me."

"Are you sure you want to do this here, in front of everyone?"

"Take off the veil."

I closed my eyes and unwound the black fabric that blurred my facial features.

"The amount of joy you take in torturing me will be repaid tenfold, *wraith*."

"Are you threatening me with a good time?" I teased.

"Vaza, please." His voice was a desperate plea as he tipped my chin up to face him. "Look at me."

I lifted my eyes and looked up at him through my lashes.

He stared at me, unblinking. "Your eyes… they're—"

"Gold. Just like yours." I wrapped my arms around his neck. "I'm in love with you, zealot, and I claim you as my Gi'dari."

"Hazi said I'd know when you accepted the bond. I've been holding my breath since the night you snuck into the palace, waiting for the cord to snap tight between us. Why didn't I feel it?"

"Because it didn't happen all at once. My eyes started changing color when you left with Zwara to give everyone a choice." I scanned the reverent faces packed into the tomb. "We all have a chance at a better future because you made them believe in you. Not a martyr and not the god of tides. They believe in *you*. Brex zurNaga. And so do I."

His lips hovered above mine for one beat, then another, as he scanned my eyes. Then his mouth was on mine. He kissed me slow and deep, like it was a prayer and a promise. Like time itself was measured by the immortal heartbeat that pulsed between us.

The smile that broke across his face as he pulled away and started unbuckling his leathers stole my breath.

"What are you doing?" I asked as he took off his scaled armor and dropped to his knees in front of me.

"It's not official unless you leave your mark, my goddess."

He tipped his head to the side and offered me his neck.

I pushed his hair out of the way and ran my fingertips along the exposed column of his throat. Not that long ago, I'd have given anything to get close enough to rip it out with my claws. Now I couldn't imagine living in a world where he didn't exist. Where we weren't connected by an irrevocable bond.

Brex held my waist as I bent forward and pressed the tips of my fangs to the soft spot between his neck and collarbone. The same place he'd marked me after claiming my pleasure for the first time.

"Do your worst, Gi'dari."

Brex's fingers dug into my hips as I bit down and pierced his flesh. Blood—sweet and warm and metallic—spurted into my mouth. Frenzy gushed from my spine as an intense wave of pleasure licked through my body.

Brex groaned as he inhaled and slid his hands to my ass. "Fuck, you're in heat. I need to be inside you. Right. Now." He lifted me as he stood. A mating frenzy flashed across both our chests. The sea of spectators parted as he carried me toward the alcove I'd been sleeping in with Tesk.

I slit the laces of his trousers with my claws and fisted one of his cocks before we made it out of sight behind the curved wall. I notched him at my entrance as he wedged me against the rough stone and thrust into me, burying himself to the hilt. The initial pinch of pain faded to an intoxicating feeling of fullness as my body stretched around him.

I reached up and wound my fingers in his hair. "You're mine."

"I've been yours since the moment Wu'uru predicted you would someday exist. All the while knowing I would only have you for a fleeting moment before your death. When the Nūkiri took my power, I fought like hell to hold on to the one gift I knew I would need to save you, to compel you to live. I never gave up searching for you, Vaza. I will love you until the stars fade from the sky and every world turns to dust. Even then, I will love you still."

I gasped his name as he curled his hips slowly, letting me reacclimate to the way his giant cock moved inside me. Tears spilled down my cheeks in the place of the words lodged in my throat. Words that weren't big or beautiful enough to convey everything I felt for him.

"It's Anzillu." His lips brushed mine as he slid his hand between us and found my clit.

I'd heard the word once before. It's what the Order had been chanting when we first entered the tomb.

"What does it mean?" A searing heat spread from my core as he fucked me harder.

"Abomination."

"I don't understand." Little quakes of pleasure had me tightening around him as my release hovered at the edge, just out of reach.

"My true name. The one whispered by the universe when it breathed me to life. I want you to scream it when you come and let everyone know that you're mine."

The name tore from my lips as he thrust into me, and I broke. His growl shook the cavern as his body jerked and he filled me with his seed.

Brex planted soft kisses along my neck as he eased my feet to the floor. "We should join the others. We depart tonight."

I pushed him back toward the pallet of blankets, and I dropped my eyes to where his second, still-engorged cock throbbed between us. "Not until I've thoroughly claimed you."

He smiled as he pulled me to the floor with him. "You shall have everything you desire. I will deny you nothing, my goddess queen."

❧

Liquid silver sluiced off Brex's hair and the form-fitting leathers as he climbed out of the narrow black pool behind me. Hazi exited the pool to my right, behind Tesk, while Zwara took her time climbing out of the one to my left with one of her guards.

Wu'uru had shown Tesk how the Nūkiri coated themselves from head to toe in the silver before unlocking the Eye. Even then, they were only able to hold it open for a short time. The Order assigned each of us a shield to protect us from being drained too quickly in hopes that we would be able to keep it open long enough for everyone to make it through.

The crowd cheered for the *ki'sikilta* as Zwara climbed the dais. I rolled my eyes as Brex wrapped his arms around me from behind.

"I can't believe you're letting her take credit for this. They're going to worship her forever if this works."

"I'll never forgive your sister for what she forced you to endure, but we need her for this. We're all on the same side."

"For now." The only side Zwara had was her own. "She'll do whatever she can to seize power as soon as we pass through the Eye."

"That's the plan," Brex said. "Issor's spy inside the Nūkiri's corps of watchers says the Nursery facility is only protected by a small security team. Our greatest advantage will be in taking them by surprise. They'll try to take out the strongest fighters first. Zwara's team of storm mages will make a show of destroying the compound while the shields protecting the queens make a quiet escape."

My body went rigid. "You're using my sister as bait?" Zwara and I had a complicated history, but I wouldn't stand by and let the Order sacrifice her. Not when Brex and I were immortal.

"It was her idea," Brex said. "She knows we don't stand a chance against the Nūkiri if the queens don't make it to Issor zurNella. The thirteen of you carry millions of Kateri in your clutches. Enough to build an army to bring down the vicious goddesses."

I turned to face him. "Zwara's a queen too."

He slid his thumb under the edge of my leathers, smoothing it over the shrinking scar on my abdomen. "She's also the only one we can afford to lose."

Zwara's icy blue eyes found mine as I pulled away from Brex and climbed the dais. She dropped to her knees in reverence, and I realized I didn't really know my sister at all. She'd never gotten on her knees for anyone. Not even Brex. I couldn't tell if it was an act for the crowd or if she actually respected me now that I outranked her.

Tesk threw her arms around me. "We won't be twins on the other side," she said wistfully. "Wu'uru said I'll be in a human husk, and you'll still be you. Now that you're immortal like the Nūkiri, the Eye can't consume you."

"Which is why she's going to keep those beautiful eyes covered," Brex said. "If the Nūkiri find out I have a mate, they'll hunt you down and torture you."

"What do we do if we're captured?" Tesk's eyes gleamed with fear.

I cupped her oil-slick face in my hands. "You do whatever it takes to survive."

My eyes went glassy as I surveyed the thousands of Kateri gathered in the cavern. Many of them would die. They all understood that. What we didn't know—what Brex and Wu'uru couldn't tell us—was what would happen to their souls outside of Eden. Would they dissipate into dust without a queen to protect them? Would the Nūkiri try to collect them? Either way, their next death would be final.

"Together, or not at all," Tesk said, offering me a half smile.

The sea nettle of guilt in my gut spread its stinging tentacles. She meant the two of us, but I couldn't stop thinking about Zwara and all the others and wishing there was a way to make them all immortal. I blinked back hot tears as I turned my face to the Eye, refusing to let anyone see my hesitation.

I felt a gentle brush at the back of my mind and glanced at Inanna where she stood on the other side of Tesk and Hazi. "They're all going to die if they stay here. You're giving them a chance to defy fate and survive." The mind mage couldn't read my thoughts, but she might as well have.

I nodded and took one more long look at each of my sisters, committing their faces to memory.

"Hemeda would be proud," Zwara said. "She told me once that we survived the wasting because fate had plans for us. I only wish she could have lived to see how right she was."

The Eye flashed as the dark shadow flitted back and forth impatiently.

Brex slid his hands over my shoulders. "It's time."

Kor's female form climbed the dais and pulled Tesk into a kiss that made my sister's bioluminescent markings pulse with need.

"Enough," Hazi growled in warning, still not used to seeing my sister as anything other than the *ki'sikilta*.

Kor flashed him a demure smile. "Crack this thing open like an egg, darling. We want to be the first through the portal to claim the best corpse for our queen."

"They're called husks," Hazi said as he wrapped his arms and shield around Tesk.

Kor waved him off with a flick of their wrist. "Apologies, darling. We're still learning the nuances of their many languages."

Brex hugged my back to his chest and wrapped his shield around me as he brought his lips to my ear. "Until the worlds turn to dust."

I nodded to my sisters and placed my hands on the Eye.

A buzzing sensation kissed my palms as Wu'uru's mushy voice crept through my head. "There you are, my *kisikilta*. I've been waiting so long for all of you to open me together. I will do my best to be gentle, but my hunger is an entity all its own."

The shadow vanished, and the gelatinous surface went soft beneath our simultaneous touch. My arms sank to the elbow, and I could feel it tugging me in toward the center where an ice-covered cavern appeared at the end of a long tunnel.

"It really is a door." Laughter curled at the edge of Tesk's voice. "Go now," she said to Kor.

"See you on the other side, darling," Kor said in unison and stepped into the Eye. The orb flared with turquoise light as their bodies disintegrated and a single ghostlike form floated into the room at the center of the orb.

Zwara screamed at the patrol of storm mages standing beside her. "What are you waiting for? Go."

The buzzing sensation bit at my skin as pod after pod of Kateri disappeared through the portal—the Eye releasing them from their physical bodies and consuming their flesh. Dark veins snaked up my bare arms, leaving blackened flesh in their wake.

A feral growl vibrated against my back as the Eye tried to consume me.

Tesk screamed beside me. "It's eating my fingers. Make it stop."

"Block her pain," Brex yelled at Hazi.

"I am. It's breaking through my shield. How many are left, Inanna?"

Hazi cursed at whatever answer she'd given him.

Brex pressed a kiss to my temple. "We're almost done, my love. You're doing great."

"You're a terrible liar, zealot." I could see the reflection of the cavern on the Eye's iridescent surface. There were still too many.

I glanced at Tesk. Dark veins slithered over her shoulders and crept across her chest, slowly swallowing her light.

"Release me and extend your shield around Tesk," I said to Brex. "I can take the pain."

"I'm not letting go of you."

The Eye made a wet belching sound and expelled a flood of bloody slime-covered clothing and bones from its underside.

"Did you just vomit on my feet?" Zwara hissed at the Eye.

"He's never eaten a whole body before," Hazi said. "We just fed him thousands. I think we made him sick."

"We need to go through before the Eye closes," Brex growled.

"Keep holding," Zwara said. "None of my priestesses have made it through."

"We go on three." Brex began counting down. On the count of two, he scooped my body up in his arms and stepped into the orb.

⇛

The whine of cleaving ice exploded inside my head. A sharp shrieking sound blared from somewhere close by. Every nerve in my body jolted awake—too many sensations too fast. Broken glass cut into my hands and knees as I crawled across the floor, blinded by the searing light.

My body went flying as an explosion reverberated through my chest. I slammed into the side of the tank, knocking it over on its side. The lid popped open, spewing a gush of warm fluid over me as a body toppled out. A female form with pale skin and flame-red hair wearing a form-fitting black bodysuit that looked almost identical to my gorzin-skin leathers rolled onto her back. Her strange round eyes caught mine as she clawed at the apparatus that covered her mouth and nose like a parasitic face crab.

"Relax," I said. "Let me help you."

The female nodded, and I slipped the straps from the back of her head. She gagged and coughed as I pulled the long tubular tentacle out of her throat and threw it to the side. She heaved over and vomited on the floor before sucking in a deep breath.

"Vaza." Her voice was slurred like her tongue was too big for her mouth.

"Tesk?" I asked tentatively, placing a gentle hand on her shoulder.

She cut me a dark look as she wiped her mouth with the back of her hand.

"Wrong sister," Zwara said with the same mushy affect as Wu'uru. "Your zealot closed the portal before all of my storm mages made it through."

"If we'd have waited any longer, priestess, we would have lost the connection." His deep voice melted through me and settled in my bones.

"Brex."

He pulled me up on wobbling legs and pulled my hair over my eyes.

"Keep your head down. We need to find Hazi and Inanna and get the hell out of here."

"I'm not going anywhere until I find Tesk and Kor."

"We're right here, darling." I turned to see Kor, somehow still stunningly beautiful in human female form with dark coils of hair clinging to their face and long neck.

Two identical male forms with the same dark complexion flanked another female with a pale hide and thick reddish-brown hair that cascaded over her narrow human shoulders. Her wide hips and thick thighs, however, were fit for a Kateri queen.

"Tesk."

My sister's new body moved faster than my eyes could track. Before I could blink, her arms were around me, squeezing the breath from my lungs. "Vaza."

I brought my palms to her round cheeks, my chest ballooning with wonder as I memorized every feature of her new face. The faint brown speckles spattered over the bridge of her ivory nose. The pursed red lips and round amber eyes flecked with gold.

"How is it that you look human, yet so Kateri?" I asked.

"The Nūkiri mated with the evolving sentient species and imbued them with the Kateri souls they carried when they left Eden," Brex said. "Humans are the resulting hybrid."

"Minus all the best parts," one of Kor's male forms grunted as they adjusted the tight form-fitting black bodysuit that matched all the others.

Tesk ran her tongue over her teeth. "I already miss my fangs."

"Zwara's storm mages are keeping what's left of the guards busy. As far as we can tell, every shield pod containing a queen made it out safely, but we tripped some sort of alarm," Kor's female form said, cutting their eyes to the flashing lights gilding the cavern in a bloody red glow. "We need to get out of here before reinforcements arrive. Hazi and Inanna are waiting for us with transport outside."

"Where'd Zwara go?" I asked, glancing around.

Brex pointed across the cavern to a lithe female form as she disappeared through a wall of silver doors, each one etched with the Kateri symbol for knowledge—an Eye with a slit pupil at its center. It wasn't the first eerily familiar thing about this new world.

"One step ahead of us, as usual," Tesk said.

"Let's go." Brex unsheathed one of the blades from his thigh and handed it to me. "If we get separated, don't hesitate to do whatever it takes to protect yourself and the others, even if you have to pull a soul from your clutch."

"Are you giving me permission to consume a soul, zealot?"

"You're a goddess, Vaza. You don't need my permission to do anything." A buzzing sensation caressed my skin. Brex extended his shield around our little group to deflect flying debris and rogue blasts of lightning from the last throes of battle at the other end of the cavern as we made our way to where Zwara had disappeared.

A different set of silver doors opened as we approached.

"Where does it lead?" Tesk asked.

Brex peered into the small room and ushered us inside. "To the surface."

Brex released his shield as the strange doors slid shut behind him. My stomach dropped at the sensation of falling and flying all at once—the same way it had when Kor grabbed me and jumped off the ledge in the ruined city. I couldn't tell if we were going up or down.

"I think I'm going to be sick," I said as I hunched over and slapped a palm against the wall for stability.

Brex turned toward me as the sensation shifted and the small room came to a cushioned halt, sending a bubble of bile into my throat.

"It's over," he said as the doors slid open. "We made it out."

Tesk screamed as an electronic popping noise erupted behind him. His body seized as it dropped to the ground next to my sister's writhing form.

Two humans in white bodysuits stood on the other side of the doors, pointing some kind of electric-shock device at them.

I lunged forward at the same time as Kor's female form. The guards clutched their throats as Kor sucked the air from their lungs and I sliced my blade and claws across their soft bellies.

Searing pain exploded across my back, sending my body into convulsions. I collapsed on top of one of the humans I'd disemboweled.

Another electronic pop, and Kor's female form dropped to the floor. Two more guards clad in white uniforms stood above us.

"Bring the collars. These two are still alive."

I couldn't understand anything they said. They flinched as the domed glass ceiling above their heads shattered. The last thing I saw as the darkness closed in were Kor's male forms flying through the hole in the roof, carrying Brex and Tesk's unconscious bodies in their arms.

Chapter Twenty-One

RENAE

"Are you sure you can't fix this?" I asked Jason as I slung the backpack over my shoulder and we hurried across the parking lot toward the hospital in Kona. He'd kept my human husk alive while I was in the Void, but just barely. All the color had leached from my skin and hair in the rudimentary biostasis tank he kept in the back of his grandfather's greenhouse.

"Not unless you want to go back into the stasis tank. Your body will need another month of gene therapy to repair the melanin-producing cells damaged by the onset of decomposition when you abandoned it. We don't have that kind of time."

"You mean when I died after you drowned me in a vat of alcohol?"

He shot me a sidelong glance, his long legs outpacing mine. "I was following orders. If it weren't for me, you wouldn't have a body to come back to. Your appearance is the least of our problems right now. We need to collect the asset and get to the compound."

"The *asset* has a name," I said under my breath as we approached the visitor desk.

"Hello," Jason said casually to the middle-aged woman behind the counter, as if we hadn't just sped across the island to get to Liam before he came out of his coma. It could be any minute, now that his soul was back inside his body where it belonged. Liam had woken up without me every day for a decade in the Void's warped time scale, and I refused to let him go through that ever again.

The woman's eyes shifted to mine, pausing too long on my pale features. The bright tang of ripe berries burst across my tongue as I unfurled a syphon and pierced her spectrum. Her energy was the first I'd tasted since escaping the Void, and I fed on her curiosity like a glutton. Unlike Liam, who could see and feel my syphons due to the bond and his enhanced sight, the woman was completely unaware. Her telltale yawn was my cue that I'd taken enough.

"We're here to see my grandfather, Ken Ito. He's in the ICU," Jason said, drawing her attention.

"Only immediate family are allowed." Her eyes flicked to mine and back to Jason's.

I plastered a sweet smile over my expression as I glared at the side of his face. "This is taking too long."

Jason's dark eyes narrowed on the woman the same way they had on me so many times before as he'd attempted to smother me with his gift. "We need two badges, please."

She checked the computer and handed him two peel-and-stick visitor badges. "The intensive care unit is on the second floor."

Jason thanked her as I pulled him toward the elevator. "Why didn't you tell me Mr. Ito was in the hospital?" I said as soon as the doors squeezed shut and we lurched upward. "You were supposed to heal his cancer."

"I'll keep my word to the old man and remove his illness when I'm done using his husk. He was my only way into the ICU to keep an eye on Liam while you were gone."

"Is he in pain?" My gut twisted at the thought of the sweet old man suffering because of me—not that I would change a single decision I'd made to cause it. If that made me a terrible person, I was willing to accept that.

"Not while I'm in control of his body and my consciousness resides inside him. I've been using my shield to block his pain and keep him in a coma-like state. I can hear everything that happens in the room he shares with the asset."

Liam's energy surged across the bond as the elevator doors chimed open.

"He's awake," I said, shoving past Jason to bolt down the hall.

I didn't bother to check in at the nurses' station when they buzzed me in. A gentle tug on the bond told me which room he was in.

A nurse rose from the desk and called after me.

"Forget about her," Jason said, diffusing the situation with his charm and gentle compulsion.

Liam's bed was on the far side of the room, hidden by a pale green curtain.

"Renae." My heart lodged in my throat at the raw rasp of his voice.

"I'm here." I dropped the backpack on the floor and scraped my fingers through the scratchy whiskers along his sharp jaw as I pressed my lips to his. It didn't matter that they were dry and cracked or that there was a thin feeding tube taped to his cheek to keep it from pulling out of his nose. He was perfect and he was home.

He brought his hand to the back of my head, fisting my hair and deepening the kiss. I unfurled all six of my syphons and drank in the milky sweet spice of him as I climbed onto the hospital bed.

"There's my greedy little reaper." His eyes fluttered open and caught mine as his hands drifted to my hips where I straddled him.

My heart lodged in my throat as I ran a palm over the velvet nap of his cropped hair. The slash of scar tissue across his forehead and every angle of his face felt sharper without his mop of amber curls to soften them. He was as brutally breathtaking as the raw power coursing through him. I studied his pupils like I'd seen the doctors do the night he'd been admitted, searching for a change in dilation or any sign that his brain wasn't fully recovered. Two symmetrical denim globes flecked with streaks of silver stared up at me, reading my worried thoughts.

"Trust me, chica, *everything's* working just fine." The scar bisecting his forehead deepened as he winced and shifted his hips beneath me. A twinge of pain shot across the bond as he pressed his hardening length against the curve of my inner thigh. "Waking up to you sitting on my cock is the best thing that has ever happened to me, even if you are kneeling on my catheter."

"Gods, I'm sorry." I'd been so consumed with the selfish need to taste him, to reassure myself that he was all in one piece, that we were still one—body, soul, and bond. I hadn't considered it might cause him pain.

He held me in place as I tried to extract myself from his lap. "I told you before—never apologize for taking what you need from me, chica."

Liam scowled at the soft scrape of metal as Jason slid the curtain shut behind a nurse. Her stiff movements and the way her wide eyes darted between us told me she was under his spell.

"What the fuck are you doing here?" Capsaicin laced my tongue, and every muscle in Liam's body went taut beneath me.

Jason cut him a dark look as I climbed off the bed.

He's our new handler. He's been tasked with delivering us to one of the Corps training facilities. I shoved the thought across the bond to keep the conversation out of the nurse's ears. The fewer memories I had to siphon from her, the better. I hated leaving innocent humans with heads full of Swiss cheese.

"I'm here to remove your Foley line, IV, and feeding tube, Mr. Riley. You're being discharged." She opened a cabinet and pulled out a handful of supplies with shaking hands. Chalk replaced the fiery sensation in my mouth as I used my syphons to lick away the woman's fear.

"That was fast," I said to Jason, wondering how he'd managed to get a doctor to sign off on discharge papers and compel a nurse in under five minutes.

"Take a deep breath and exhale slowly," the nurse said to Liam. I averted my eyes as she made quick work of removing his catheter and moved to the far side of the bed.

"Your discharge is complete." Monika, Liam's human ex-girlfriend, rounded the curtain waving a slip of paper, lips curling in a smirk that looked out of place on her round face.

I cocked my head as my syphons swept toward her. The sour sting of champagne vinegar exploded on my tongue as she allowed my syphons to burrow into her.

"Hello, reaper. You've looked better," she said, eyeing me from head to foot.

"Monika, what are you—" Liam's voice cut off as he read my mind. *That's not Monika. Not anymore.*

His wide-eyed nurse squawked as Liam lunged from the bed stark naked and took two steps before collapsing under his own weight, taking Monika's body down with him. Alarms sounded from the monitors above the hospital bed as he wrapped his fingers around Monika's throat.

"Release her."

"I can't," Cyrena gasped in Monika's velvet voice.

The hair on the back of my neck lifted in warning as Liam charged his gift. He placed a glowing palm on her chest.

"I'll stop her fucking heart and restart it if that's what it takes to exorcise you from her body. You can't have Monika." He bit the words out through clenched teeth.

"Let Cyrena go," Jason said as he wrapped his shield around me like a protective blanket. "If you disobey the Nūkiri, Renae will pay the price. You may be willing to gamble with her life, but I'm not."

Liam's eyes blazed with fury as they snapped to where Jason put his hand on my shoulder. The bleating alarm coming from the monitors above his bed strangled out a final plea, and the lights flickered as Liam pulled power from the room.

"If you value your life, pretty boy, you'll take your hands off my Gi'dari." Liam lifted a lightning-wreathed arm toward Jason. Blood ran down his forearm where the IV had ripped out during his violent lunge toward Cyrena's new form.

Jason's protective shield shattered under Liam's crushing will.

I crouched next to Liam and placed my hands on his arm as I siphoned the peaks off his anger and grief. "Look at me. You need to set your emotions aside for a moment so we can get you out of here. I brought you some clothes. We have a plane to catch, and you need to get dressed."

Cyrena wheezed as he released his grip on her throat and leaned against the bed. "Why did it have to be Monika? She has a family and a whole life plan. She didn't deserve to get dragged into this. It's cruel."

"The Nūkiri gave me no choice," Cyrena said in a voice that sounded like a cracking flame. "They made Lucy give them her bond so she can never betray them or act against their will again. This body was my punishment." Cyrena stood and used the baggy T-shirt she wore to wipe Liam's blood off her neck.

They'd demanded Lucy's bond—taken her free will. She'd be a slave to their whims for eternity. I clenched the bedrail with a sweaty palm. If Liam had let me defend myself to the Nūkiri, I might have been able to spare her.

"Why the fuck would they want you to possess Monika?" Liam asked. "She has nothing to do with this."

"To remind you that if you disobey them, they won't hesitate to take away everyone you care about." Cyrena's dark eyes faded to green as her skin paled and her mahogany hair went black. She still wore Monika's clothes, but she looked like herself again. "I can't release the girl's body without killing her, but I won't force you to look at her."

"Don't bother hiding behind a projection," Jason said. "I have a feeling he's going to need a daily reminder."

Liam scratched at the bite marks on his neck as he banked his power. The monitors came back to life and resumed their incessant beeping.

"Can someone turn off the goddamned alarms?" Liam barked as I led him back to the bed, where the dripping IV line hung off the edge, creating a puddle of clear fluid on the floor. The only tube still connected to him was the one taped to his face. Liam pinched the tube in his nose as he tipped his head back.

"Wait, let the nurse—" The complaint died on my lips as he pulled the feeding tube out on his own.

"Get dressed. Our flight leaves in an hour." Jason picked up the backpack I'd dropped on the floor and tossed it to Liam. "Renae, can you escort the nurse into the hall and help her with her memory while I see to my grandfather?"

I put my arm around the poor woman's trembling shoulders as I dug through her spectrum with my syphons and sucked out the glowing strands from the last twenty minutes of her life as if it were spaghetti. Her memory of everything that had happened inside the room was safely locked in the vault at my core by the time we reached the door.

"Can you tell me where the closest restroom is?" I asked.

The woman blinked three times before responding cheerfully. I thanked her for her assistance and watched her scurry down the hall before I slipped back into the room and joined Liam in the bathroom.

"What the hell is Jason doing here?" he asked as he tugged his jeans over his incredible rear. He'd recovered from his initial stumble inhumanly fast. He certainly didn't look like someone who'd been in a coma for six weeks.

"Jason's *our* new handler. So maybe refrain from threatening to kill him."

"I don't trust him." Liam found the toothbrush and toothpaste I'd thrown into his bag with the rest of his things.

"Well, I do, and so did your mother." I crossed my arms and leaned against the door. If he hadn't been obsessed with throwing away his freedom to spare me a punishment, Ziggy might have been here to tell him so herself and Monika might have been spared.

Liam's eyes met mine in the mirror as he rinsed his mouth. "And maybe you could try not thinking so loud."

"We're not in the Void anymore. I get that it's going to take some time to adjust to being around people again, but you can't just wield your gifts in front of humans. Anonymity is one of the Corps' major tenants. You can't blow your cover."

He wiped his mouth with the back of his hand and leaned against the sink. "Is that what you're pissed about? That I used my gift in front of the nurse?"

"All I'm asking is that you keep your reactions in check."

"Cyrena stole Monika's life, and our *handler* tried to restrain you."

"You can't go feral every time someone touches me."

Liam closed the distance between us and slapped his palm against the door above my head. "No one touches you but me."

He'd been annoyingly possessive before we'd consummated the bond. All those feelings were now amplified. For both of us.

I ran my fingers over the scars on his neck. "Why did they bite you?"

"They said my power belonged to them after they fed on me. It's just another intimidation tactic, like taking my mother and then Monika. A reminder that they're in control."

My stomach hardened. I told myself it was because I hadn't eaten any real food yet. Not because three beautiful immortal entities had fed on his energy, tasted the sweet spice of his power, and claimed it as their own.

Liam's mouth curled as he read my thoughts. "Your nose scrunches when you're jealous."

I glared up at him through my lashes. "Don't tease me."

He leaned in and hovered his lips above mine. "Every part of me belongs to you. Nothing will ever change that."

My heart pounded against my ribs as Jason pounded on the door behind my head. "We're in the middle of an alien invasion. You two can make out later. We need to go."

"What the fuck did he just say?"

"Come on. Jason will brief you on the way to the airport."

⸙

Apparently, living gods were deemed too dangerous to fly commercial. The Corps wasn't taking any chances with Liam's volatile power by putting him on a plane with hundreds of unwitting humans. I was more than happy to not be packed into another small space with so many people without the little blue pills Ziggy used to prescribe. I made a mental note to ask Jason for a refill when we got to the compound.

He plopped down next to Cyrena in the booth-like nook as we combed through video footage of the attack on the New York nursery where I'd trained. The facility had been decimated in the battle.

"Whoever these souls are, they know how to fight," Liam said as he traced an idle circle with his thumb on my palm beneath the table. He sat close to me, the side of his thigh pressed to mine. His knee bounced as he studied the tablet propped up in front of us. "They're moving through the compound like they know exactly where they're going. Which means—"

"They have someone on the inside." Cyrena's thin eyebrows knit together over her vivid green eyes. She was still projecting her own appearance over the body she'd stolen from Monika. She clearly didn't want to cause Liam any more pain than necessary. She'd been watching him from the shadows his entire life. For all her snark, it was obvious that she cared about him—even though she'd tried to kill him. Twice.

"Why are the Corps' guards holding back?" Liam asked as we watched one of the invaders take out a dozen assets alone.

"They're not," Jason said. "The aliens' gifts make ours look like child's play. The readings we've gotten from the trackers embedded in the husks they stole are off the charts. The only way we can take one down is with a combination of tasers and tranks. You might be the only one of us who can go toe to toe with one and survive."

"How am I supposed to take on an entire alien army on my own?"

"You won't be alone. You'll have a patrol of trackers and the Corps' arsenal at your disposal. We're modifying all of our weapons now that we know how to immobilize them."

"Are we sure they're alien?" I asked. "Their gifts seem to function the same way ours do. They're wielding wind, ice, and lightning like forecasters. And this group—" I pointed to the screen where half a dozen husks huddled under the protection of a shield as they made their way to a bank of elevators.

"Yes." Jason pulled up footage from inside the elevator of a female with dark blue hair draped over her face. He zoomed in on the giant male next to her. "These two came through one of our Astrals with their physical bodies intact."

I grabbed the tablet to get a closer look. "That's not possible. Physical matter can't pass through a portal."

"Unless you're immortal." Liam scooted forward in his seat. "Look at his eyes. They're the same as the Nūkiri's."

I zoomed in on his face. I'd only seen the Nūkiri once, and it wasn't up close, but there was no mistaking those glowing golden eyes.

"We have his female companion in custody and one of the hijacked husks in custody."

"What do they want?" I asked.

"We're still trying to figure that out. Our linguists are trying to decode their language. The only information we have so far is what we've managed to extract from their minds. They call themselves Kateri, and their visual memories indicate they're a low-tech, highly ritualistic species with at least one Astral." Jason switched over to a live feed of a prison cell containing a female husk with ebony skin and hair.

"Why is she wearing a collar?" I asked.

"It's a power suppression device."

I watched as the prisoner clawed at the collar with bloody nails. "Is it hurting her?"

"Only if they attempt to use their gift. As far as we can tell, each Kateri wields a single power. This one's a mimic."

"How can you tell if you're suppressing it?" Liam's brows knit together.

"The trackers embedded in their husks give us all sorts of biometric ratings, including the energy signatures that reveal their gifts. According to the memories we've extracted from the blue-haired female, we think she may be a breeder without any gifts."

The mimic's lips peeled back, and a swath of brilliant white cut across her face. I flinched as she lunged for the Corps agent in the cell with her. The collar around her neck flashed, dropping her to the floor in a heap. Her eyes rolled back, revealing only the whites as her body convulsed.

"Turn it off." I shoved the tablet across the table. The Corps trained its operatives to be spies and assassins. I wasn't naive to their tactics. That didn't make it any easier to watch.

Liam stood and paced the narrow aisle between the table and television console nestled into the airplane's curved wall. He scrubbed a palm over his golden halo of cropped hair. "I thought torture was against the Geneva Convention."

Cyrena turned the screen toward her to get a better look at the prisoner. "Human laws don't apply to the Corps. Our directives come directly from the Nūkiri. You'd all do well to remember that."

Jason stood and stretched, still looking a little green. "It's a long flight. I suggest we try to get some sleep. There won't be much time for rest in the coming days. The seats recline and two couches fold into beds. There's a shower in the bathroom at the back of the plane and a stocked kitchen up front if anyone's hungry."

Jason pulled blankets from the credenza beneath the flat-screen television and handed one to Cyrena, whose legs were already sprawled across the overstuffed seat he'd vacated. I declined a blanket and made my way to the kitchen with Liam. He locked the pocket door behind us and immediately folded me into his arms.

He let out a heavy sigh that was equal parts exhaustion and relief. My body relaxed for the first time in weeks as I leaned into him. I curled my syphons around him as I breathed in the faint salt and cedar scent that clung to his clothes.

"I'm sorry I couldn't save Ziggy or your sister from the Nūkiri's retribution."

Acid burned beneath my sternum as his guilt flooded the bond the same way it did every time he looked at Cyrena.

"It's not your fault. There's nothing more you could have done to save them."

Liam kissed my temple.

"How are you feeling?" I asked as I pulled back to examine his pupils again. Jason had scanned Liam with his healing gift and declared he was fine. Physically, anyway. I was more concerned with the damage he couldn't see.

"Like there's no way in hell I'm gonna be able to fall asleep. Wanna help me raid the fridge?"

"If it's stocked with salmon and rice, I'm going to scream."

I surrendered a little moan as I opened the narrow refrigerator. No salmon or rice in sight. I grabbed two fizzy waters, a couple of prepackaged sandwiches, and a giant bag of waxed cheese rounds.

Liam went through the cabinets and piled packs of fancy crackers, cookies, nuts, and granola bars on the table. He opened a drawer packed with mini liquor bottles. I didn't miss the pause he made before moving past it.

I untwisted the mesh bag containing the cheeses and wound the tie around my pinky before dumping them onto the pile.

"Fuck." Liam groaned past a mouth full of Oreos as he leaned back in his chair.

I popped one of the peeled cheeses into my mouth and whimpered at the salty ecstasy that exploded on my tongue.

We didn't speak as we decimated the mountain of snacks. He grabbed my wrist as I went to snatch the last chocolate cookie. His brow arched as I closed my fist around it.

"You've already eaten four packs," I said. "This one is mine." If he wanted it, he'd have to pry it from my hands.

Liam pulled me around the table until I straddled his lap, still holding my wrist hostage.

"I have no intention of taking it from you. I want to watch while you eat it." He dropped his hands to my hips, and I twisted the two halves of the cookie apart. Liam's eyes dropped to my mouth as I licked the vanilla crème center.

Heat built at my core where he pressed against me. I rocked against him as his hands slid around to my backside where I'd stuffed his cell phone and charger down the back of my jeans to hide them from Jason when we'd gathered Liam's things.

Liam read the thought and pulled out the phone. "Why did you need to hide it? I thought you trusted him."

I wiped the cookie crumbs from my lips. "They'll confiscate it when we get to the compound, but I thought you might want to call your brother."

Liam kissed my forehead. "I love you."

"I encrypted it and got rid of your SIM card, but the Corps may still be able to track it. Don't text and don't power it on unless you need to use it. Keep your Wi-Fi calls under two minutes," I said, pointing to a sign on the wall with instructions for making Wi-Fi calls during the flight.

"I'm guessing the Corps has rules about what I can say."

"Connor sat by your side for weeks. Jason said he only went home to try to arrange to have you moved to New York. He'll be thrilled that you're awake, but he'll have a lot of questions. Everything you say will become an official part of our cover story, so keep it vague."

"How am I supposed to say what I need to say in under two minutes?"

"I'll give you some space to collect your thoughts." I crawled off his lap, and he pulled me between his knees.

I cupped Liam's stubbled face and turned it up to mine. The inner corner of his eyes glistened with unshed tears as he attempted to hold everything in. After a decade alone, he'd been dragged through the claustrophobic city of the dead, bargained for his life, and he'd lost his mother and Monika in the span of a day. His anger had finally given way to grief.

"Do you want me to take the pain away so you can get through the conversation with Connor?" I asked, running my hands over his short velvet curls.

He nodded and hugged my middle as I pierced his spectrum with my syphons and drank in the heady sweet spice of him until I finally felt his shoulders relax.

"I might need some space to get my head straight before I make the call."

"Take as much time as you need. I'll be right outside." I grabbed a handful of snacks and gave him the privacy he craved after being around people all day.

Unease was a hard ball in my stomach as the lock clicked behind me. The only time he'd kept me out in the Void had been to self-medicate. I shoved the thought down into the tomb at my core along with the other unhelpful feelings I had about his lapse in sobriety.

"Where's Marcella?" I asked as I tossed a protein bar to Cyrena. Her Gi'dari's ghost never strayed too far from her side. It was strange that she hadn't made an appearance.

"I'm not completely heartless. I asked her to stay behind and watch over Monika's family."

I nodded as she took a bit of the peanut butter flavored brick and went back to watching replays of the prisoner interrogation sessions. Jason had reclined in one of the chairs and was already snoring. He'd dimmed the lights and pulled out both beds, presumably for Liam and me.

I chose the one at the back of the plane and sighed with relief as I pulled my bra off through the arm of my shirt and tugged off my jeans. My old clothes felt stiff and confining after weeks of sleeping naked with Liam. I tucked the blanket over my lap and settled in with my pile of snacks and another tablet to rewatch the attack on the nursery from every camera angle. The prisoner I'd seen in the shock collar had been one of the first to emerge from the stasis pods. She and two identical male husks went from tank to tank as if they were looking for something—or someone—in particular. I zoomed in on the one pod that caught their attention and watched as my spare husk came to life. Every Corps agent had a backup body in case we were killed and we needed to be reinserted into a mission immediately.

The prisoner embraced my doppelganger's face as they exchanged words I couldn't hear, and then the three of them closed ranks around her. They joined the two immortals who looked like the Nūkiri—eerily human aside from their glowing eyes. The way they all circled around my doppelganger struck me as odd. The readings from her tracker indicated that she was a reaper, but she didn't join the fight. The others huddled around her and snuck her out toward the exit. It was like they were intentionally avoiding drawing any attention to her.

My eyelids grew heavy as I watched the interaction over and over. I lay on my side and propped the tablet against the wall. Liam was right. The underground tunnels of the compound were extensive. It would be easy to get lost. The stolen husks didn't make any wrong turns. They navigated the compound like they had maps in their heads.

"Scoot over." The clean scent of soap and wintergreen mouthwash tickled my nose as Liam cuddled up behind me under the blanket. He pushed the hair away from my neck and kissed the tender flesh behind my ear.

How did your conversation go?

Liam read my thoughts and projected his voice into my head. "Too quick. He lectured me the entire time about getting on a plane less than an hour after being discharged."

I rolled onto my back to face him. *Why would you tell him that?*

"Because he threatened to come to Hawaii to examine me himself. I had to tell him something, so I told him I was coming to find you. That you had family in upstate New York."

You couldn't have said Texas or Colorado? If he knows you're in New York, he's going to want to see you.

"Yeah, he said that too." Liam wrapped a lock of my hair around his finger. "I'm new at this clandestine shit, and I've never been able to lie to him. It was the hardest conversation I've ever had."

The grief and anger I'd tasted earlier were gone, replaced by an aching hollowness I knew all too well. The empty feeling that came after your entire life had been ripped away from you.

I ran my fingers over his smooth cheek. *You took a shower.*

Liam brought his hand to mine and pressed a kiss into my palm. "What's this?" he asked, toying with the twist tie that was still wrapped around my pinky.

"An old habit. I was forever losing the twine ties as a kid, and my mother wasn't fond of stale bread. She made me tie them to my finger when I helped her in the kitchen because I tended to lose things as soon as I let go of them."

He unwound the white wire tie from my pinky. The tips of his fingers lit as he melted and reshaped it with his gift.

"Sometimes I forget that you lived an entire life before I was born." Liam rolled a thin glowing ring between his fingers as it cooled. "I'm hanging by a thread, and you're my only anchor. Please don't let go of me." He held up the band like it was a question.

My heart lodged in my throat as he slipped the ring onto my finger.

"I'll always help you find your way home," I said aloud.

He slipped a hand under the blanket and traced the exposed strip where my T-shirt had ridden up above the waistband of my underwear. "I don't know how much time we'll have together once we land."

My nipples tightened as his fingers drifted lower, leaving a scorching path over my skin.

"We're not alone," I said, glancing toward the other end of the dark cabin.

"They're both sound asleep."

"What if they wake up?"

"I compelled them both into a deep sleep. They won't wake until I allow it."

I sucked in a breath as Liam traced the seam between my thighs through my damp panties. He silenced my whimper with his mouth. Heat spooled in my core as his tongue swept into me, teasing and tasting. His bicep flexed under my grip as he pressed the heel of his palm against my throbbing center.

He knew exactly how to turn me into a writhing pile of need. The need to feel him anchored inside me and the even greater need to use my body and my love as a shield. To wrap it around him and ease the pain of the last day—the last decade of his life. To reassure him that I wouldn't ever disappear. That we would always be together in this life and the next.

Liam read all of that and more as I lifted my hips and let him peel off my panties. He fisted the back of his T-shirt and yanked it off over his head. His body was incredible. All chiseled muscle and sinuous lines. I ran my hand over the dragon tattoo inked across his shoulder and chest, letting my syphons unfurl and lick the dips and valleys of all that taut flesh.

He pushed my shirt up my torso and leaned back to stare at me. He traced the contours of my body with his eyes and then his hands, as if he were committing it to memory.

"You're beautiful."

My skin pebbled as he sent a rush of cool air skating across my skin. I palmed my breast and pushed it toward him. Liam bent and sucked the sensitive bud into his mouth, circling it with his tongue as his hand slid down my belly into the soft curls that were as pale as the ones on my head. My insides went molten at the pleased sound he made as he parted me with his fingers.

I traced the V-shaped indents from his hips to the waistband of his sweatpants. He groaned as I freed his rigid length. I stroked him from base to tip as he hooked my leg over his body and slid his palm down the back of my thigh.

I angled my hips as he positioned himself at my entrance. Liam worked himself into me with slow, shallow strokes. My body stretched to accommodate him as if it were the first time. He filled me in a way that felt familiar and new all at once.

Liam rolled his thumb over my throbbing clit, bringing me to the edge of release, and held me there with his gift in the most exquisite form of torture.

"Liam, please."

"We break together." His mouth found mine as he lifted my leg higher and pumped into me until our bodies and breath and our pleasure were one. I clenched around him as the orgasm ripped through us at the same time, and all we could do was cling to each other as we shattered.

Chapter Twenty-Two

LIAM

A young girl ran up to Renae and threw her arms around her as we entered the communal dining hall. The compound, with its crystal-clear mountainside lake, manicured landscape, and elegant glass and gray stone buildings, looked more like a goddamned resort than a secret base for an army of supernatural sleeper agents.

Renae smoothed her hand over the little girl's hair. "Lucy, I'm so sorry. It's my fault the Nūkiri forced you to come back to Earth against your will, and in the body of a child."

Lucy pulled away and straightened her glittery unicorn T-shirt. "I've been born seventeen times and haven't lived past the age of twenty in any of them." She spoke with the same heavy French accent she'd had in Almega. "It's more of a cruel joke than a punishment. A reminder that we were created for their amusement alone."

She'd been Renae's sister in their previous life. I wasn't sure how the whole past life family dynamics worked. My head was still wrapping itself around the fact that she'd lived seventeen lives and never made it to adulthood.

Lucy turned to me with a gap-toothed smile. "Hello, Liam. Welcome to the Corps. You may leave your personal items with security before we tour the facility."

I tightened my grip on the strap of my backpack and gave her a weak smile. "I'm good." No one had attempted to search it yet, and I sure as hell wasn't going to hand it over to guards. Not with my contraband cell phone and the stash of mini liquor bottles I'd stolen from the plane hidden inside. I didn't even know why I took them. To test myself? Because they were there?

Lucy dipped her head and swung her outstretched hand toward the exit and the seven isolators who'd been assigned to escort me around as soon as we'd arrived. "Right this way."

An icy sensation slid down my spine as Cyrena projected her voice into my skull. "They'll search your bag before you enter the nursery."

I'd forgotten she could read me like a damn book and knew all my tells.

Stay the fuck out of my head, succubus. Her smirk told me she'd read my thoughts loud and clear.

"Go ahead without me, darlings," Cyrena said aloud. "I'm going to grab some breakfast. If memory serves, the head chef makes a heavenly omelet. I'll see you at the debrief in an hour." Her gaze cut to mine. "I'd be happy to deposit your bag in your room for you so you don't have to carry it around all day."

Cyrena's voice split through my head again. "Last chance. If you want to keep what's inside, I suggest you give me the bag... unless you want your girlfriend to see all your little souvenirs." The corner of Cyrena's thin lips quirked up in a smirk as she spoke inside my head. "Your secrets are safe with me, darling."

I hadn't had any withdrawal symptoms yet, but I was getting desperate for something to take the edge off. Fucking Renae and letting her feed off me helped, and gods knew I wasn't opposed to the idea of putting my dick inside her three times a day if she'd allow it. But I'd been an addict and alcoholic long enough to know that using sex as a temporary coping mechanism would only work for so long. It wouldn't fix the real problem. It wouldn't alleviate the guilt festering inside me.

I wove my fingers through Renae's and eyed the guards who'd closed rank around us as we followed Lucy's small form down a long sterile hallway lined with blue LED lights.

The cavern housing what was left of the stasis pods sat deep inside the bowels of a mountain. A high-speed elevator took us straight to the bottom. My stomach went weightless for half a second as it came to a soft stop and the doors opened to what could have easily been mistaken for the aftermath of an earthquake. Forecasters clad in white uniforms with the bright blue mark of the Nūkiri—a diamond-shaped star with an eye in the center—manipulated air currents to move chunks of rock, ice, and twisted metal into the deep beds of dump trailers.

It was the same massive cavern I'd visited the first time my traveler ability manifested before I fell into the Void and time sped forward for me. In reality, it had only been a few weeks since I'd stood here with Cyrena, searching for Renae's doppelganger.

The domed ice ceiling that had sparkled like the night sky lost its luster with the glare from the emergency lights that had been brought in to aid the round-the-clock cleanup effort. A steady stream of trucks moved in and out, some carrying away debris, others bringing in new stasis pods, electronic equipment, and massive coils of conduit. Three days had passed since the attack, and the cavern was already well on its way to being rebuilt.

"Where did all these people come from? There were only a handful of guards here during the attack."

"We mobilized every sleeper agent we had on the east coast."

"Imagine what FEMA could do if they had an army of forecasters at their disposal," I said, shaking my head.

"Humans can't be trusted with the knowledge we keep," Lucy said.

"Seems to me the Corps can't be trusted with its own secrets," I said. "They had to have inside information to pull this off. You need to find your mole before they come back and finish the job."

"We think Ziggy may have given them the building blueprints," Jason said.

"She would never aid an alien invasion," Renae snapped back.

"She may not have known what they were planning," Jason said in a placating tone. "Her primary focus was on manipulating you to keep an eye on her son."

"We've shut down all the Astrals and placed every nursery on high alert. We're ready for them this time. They won't be able to attack again without taking heavy losses. Their gifts are stronger than ours, but they're no match for our advanced weapons." There was a disturbing ring of excitement in Lucy's little girl voice.

Jason scowled. "They only made it out with eight hundred husks and destroyed the rest during the attack."

"How many have we recovered?" Renae asked.

"Twenty-seven."

"Dead or alive?" I asked.

He gave me a sidelong glance as we made our way into a tented off section. "They knew about the trackers. Most of the invaders removed them before we were able to get the system back up and running to send out the kill signal."

Jason parted a thick plastic flap and led us into a makeshift morgue. Naked husks were stacked in rows like fucking logs, waiting to be repaired by healers hunched over metal worktables. They wore the same stark white uniform as the others, the symbol on the back a dark red instead of blue.

I covered my nose and mouth to block the stench of death.

"They'll need a few weeks in the new stasis tanks to reverse the cell degeneration," Jason said, dragging his eyes from where Renae clasped my hand. "When you go hunting, try to use nonlethal force to apprehend them. It will make it easier for the healers to recycle the husks if you don't fry them with your lightning."

"How many have you recovered alive?" I asked.

"Only the two," Lucy said. "But that will change now that we have you."

"I appreciate your confidence, kid, but I haven't met one of these things up close yet. I have no idea if I can take one out."

"Then let me introduce you to our guests," Jason said. "Follow me."

He led us down a short hallway to another cavern filled with a fleet of cargo vans, armored trucks, and ATVs. We hopped into one of the golf carts lined up along the wall. Jason drove, and Lucy called shotgun. I hugged Renae tight to my side. The need to touch her, to be in constant contact, moved like a living thing inside me. All teeth and claws and unable to settle when we were around other people.

Wind tugged a stray hair from her silver braid as we sped down a wide stone tunnel that was too straight and smooth to be a naturally occurring formation. I had no doubt that, like the arena in the city of the dead, the inside of the mountain had been melted and reformed to suit the Corps' needs.

While the above-ground facility could easily pass as a bougie resort, the sprawling underground compound was a straight-up military base. Directional signs pointed out entire wings dedicated to the housing and training of recruits for each supernatural gift. I clocked the locations of an armory and the electronics operational center as we zipped past.

"How long were you stationed here?" I asked Renae.

"Three years. I was transferred to Hilo under Ziggy's supervision after I passed my trial."

My chest tightened at the mention of my mother. A nagging thought pricked at the back of my brain. If the Corps' security was so tight, how had she managed to work against them and hide in plain sight for thirty years? She'd stolen secrets and sold them to my father and his research partner. She was a traveler, able to send her consciousness to far-flung places. Did that include other worlds? Had she sold information to the

Kateri? If she was the mole, it explained why the Nūkiri were so quick to turn her into an Astral and imprison her spirit inside a gelatinous blob.

"Any progress on finding the mole?" I asked Jason as I pushed my awareness past the walls of his isolation shield. His spine stiffened as our eyes met in the rearview mirror. The last place I wanted to tread was inside Jason's head. He had a thing for Renae, and his vivid imagination made me want to cave his skull in. The only thing stopping me was her genuine affection for him and the knowledge that if shit ever went sideways, he wouldn't hesitate to protect her. But he'd worked for my mother. If Ziggy had been selling secrets to the Kateri, he would have known. I was suspicious of his sudden promotion. Did he earn it by selling her out?

We have rules here against intruding into the minds of fellow assets without consent. The pretty boy's thoughts were an easy read.

I projected my voice into his head. "Do I look like I give a fuck about any of your rules?"

His eyes skated to Renae and back to me as he spoke aloud. "Finding the leak is our number one priority. The interrogators have been instructed to extract the information from the prisoners by any means necessary."

"Is there any indication that the other facilities may be targeted?" Renae asked.

"The intelligence we've gathered from the prisoners doesn't indicate that, but we aren't taking any chances," Jason said. "Measures have been put in place to prevent them from hijacking any more husks."

"What's stopping them from taking humans as hosts like Cyrena?"

"Nothing." Jason shook his head. "Their energy vectors are off the charts. If they start snatching unmodified human bodies, they'll burn through them in a matter of hours. They'll toss each one aside like a wet sock and move to the next host. We're monitoring law enforcement channels for unusual upticks in unexplained deaths. Hopefully one of them will leave a trail we can follow to Issor Nella."

I glanced back at the isolators following us and shoved down my next question, not wanting to know how long it would take for Cyrena's energy to destroy Monika's unmodified body.

My knee bounced, and Renae's syphons licked over my shoulders in a gentle warning to dial my emotions back. The golf cart took a sharp turn and curved around the outside of a spiral shaft that led deeper into the mountain. I leaned out and looked up at the circle of blue sky high above us. It was the only exit I'd seen, aside from the elevator that had brought us down to the nursery floor after we'd gone through security.

As far as I could tell, the entire underground base was built around the center shaft, with tunnels jutting out like spokes on a wheel. We exited the spiral ramp several levels below where we'd started and parked in front of the detention center.

The brief interrogation I'd watched on the plane did nothing to prepare me for what greeted us in the Corps' prison.

The acrid scent of ozone and burnt hair hit me as a guard opened the heavy door leading into the interrogation room. A sizzling hiss floated toward us like someone had just walked through with a plate of fajitas. I'd experienced every scent and sound of Renae's first death each time I walked through her nightmares, and there was no mistaking the smell of charred human flesh.

Renae's eyes went wide as I twisted her to face me and wrapped an impenetrable barrier around her to block the smell and sound of what the forecaster was doing to the writhing husk on the floor in front of him. The contents of my stomach pressed at the back of my throat as I extended my shield over the helpless prisoner, blocking the attack. No one deserved to be tortured.

"*Mon dieu*," Lucy whispered, covering her mouth and nose with a hand as the last of my security escort filed into the room and blocked our only exit.

Renae struggled against my hold and tried to follow her sister's horrified gaze.

"Do not turn around," I commanded. I hated myself for compelling her to obey, but it was the only way I knew how to protect her from the god-awful scene in front of me.

I pulled her rigid body against mine and scanned the room in vain for another exit as Jason barked at the interrogator to stop frying a million-dollar husk. As far as I could tell, the Corps seemed to have an unlimited pool of resources. It said a lot about his priorities that their bottom line was his first concern after watching someone, alien or not, get torched.

"Liam, let go of me. What's going on?"

"Trust me, chica. You don't want to see this." There was no way I was letting her come face to face with another charred body.

"The immortal bitch attacked me first," the forecaster said as he pulled all the water from a giant tank and dropped it on the prisoner with a cruel smirk. "I acted in self-defense. It's not like she won't heal. Eventually."

Steam rose from the husk's blackened shoulders as she pressed up to her hands and knees, her back rising and falling with shallow gasps. What was left of her dark hair hung in limp strands around her face. She reached up and yanked the melted collar off her neck.

"The power dampening device won't," Jason said. "You're lucky this one doesn't have any gifts."

A sheet of ruined flesh sloughed off the prisoner's cheek, revealing the muscle and bone beneath as she lifted her head and pinned me with a pair of piercing yellow eyes. Her blistered lips curled into a wicked grin as she rose and dipped her chin in my direction.

It was the only warning she gave.

Cold power prickled across my skin, raising the hair on my arms and the back of my neck.

"Get down!" The words bellowed from my chest in slow motion as she turned her attention to the interrogator.

I forced my vision to shift and sent a cyclone of air spinning around the room, toppling Lucy, Jason, and my escort of isolators like bowling pins as I shoved Renae to the floor.

The puddle of water at the female alien's feet whined as it froze and cracked into razor-sharp shards. I yanked up my shield as something whizzed past my ear.

There was something not right about her power. I studied her aura with my enhanced sight. Her energy flashed like lighter fluid on a smoldering fire, burning too fast and too bright, like she wasn't in complete control of her gift.

A wet gurgling sound drew my attention back to the interrogator. The bloody tips of a dozen ice daggers protruded from his back. His husk slumped to the floor, and I watched the soul leave his body and float up toward the ceiling, where it passed through the stone and disappeared.

The prisoner was hissing what sounded like an irreverent curse punctuated by hard inflections and clicks in a language that wasn't even remotely human. I stared at her in awe, realizing that I was standing in front of an entity from another world. Her eyes were full of intelligence, and I had the sudden urge to *know* everything. Where did they come from? Why were they here?

But I didn't get the chance to ask. Her power fizzled out as quickly as it began, and her eyelids shuttered. I sent out a gust of air to cushion her fall as her unconscious body slumped to the floor.

Chapter Twenty-Three

VAZA

I gasped Brex's name as I sucked in a breath.

A familiar buzzing sensation kissed my skin as I locked eyes with the golden-haired male restraining me against the examination table with his shield while another healed my burns.

I'd been held down by hundreds of males. There was only one whose gift felt like a tingling caress as it coiled around me. And this human wasn't my Gi'dari.

"Jason, she's awake."

I couldn't understand his mushy language like Kor could, but I recognized the power coursing through him the second he dropped his shield over me in the torture room.

"That gift doesn't belong to you," I hissed. My chest lit with rage as I pushed back against his stolen magic.

"Can you work any fucking faster?" He scowled at the healer. "She's killed three guards. The sooner we get a collar back on her neck, the better."

"Almost done."

I flashed my fangs at the dark-haired healer as he ran his fingers over the mark where Brex had claimed me.

"Her skin is tougher than a human's, and whatever metal they used to seal these puncture wounds is resisting my gift."

"They look like the bite marks the Nūkiri gave me in Almega." I cut my eyes to the blue-eyed male, not sure if I'd heard him correctly. Was he talking about the goddesses?

"Maybe *you* can explain how they ended up on my body in the hospital." He pulled the neck of his tunic down to show the marks where he'd been claimed to the healer.

Why would the goddesses give the power they stole from Brex to a human?

The healer glanced at the other male's neck. "I'm curious about that myself. Renae said you tried to save Ziggy when you made your deal with the Nūkiri."

The blue-eyed male's face pinched with something that looked like shame as he scratched at the scabs. I knew that look. It was the same one that had twisted Brex's beautiful face when he told me the story about how the Nūkiri and the god of tides—when he tried to tell me what he was.

You'll never stop feeling responsible for the ones you couldn't save.

My chest ached where the bond tugged. I couldn't stop seeing his body convulse on the ground next to Tesk's. I'd spent the last three days testing the durability of the shock collar by goading the interrogators to attack me. Being submerged in water didn't affect it. But apparently the combination of wet hair and lightning was enough to short out the device long enough for me to pull an ice mage from my clutch and freeze the device until it was brittle enough to shatter with my hands.

If I could replicate the process, I'd have a chance of getting Kor and myself out of here and finding Brex.

"Can you hold her a few minutes longer? I'd like to use my gift to look inside her body to see how different their anatomy is before we put her back in her cell."

"Yeah, I think she's losing steam."

Heat pulsed from the healer's palms as he ran his hands over my bare chest, following the light across my bioluminescent markings. "She's truly incredible. I can't believe I'm the first person to examine an alien."

The blue-eyed male scowled as the healer inspected my breasts. "Do we have any idea where the Kateri came from?"

"Someplace with a lot of water." The healer closed his eyes as he traced his fingers over my ribs. "These scars used to be gills. They're connected to her lungs."

I glanced around the sterile white room and smiled as my eyes landed on the tray of scalpels next to my new collar. If I could get the blue-eyed male to drop his shield for one second, I might be able to grab the collar and snap it around his neck. Then, I'd cut off the healer's fingers for touching me like he fucking owned me.

"You might want to hurry up with that. I don't think she likes your bedside manner. She's currently contemplating ways to maim you."

"You can read her mind?"

"Her thoughts keep flitting back to the male with yellow eyes. I think he's her Gi'dari."

My light flared at the familiar word.

"Shit, I think she understood me."

He pushed a fuzzy image of Brex into my head. "Is this your Gi'dari?"

"Where is he?" I growled.

"Can you please stop pissing off my patient?" The healer slid his hands over my abdomen and stopped above my clutch. "Liam, read my thoughts. You need to see this."

The blue-eyed male projected a different image into my mind. "What the hell is that?"

"I believe it's called spawn." The healer smiled down at me. "This beautiful creature is pregnant."

CHAPTER TWENTY-FOUR

LIAM

THE HANGAR HELD TWO small prop planes, a helicopter, and a fleet of drones. Renae's body twitched with anticipation as she stood too close to Jason and watched the live footage playing out on one of the flat-screen monitors mounted to the wall. The black eye on the back of her skintight uniform glared at me. At least that was the way it felt as I treaded through her stream of consciousness. She wouldn't thank me for intruding on her thoughts while she was already seething, so I kept my steps light.

She was furious that I'd barred her from the examination room an hour earlier and denied her the opportunity to inspect the alien up close. It didn't help that Jason was all too happy to gloat and insert himself at her side while she was grumpy with me.

From the moment I met her, I knew we were the same. Stubborn, Impulsive. Prone to self-destructive behavior. Admittedly, her coping mechanisms were better than mine. While my first instinct was to drown my anger with drugs and alcohol, Renae preferred to chase hers off with adrenaline—running on lava, throwing herself out of an airplane to remind herself that she was alive.

Renae ripped a hole in the goddamned fabric of reality to be with me—a possessive, overprotective junky. How long would it be before she regretted that decision? She'd never forgive me if she found out I'd had the opportunity to save Ziggy from her fate. That I'd been selfish and taken the deal that worked best for me. The one that kept her irrevocably bound to me.

She was my anchor. Renae would never need me in the same way. Her unyielding independent streak was the thing I loved most about her. For all my Anzillu powers, Renae was the strong one, and I couldn't shake the feeling that I was one lie away from losing her.

I forced my attention to the petite white chick with pink hair who was controlling the drone on the screen. She thumbed an X-Box controller, dropping the camera closer to an abandoned church. Graffiti covered the boarded-up windows and doors, and the roof sagged in the middle around a gaping hole.

"They cut out their trackers, but a police dash cam in a town just over the border in Vermont pinged a facial match to one of the stolen husks," she said around a wad of gum. "It didn't take me long to find them. The church sits right at the edge of the town. They've been holed up there for the last six hours."

"How many?" Renae asked.

"Five." Pink hair chick clicked something on the controller, and five dossiers popped up on the screen. "These two are a mimic with forecasting as a secondary gift," she said, pointing to two identical male husks. "The blond female is a telepath. The redhead is a reaper, and the other male husk is a shield."

"What's the plan?" I asked.

"We'll drop the team a half mile outside the town at dusk. You'll approach first on foot and sneak into the building. Once you've immobilized all five targets, we'll send in the rest of the unit for the extraction."

"You want me to apprehend five powerful aliens... by my fucking self?" I'd used my gift on the pregnant one in the prison morgue easily enough while Jason healed and examined her. I had no idea if I could take one on in the wild, though, let alone five.

"These things are monsters. You can't send him in by himself." The way Renae shifted closer to me made my chest tighten. "Liam might have the power of a living god, but he's not a soldier. He's never been trained as an asset and doesn't know anything about tactics. If they take him out, we'll lose the best weapon we have."

"She's right," Jason said. "When the prisoner ripped off her collar and attacked us, Liam's immediate instinct was to protect everyone else in the room when he should have eliminated the threat first. She almost took him out. We can't afford to lose him. If he dies, the Corps doesn't have any backup husks for him to inhabit, and he'd burn through an unmodified human host in a matter of hours."

"What do you suggest?" Cyrena asked.

"Liam will go in with the isolators as backup. Renae will stay back in the van with me."

"What?" All six of Renae's syphons uncoiled and pitched toward him. Jason took a step back instinctively, even though I was the only one who could see and feel them, thanks to the bond.

"You're a distraction. One that could compromise the entire team. If I send you in with him, your safety will be his only priority."

"I'm a reaper, not tech support." Renae's voice came out strained as she glanced toward me, those golden eyes all but begging me to stand up for her and argue that she be allowed to put herself in jeopardy.

As much as it pained me to admit, I agreed with Jason. I wouldn't be able to focus if I was worried about her safety. "Sorry, chica. I vote you stay in the van."

She balled her hands into fists and reeled in her syphons. A cold mask of detachment plastered her features. The same look she used to keep me at arm's length when we first met and she was desperate to sever our bond.

"Let's go," Jason said with a smirk. "It's a two-hour drive."

I climbed into the back of a blacked-out SUV with Cyrena and three isolators with gray emblems on their backs. Lucy took the front passenger seat, even though she could barely see over the dash. A lanky teenage boy climbed behind the wheel. The black eye on his uniform marked him as a reaper, and he moved with a fluid confidence that defied his youthful appearance. An old soul in a fresh husk.

Jason guided Renae to a mobile comms unit disguised as an Amazon delivery van. The way Jason's palm slid to the small of Renae's back as he helped her step up into the vehicle made me want to break his damn wrist.

"Jealousy will poison all that bonded bliss," Cyrena said as she followed the line of my focus.

"I'm not jealous."

"Clearly."

"Stay out of my head, succubus."

"I've watched over you your entire life, darling. I don't need to probe your mind to see what's written all over your face. Bond or not, if you don't ease your grip, you're going to drive that woman away from you."

I glared at the false projection she wore, unable to forget the human face she hid behind it. *Don't get in my way today. It will take very little for me to rip the air from your lungs.*

Cyrena read the thought and projected her voice into my brain. "Idle threats don't suit you, Liam. Best leave the violence to those of us willing to wield it without remorse."

I shoved her out of my head and yanked up my shield. She didn't know shit about what I was willing to do. Especially when it came to protecting Renae.

The landscape was a blur of gray rock and patches of snow in the shadows beyond the reach of the late afternoon sun. The bleak two-hour ride gave me plenty of time to think. It struck me as strange that the cell we were going after hadn't made it very far in the three days since the initial attack.

According to the reports I'd read, all the other facial recognition sightings had pinged much farther away. Never staying in one place long enough for the Corps to track them down.

Whoever the mole was, they had to be providing the Kateri with money and resources in addition to information to keep them on the move. If they were here to become our alien overlords, why would they scatter? Were they planning some kind of terrorist attack on multiple targets?

If I survived this, I needed to dig through the pregnant alien's head again.

The setting sun painted the surrounding mountains blue and purple as we weaved through the town. Jason pulled into a strip-mall parking lot as we continued ahead. I closed my eyes and forced my gift to go ghost mode, sending my shadow body inside the surveillance van.

Renae sat at a com station, watching live drone footage of our black SUV. The thermal image showed six glowing bodies within. One of them was mine.

She flicked her pale gold eyes up to where I hovered next to her, instantly aware of my presence.

Are you trying to prove him right? She tipped her head to Jason as I read her thoughts.

"About what?" I asked, knowing Renae was the only one who could see and hear me in ghost form.

That I'm a distraction. She focused her attention back on the screen.

I crouched next to her so that our eyes were level. "You're my reason to breathe. Everything else is a distraction."

She bit back a smile as she turned toward me. *You don't suck at apologizing.*

"When we get back to the compound, I plan to show you all the things I don't suck at."

Her pale face went somber. *Promise you'll come back.*

I ghosted my fingers over her cheek. "Chica, not even death could stop me from finding my way back to you."

"Wake up, darling. We're here." Cyrena projected the shock of ice water being dumped over my head to snap me back into my body.

I rubbed at the sudden tightness in my chest as the SUV pulled onto a dirt road hidden by dense trees.

"The church backs up to the other side of the woods," Lucy said, handing each of us something that looked like a silver kidney bean. I copied the others and shoved it into my ear as I hopped out of the vehicle.

A tickling sensation crawled through my ear canal. "What the—"

"It's a neural-lace pod." Renae's velvet voice sounded in my ear. "The nano filaments connect with your neural network and allow Jason and me to see and hear everything you do. They act as two-way mics for the team. Also, your ass looks hot in spandex."

I threw a glance up at the drone hovering above us. "I don't know how we're supposed to sneak up on them. These white uniforms don't exactly blend in."

"The high visibility uniforms hardly matter. I already have the targets under my projection. They'll only see and hear what I show them." Cyrena brushed past me. "This would be much easier if you could stretch your isolation net over them from here as well."

"I can't control anyone outside my visual range."

"We need to work on that, darling."

"Can the rest of you extend your shields that far?" I asked as I followed Cyrena's footsteps through the ankle-deep snow.

"Yes," Lucy said, pigtails bobbing on the side of her head. "I'm blocking their auditory senses. They won't hear a thing as we approach.

They will, however, notice if we try to lock down their will and immobilize them."

"The blond telepath and the shield with gray hair just moved outside to the cemetery behind the church. You'll have to walk right past them to get inside," Jason said as the trees thinned and the church came into view.

Cyrena held up a bony hand, and the entire team halted as a guy with a man-bun pulled a woman with long blond hair to his chest.

He spoke to her in a low, guttural tone as he walked her back against a stone monument and sank his teeth into her neck.

"Did he just... did he just bite her?" Renae asked.

I scratched at the scabs on my throat as the male dropped to his knees in the snow and started unbuttoning the chick's pants.

"Keep moving," Jason said. "Cyrena will take care of these two. Your primary objective is to take out the reaper and the two mimics inside."

Snow crunched beneath our feet as we made a wide arc around the pair to hide our tracks.

Renae's voice sounded in my ear. "I'm looking at the thermal images. Two husks appear to be sleeping on pews in the sanctuary. The other is standing watch at the front. Go to the north side of the church. There's a side door that's been kicked in. That looks like your best entry point."

Lucy and the gangly reaper who'd driven the SUV flanked me as we stepped into an old kitchen missing a chunk of its floor. The dusty boards creaked under my weight and sent something way too big to be a rat scurrying across one of the counters in the dark.

"Raccoon," one of the isolators said at my back as we moved into the hallway.

Male voices floated toward us, carrying a conversation in a language that didn't sound like it was meant for the human tongue. One of them hissed like a damn snake as another laughed. That was universal, at least.

I pressed my back to the wall and peeked into the sanctuary from an arched door next to a giant pipe organ. I only clocked one target. The reaper—a middle-aged woman with red hair.

She didn't resist like the one in the morgue or even seem to care when I wrapped my shield around her. A prickling sensation ran over my scalp. This was too easy.

"I disabled the reaper, but I can't see the twin mimics."

"They're still lying down in the pews," Renae said. "You need to do something to bring them into your visual range."

"Got any suggestions?"

"There's a lot of snow on the roof. Try gusting it down through that massive hole right above them."

I forced my vision to shift and focused on the air currents above the church as I stepped through the door. Wind howled against the roof, blowing a spiral of snow through the ceiling.

A dark figure shot up from the row of wood benches faster than I could track and disappeared into the night.

"Cyrena, watch your back. You've got a hostile incoming," the reaper who'd driven us said, shouting through the comms.

"I see him."

"Help me out here, chica." I flicked my wrist and summoned the static from the air. It circled my forearm, painting the ends of the pews in blue light as I moved down the center aisle. "I need eyes on the other mimic. What do you see on the infrared camera?"

The electronic whizz of propellers drew my eyes to the ceiling as the drone crashed through the hole. I lunged to the ground between two pews, escaping a nasty slice from one of its blades before it slammed into the floor.

"Fuck. We lost the drone." Jason's voice boomed in my ear.

"No shit. It almost took my damn head off." I caught a glimpse of white sneakers kicking back and forth as a body slithered away from me under the pews. *Gotcha.*

I threw out my shield, but it didn't stick. He moved out of sight too fast.

The sanctuary went silent. I crawled to the center aisle and peeked around the end of a bench. Lucy, the driver, and the other three isolators were clutching their throats as the mimic drew the air from their lungs.

They slumped to the floor as I slammed my shield down on him. His lips curled into a sultry smile as his eyes cut to mine. He didn't even try to push back.

"Liam, behind—" Lucy's gasped warning cut off as my body lifted into the air and catapulted toward the front of the church. The organ groaned like a metal beast as my head slammed into the keys, snuffing out my power.

I struggled to get to my feet. The room tilted sideways as a shield clamped around me. The first mimic who'd escaped through the roof stalked down the aisle, followed by the redhead and the dude from the cemetery. The cemetery guy and one of the mimics bound my hands and hauled me out the way I'd come in, leaving Lucy and the others at the mercy of the redheaded reaper and the other mimic.

My body went hot and queasy as we stepped outside. The telepath used her toe to nudge Monika's motionless body. I thrashed against the shield restraining me, unable to produce more than a muscle twitch under his compulsion.

A rapid succession of soft pops echoed across the cemetery. The telepath chick and the shield next to me dropped to the ground. Darts protruded from their chests, delivering an electric shock that made their bodies convulse. I snapped my head up, free of the shield, and saw Jason standing at the edge of the woods with a trank gun pointed at my head.

The mimic who'd helped drag me outside used me like a human shield, pulling me back toward the church. A ghostly figure shot toward us from the tree line, hair whipping behind her like silver flames.

He sent a column of air toward Renae, toppling headstones in its wake. Pain scraped the inside of my brain as I tried and failed to raise a shield around her. The throbbing concussion from my collision with the organ must have knocked out my gift.

She darted away from the attack as I threw my head backward and connected with the asshole's nose. He uttered what sounded like a curse and shoved me to the ground. With my hands bound behind me, my face hit the snow with an audible thud.

Renae leapt over me and slammed into the male, taking him down. When they stopped rolling, he had her pinned beneath his heavy body.

His mouth curled into a feral smile. Renae's eyes went wide as panic exploded across the bond between us and she stabbed her syphons into his back.

The air between them rippled like a silvery-blue mirage as Renae sucked the soul from the mimic's body. The husk went limp and collapsed on top of her. She shoved him off and wiped her mouth on the back of her hand as Lucy came bounding out of the church.

"We have the redhead, but the other mimic got away."

I couldn't take my eyes off Renae or the way her moon-kissed skin glowed.

"Stop staring at me like I'm a monster. He was going to kill you." She crawled to me and untied my hands.

I pulled her into my arms. "I'm staring at you because you're the most beautiful fucking thing I've ever seen."

Chapter Twenty-Five

VAZA

Light pulsed across my chest as I sat crossed-legged on the cot in my cell. I ran my fingers over the smooth skin on my belly where there should have been a scar—where the knife had punctured my clutch.

"Are you sure?" Kor asked through the bars separating us.

I shot them a sidelong look. "I've spawned many times. I know my body."

The burns had masked the subtle change in my scent, but there was no mistaking the feeling of fullness and draining fatigue. My stomach would swell over the next tide until my clutch couldn't hold the thousands of developing eggs.

In Eden, I would have spent the two weeks following a mating rite lounging in bed, eating, and reading in a pheromone-infused bliss until it was time to release my spawn into one of the incubation pools. Once they hatched, the male who'd impregnated me would take his pick of the younglings and leave the rest for the high priestess to divide between the noble and working houses based on their gifts.

"I don't understand how this happened," Kor said.

"I was in heat when Brex returned from Eden. We both went into a frenzy and—"

"Darling, I know *how* it happened. I just don't understand how your body healed itself."

"Brex told me it might be a possibility after I accepted the bond and became immortal."

"We've seen the male naked. He's covered in silver scars. So are you. Why is this the only one that healed?"

No silver. She has enough reminders of what's been taken from her. The memory of Brex standing vigil at my side while Zwara healed me floated through my head.

"He knew." My chest went tight as I squeezed my eyes shut. Brex knew the silver would keep my womb from healing if I accepted the bond. I'd shown him nothing but contempt and given him no reason to expect I would *want* to spawn again or do anything other than reject him as my Gi'dari. Still, he'd made sure I didn't lose that choice.

Hot tears spilled down my cheeks. "Brex didn't let Zwara silver it."

"Are we happy, mad, or..."

I pressed a protective hand to my stomach. "We need to break out of here. I have less than a tide before I spawn, and I will not let these humans take what's mine."

"If you want to keep this brood, you need to stop baiting the guards into attacking you."

I scrubbed my hands over my face. The pristine new skin wasn't even tender where the blood mage had repaired it.

"Brex told me Issor zurNella has a spy among the humans. Any idea how we might find them?"

Kor's dark eyes went bright with excitement. "They'll have placed themselves close to the key players without making it obvious. It will likely be someone in a support position with access to information without putting themselves in harm's way."

Cool metal pressed against my spine as I leaned against the bars. "The Nūkiri gave the god of tides' power to the human who brought me back to the cell."

"That makes him *the* key player. Whoever the spy is, they'll be in his circle. The interrogators keep asking the same question over and over. They think we know who the spy is."

"Maybe we should give them an answer," I said.

"Tell them it's the male with Brex's power. The real spy will be the first to support the accusation to protect themselves. As soon as we know who it is, we can attempt to make contact. They're our only way out of here."

It was a risky move that could just as easily get the real spy killed, but it was our only option.

We spent hours contemplating the best way to communicate with the spy until my head grew heavy and my body gave up fighting off sleep.

⁂

I rolled over on my cot in the early hours of the next morning and mentally prepared myself for another round of torture as six guards marched down the hall, followed by a female with pale skin and silvery blond hair. Her human husk was the ghostly twin of the one Tesk wore.

Kor's eyes lit in recognition.

"It's not her," I said. Tesk moved with the lazy gait of a pampered queen. This female moved like a predator.

"Bring them both to the morgue." I didn't understand the command she made to the others, but the amusement in her tone set my teeth on edge. "Let them see what happens when they threaten my Gi'dari."

I cut my eyes to Kor. Their silent nod confirmed I'd heard the female's mushy pronunciation of the Kateri word correctly.

Panic tightened my nerves.

The mind mages had trespassed on every intimate memory I had of Brex, and the male who possessed his power had already guessed what he was to me. If they'd found him...

"Take your hands off me." I clawed at the shield guard who grabbed me by the arm and yanked me out of the cell. There was no collar in the world that would stop me from unleashing my wrath on anyone who attempted to harm my mate.

The pale female barked another order at another guard. They grabbed Kor and dragged us down a corridor toward the room where the human blood mage had healed me.

Kor choked on a sob as they entered the room. An awful sense of relief settled over me at the sight of Kor's lifeless male form on the examination table. It wasn't Brex or Tesk.

The feeling was short-lived as I glanced around the room. Zwara, Hazi, and Inanna stood between the male who'd healed me and the blue-eyed male. All three wore collars on their necks.

"Where's Brex?" I asked, my ribs suddenly too tight. He would never let Inanna and Hazi get captured. If he wasn't here...

I couldn't breathe.

"He and Tesk are with Issor zurNella," Hazi said. "When we left, they were planning to attack the compound to get you out. We were on a mission to apprehend the Anzillu."

"Unfortunately, the information we got from the spy was incomplete," Zwara said. "The humans use their queens as soul-reaping weapons instead of guardians of the dead."

I felt a gentle brush at the back of my mind and glanced at Inanna. The interrogators didn't ask for consent or announce their presence like Inanna before digging into my brain for information. But it couldn't be Inanna. Not with a collar around her neck.

The blue-eyed male dipped his head to me as he projected the image of the human queen inhaling Kor's soul the same way I'd consumed my first mate.

I pressed a hand to my belly to quell my lurching stomach. Why was he showing me this? The male watched me intently like he was trying to gauge my reaction.

"The pale one is a queen," Zwara said to Kor's female form. "Your severed soul isn't gone. It's inside her clutch. Your remaining half flew back to Brex."

Kor's female form lunged for the human queen next to me and crumpled to the floor as the collar shocked them. I sank to my knees and cradled Kor to my chest as they keened for the lost piece of their soul.

Violent light pulsed across my chest as my body flashed hot. "I promise I will find a way to make her release it, even if I have to cut out her clutch."

The healer took a step closer to the human queen. "The only pain comparable to a mimic losing a piece of their soul is losing your Gi'dari." He glanced at one of the guards. "Take her back to the cell so she can grieve in peace."

I wished I could understand what they were saying. Kor was too distraught to translate.

The blue-eyed male followed my gaze as I cut my eyes to Zwara.

"We need to identify the spy. When you were with Issor zurNella, did he tell you who he had on the inside?" I asked.

She shook her head. "But he took Brex and me to a human healing facility. Someone met us there to deliver information about the mission that got us captured."

"Do any of the humans in this room look familiar?"

Zwara's eyes darted to the healer. "Yes. The pretty male. They could be twins, but his other form is much older than this one."

Chapter Twenty-Six

LIAM

I PACED THE GLEAMING white floor of the above-ground infirmary while Jason fixed the goose egg on Cyrena's head where the male from the cemetery had knocked her unconscious.

"Come to gloat, darling?" Her eyes narrowed as she attempted to break through the walls I'd erected around my mind. I couldn't let my guard down until we were well out of range of everyone else in the compound.

"You and I need to have a little chat." I glanced at Jason and projected the next word into Cyrena's head. "Alone."

"You should be celebrating your victory with the others. I hear our little reaper was quite the hero. I'm sorry I missed seeing her in action."

"She's also drunk," I said. "Someone gave her a dozen mini liquor bottles."

"She took a life today, Liam. Give her a little grace," Jason said. "She needs to blow off some steam. With her high metabolism, she'll be sober in an hour."

"Shouldn't we be doing some kind of debrief about what happened at the church?"

"What's there to discuss? We captured three hostiles and recovered a husk without losing a single member of the team. Only one of theirs got away. The mission was a success."

"They knew we were coming. It was a trap, and we fell right into it."

"Stay in your lane and let the intel team do its job. You're the muscle in this operation, not the brains," Jason said.

"I have a PhD."

"Yes, in stargazing." He cut me a sharp glance as he finished fixing Cyrena's head. "I have six medical degrees between my past lives. You don't see me sticking my opinion where it doesn't belong."

"In astrophysics, you asshole." I clenched my fists to keep them from flying.

"If you boys are done swinging your dicks around, I'm going for a bit of fresh air." Cyrena hopped off the exam table and shot me a pointed look. "Why don't you join me, Liam? There's no light pollution to ruin the magnificent view of the night sky."

I followed her outside to the lake nestled between the mountains and had to admit the view was spectacular. The entire fucking Milky Way cast a glittering reflection in the water.

"What was so urgent that you needed to drag me out in the cold?" Cyrena asked as I stalked to the end of a wooden dock. "If it's about the booze, don't expect me to apologize. I did you a favor."

She was 100 percent right. I fisted a hand through my hair. I still hadn't had any physical withdrawal symptoms, but my body was strung tight. I needed Renae to siphon off the sharp edge.

Cyrena had watched my whole life play out while she used me as bait to try to catch Issor Nella. She was vicious and toxic as hell, but aside from my brother, she was the only constant in my life. She knew me better than anyone. Better than I knew myself.

And the only person I trusted aside from Renae. I glanced back at the compound, wondering what was taking her so long.

"Jason's the spy," I said.

She rolled her eyes. "I know you'd rather see him at the bottom of this lake than anywhere near Renae. You can't throw a serious accusation like that around and expect it to stick without evidence."

"He zip-tied Renae in the van during the raid."

"That doesn't prove anything. The two of you agreed about wanting her to stand down."

"That was a mistake on my part. She's my Gi'dari. My first instinct is to protect her. I didn't realize how good she was at the reaper thing until I saw her in action. Her gift is as strong as any that I have. Jason knew exactly what she was capable of, and he intentionally held her back. He knew it was a trap, and he set us up to fail."

"Why would he do that?"

"To kidnap Liam and take him to Issor Nella," Renae said, unsteady on her feet as she stepped onto the dock. "He didn't give Liam seven random gifts in an experiment to turn him into a living god. He was using Liam's genetically modified body to incubate the powers stolen from an actual god."

Cyrena cocked her head from side to side, cracking her neck. "And how did you come by this knowledge?" she asked skeptically.

I exhaled as Renae sucked the edge off my need. When she used her syphons to pump her energy inside me, it was better than any drug I could put in my veins. As long as she was by my side, I knew I could do anything.

"My gift resonates with the immortal female we have in custody. Her name is Vaza, and I can understand every thought that passes through her head when I read her. I think it's because my power belonged to her Gi'dari. Renae and I did a little experiment with the prisoners after the mission while you were laid up. We brought them all into the morgue with the one Renae killed to see if I could pull any more leads from Vaza."

Cyrena crossed her arms against the cold. "Don't keep me in suspense. What did you find?"

"Jason's doppelganger, Mr. Ito," I said, pulling Renae's shivering body to me. "Jason's been going out of his way to remind us that he's a healer, but he's also a mimic. Every time I dig around inside his mind, it's blank, as if all his memories and thoughts are held in a different head."

"The old man from the hospital?"

"I didn't want to believe it at first either," Renae said, leaning back against me. "Not until Liam showed me what he pulled from the Kateri's minds."

"They were discussing the spy, so I dug around in their visual memories. One of them witnessed Jason's elderly twin deliver info to Issor Nella." I projected what I'd seen into Cyrena's mind.

She paced the dock, chewing her nail. "We definitely have enough evidence to convince the Corps to open an investigation. They'll interrogate Jason and put out an APB for his doppelganger. That will take a few days. Enough time for Jason to cover his tracks."

"I don't give a shit about catching Jason or the old man. I made a deal with the Nūkiri to hunt down Issor Nella in exchange for Renae's freedom. He's the target."

"I've spent thirty years trying to bait him out of hiding," Cyrena said. "He changes his appearance every few years. No one even knows what he looks like."

"I do. And I know exactly where to find him." I projected another image I'd pulled from the redheaded prisoner's memory of Issor Nella sitting in the back of a limo with my brother.

Cyrena's eyes narrowed. "How did your always-do-the-right-thing perfectionist brother get involved in an alien invasion?"

"I don't think Connor's involved. At least I hope not. In the memory I read, he referred to Issor Nella as *Allen Rossi*. The biotech billionaire that's been funding some of NYU's more unusual research endeavors. I think the Kateri targeted Connor to get to me."

"What's the plan?" Cyrena asked.

"The pregnant alien's immortal Gi'dari is going to attack the compound in a few days. I saw their plans when I read the male with the man-bun's mind. We need to go after Rossi while he's unprotected."

"You've been in the Corps longer than any soul here," Renae said. "We need you to use whatever pull you have to get the Corps to evacuate the compound and get us to New York City as soon as possible."

She shook her head. "The Corps has already reinforced security. If we warn them, they'll want to know how we got the information. We can't reveal that Liam can communicate with Vaza or that he read their minds without tipping off Jason."

"So we don't warn them," I said.

Renae jerked away from me. "What about Lucy?"

I ran my hands over her shoulders. "We take her with us."

Renae let out a heavy breath and nodded.

"I can't take three assets on a mission without disclosing the details to their handler."

Renae thumbed the makeshift ring I made for her on the plane. "We're not going on a *mission*. We're going to elope."

Cyrena sucked her teeth as her gaze cut to mine.

"I called Connor an hour ago and told him the good news. He's agreed to be my best man and is expecting us in two days."

"Jason won't deny us leave," Renae said. "He'll be thrilled to have Liam out of the way when the Kateri attack. One less weapon to contend with."

"Let's hope you're right," Cyrena said. "There's also a good chance he sees right through this half-baked plan. Keep your shield up, Liam, and *do not* tell Lucy about the mission. She betrayed us once before. Leave the rest to me."

"Where are you going?" Renae asked as Cyrena retreated.

"To plan a fucking wedding for the two most impulsive people I've ever met. We leave first thing in the morning."

Renae clasped my hands. "I knew she'd be willing to help when she brought me the bottles you took from the plane." Her warm, whiskey-scented breath kissed my face and neck. The thought of tasting that sharp spice on her lips had me half-cocked.

"I thought we agreed you'd only pretend to be drunk."

"The tracker in my husk alerts Jason to changes in my blood chemistry. That part had to be real to keep him from getting suspicious."

I pulled her against me. "That's not the only part of this that's real for me, Renae. I want you to be my wife."

"Marriage is just a piece of paper, Liam. You and I are already so much more than that to one another." She slid her hands up my chest to the back of my neck and snaked her finger through my hair. "But I'd be lying if I said I didn't want it too. I thought I was going to lose you all over again at the church. I get it now. The possessiveness and obsessive need to protect me. I would have killed every single one of those monsters if I'd had to, including Jason."

A stab of rage shot across the bond as her eyes darted over my shoulder.

"I can't believe I ever trusted him. He's been watching us from Ziggy's old office window since I came out here."

"He's probably just staring at your ass." I grabbed her backside and pulled her against my hardening cock. "I can't blame him for that. It's a goddamned distraction in this skintight uniform. You should take it off so I can fuck you."

Her gaze came back to mine. "It's thirty-five degrees out here."

I pulled in a charge and forced it beneath my skin with my shield, kicking my body temp up to keep her warm.

Renae snuggled her body closer to me as her eyes darted over my shoulder again. "He's still watching."

"Eyes on me." I tipped her face up to mine and devoured the lingering taste of whiskey on her sweet, intoxicating mouth.

She whimpered as I unzipped the front of her uniform and slid a warm hand inside to palm her full breast. My balls tightened with the ache to unload inside her. To fill her with so much cum that it dripped down her thighs.

I wanted the pretty boy to watch—wanted him to see how she begged for release as I licked it off her. He needed to learn that Renae was mine.

"This place has more security than Fort Knox," she said, pulling away. "We're under constant video surveillance. Even outside."

"Feeling camera shy?" I asked as she backed toward the end of the dock.

"No. I just thought you should know we're being recorded before you take off your clothes. Everyone in the compound will have watched it by morning."

"Then we should give them a show."

She toed off her boots, and I couldn't take my eyes off the upturned buds of her pink nipples as she peeled herself out of the white uniform.

My chest hitched at the sight of her naked body in the moonlight. She looked like a fucking goddess surrounded by black water and glittering stars.

It could have been ten below and I wouldn't have noticed. Not with the way my skin blazed where Renae's syphons licked over me, tugging me closer. If this went as planned—if we delivered Allen Rossi, Renae would be free.

She unzipped me from neck to groin and wrapped her cold fingers around my throbbing cock. The shock sent a zap of pleasure straight to my spine as she dropped to her knees and took me into her mouth. The same mouth she'd used to suck the soul out of a husk. I almost lost my load then and there.

I grabbed the back of her head, holding it steady as I slowly pushed into her throat. My cock twitched as she gagged and tightened around me. She shook her head and dug her fingers into my hips as I tried to pull out.

Renae looked up at me with hungry eyes as she swallowed me even deeper.

"I love it when you're greedy for my cum, reaper."

Static prickled over my scalp as I fucked her mouth.

She vibrated around me as she groaned. My pleasure snapped like a rubber band at the base of my spine. My body went white hot as I spilled down her tight throat.

I sucked the cold air into my lungs, taking a full breath for the first time in a decade.

Chapter Twenty-Seven

RENAE

I'D NEVER BEEN HAPPIER to see sunlight than when we climbed out of the packed subway five blocks from the hospital where Connor worked. Liam had used his shield to keep the crowd of bodies away from me on the train.

"We'll take a taxi when we go back to the hotel to get Lucy." Liam pressed a gentle hand to the small of my back, guiding me onto the sidewalk and away from the curb as if he were a barrier between me and the overwhelming press of the city against my nerves.

His emotions were harder to read with his shields up, but the way he kept a hand on me at all times was enough to tell me I wasn't the only one on edge. We hadn't talked about the alcohol he'd taken from the plane. Or how much I enjoyed getting him off and siphoning him to keep his cravings at bay. It hung like a phantom between us that neither of us was willing to look at too closely. Not when we had more pressing problems to deal with.

We'd be married in less than ten hours, and the billionaire geneticist who'd manipulated Liam's mother into stealing DNA from the Corps to create a living vessel to hold the powers of an immortal god was invited to the ceremony.

I wasn't even sure which part I was more anxious about—saying "I do," or murdering Allen Rossi during the champagne toast.

We'd applied for the marriage license the day before. My stomach did a nauseating little flip. The dress, bouquet, and rings would come tonight.

"I'll scope out security at the venue while the two of you meet with Connor to discuss the details," Cyrena said as she cut a path through the pedestrians ahead of us.

"Connor will want to examine me. What am I supposed to tell him about my miraculous recovery?"

"Stick to the cover story and try not to embellish. He knows you better than anyone and can spot your tells when you lie. Let him give you a full medical workup if that's what it takes to put his mind at ease." Cyrena pulled her hood up against the whip of cold air cutting between the buildings.

"How are you going to snoop around Rossi's restaurant without being noticed?" I asked as we stepped around a delivery person pushing a dolly of cardboard boxes.

Cyrena glanced back at us as her face and clothing morphed to match the man we'd just passed—right down to his wind-chafed skin and brown uniform.

"This isn't my first rodeo, darling." She winked and disappeared into the fray of people crossing the street.

"Thank the gods she's on our side." Cyrena had the kind of personality that thorned its way under your skin and festered into an odd kind of affection. Liam would still be in the Void without her help. She was the only other person I trusted with his life.

"I hate lying to my brother. It's the one thing I told myself I'd never do again." Liam raked a hand through his halo of amber curls.

"Stick to the truth. Let me feed him the lies. It's the one thing I excel at."

"Agree to disagree, chica. You excel at a great many things." The corner of Liam's mouth twitched as we entered the medical complex.

Connor met us in the lobby, looking thinner than the last time I'd seen him. He was still just as striking, with his chiseled cheekbones and dark hair. The only resemblance between him and his brother stopped at those chiseled cheekbones and heart-stopping denim eyes.

"Jesus fucking Christ, Lee. I sit by your side for weeks, and you go and wake up the minute I fly home to arrange a transfer for you." Liam's brother yanked him into a tight hug.

"If I'd known you wanted to witness the miracle firsthand, I'd have waited for you to come back." Liam feigned an annoyed smirk as Connor gripped the sides of his head and studied his pupils. "I'm fine. The docs released me with a clean bill of health."

"I'm aware. I read the discharge paperwork. The neurologist's notes were nonexistent, and there's no record of a CT scan or order for follow-up care. I'm preparing a complaint for the Hawaii board of health."

"Please don't," Liam said, pulling away from him. "I declined the follow-up scan. Do you know how much a single day in the ICU costs? The medical bills are going to bankrupt me."

"You know Patrick and I will help you with that."

"You found us a wedding venue on short notice. That's more than enough." I unfurled my syphons and licked the acidic edge off Liam's guilt. He hated himself for dragging his brother into the middle of our trap to capture Rossi by asking him to call in a favor from his billionaire friend.

Liam reached for my hand and wound his fingers through mine.

"Renae." The sour twinge of rotting fruit slicked my tongue as Connor's gaze landed on me. He thought I'd abandoned his brother after that first night in the hospital when I disappeared to follow him into the Void.

"Thank you for taking care of Liam when I couldn't. I..." I dropped my eyes to the copper stripe on the floor. "My family was killed in front of me when I was a child, and seeing Liam like that in the hospital triggered my PTSD. I couldn't handle seeing him like that."

Liam wrapped his arm around my shoulders and pressed a kiss to the side of my head. "It's okay, chica. You don't owe anyone an explanation. We all process trauma differently."

The unpleasant bite of Connor's mistrust faded as he studied us. "You're right. I've had patients whose family members find it difficult to remain in the hospital with them. I'm glad you're here for him now. He needs someone to keep an eye on him. Have you noticed any side effects since he woke up? Headache, confusion, lack of—"

"Can we not do this in the lobby?" Liam gave his brother a warning scowl.

"Fine." He held up his hands in defeat. "The interrogation can wait until we're in my office. Follow me."

The excuse I'd given Connor about my unease in hospitals hadn't been a complete lie. The frenetic energy tugged at my useless healing gift. Jason might be a traitor, but I couldn't deny the respect I had for how he'd completely healed the pregnant alien after the interrogators tortured her. A part of me still found it hard to believe that he was the spy. I had to keep reminding myself that the evidence was clear.

He told me it was for my safety when he'd zip-tied my hands and feet inside the van. If it had taken me a second longer to break the restraints by sawing them against each other, I would have been too late. He was hiding in the woods like a sniper. He only shot the Kateri to save his cover when he heard me barreling through the woods.

Liam sat on the edge of an immaculate desk while Connor examined him.

"Thank you again for arranging a venue for us on such short notice," I said while he shined a penlight in Liam's eyes. "I understand the owner is a friend of yours."

"Allen is more of a benefactor than a friend. He owns an obscene amount of real estate in the city. He was more than happy to offer one of his restaurants for the evening. I hope you don't mind that he'll be attending."

"Not at all," Liam said as he offered me a soft smile.

Connor checked the pager attached to the waist of his scrubs. "I'm sorry, but I need to cut our visit short. I just got a bypass surgery consult from the ER. Lee, I'll see you at the condo at four to get ready. Patrick has a suit waiting for you at home. Renae, I'll see you at the restaurant at seven."

"Do you mind if I use your private restroom?" I asked as Connor moved to shuffle us out of his office. I'd had five cups of coffee since leaving the compound at three in the morning to make the five-hour drive into the city.

"Sure, see yourselves out when you're finished." He gave me a quick kiss on the cheek and clapped Liam on the shoulder before rushing out.

I had to pee so badly I didn't bother shutting the door. There was no modesty left between us after everything we'd been through. I stared at the dark circles under my eyes in the mirror after relieving myself and washing my hands. I felt Liam's anxiety swell through the bond, and I couldn't help wondering if Cyrena was right—that we'd been too impulsive. We'd thrown this mission together in less than forty-eight hours.

"You okay in there, chica?"

"I just need a few minutes to collect myself." I took a deep breath and counted backward from ten, telling myself this wasn't all happening too fast.

I emerged from the bathroom and found Liam sitting in Connor's chair and rifling through his desk.

"What are you doing?"

He startled and attempted to stuff something into his pocket.

Sulfur laced my mouth as a crumpled piece of paper fluttered to the carpet.

Liam closed his eyes as I stooped to pick it up.

"Why would you take a blank prescription?" I asked, even as I tied the loose threads of my confusion together.

Liam hunched forward as if the weight of the world hung around his neck, and I suppose it did. He braced his elbows on his knees, clasping his fists tight between his spread legs. His head lolled between his bare shoulders. I'd never seen him look so defeated.

"Because it was there and I'm a junkie. I'm struggling to hold my shit together right now. I know you've been suppressing your doubt about my ability to stay sober and your own overprotective need to save me from myself. It's killing me that I can't be strong for you or the kind of partner you can count on. You're my anchor, but I don't want you to become my crutch."

I didn't know what to say. Trying to convince him that everything would be fine, that he was strong enough to fight this and an army of aliens felt wrong.

"Tell me what I can do to help."

"When this is over, I need you to stop trusting me. Don't give me any slack. If you think or even suspect that I'm slipping, call me out."

"Okay." I bit back hot tears as I put the prescription back in the drawer and moved to stand between his knees.

"I'm sorry." Liam hugged his arms around me, and my insides ached with something that felt hollow and too full all at once. Like a balloon trying to expand inside a steel cage. I loved him and would do *anything* to take his pain away. But he was right. The same way my father had been right when he forced me to climb up that cold, muddy riverbank by myself without a crutch.

Our connection wasn't woven from sunshine and rainbows and happily ever afters. We were fused together by sinew and scars and the overwhelming need to fix in each other what we couldn't fix in ourselves.

"I know you're having cold feet. We can still go after Rossi tonight without going through with the wedding," Liam said. "I don't want marrying me to be something you regret."

The tears I'd been holding back streamed down my face as his wet eyes found mine.

"I want to live a thousand lifetimes with you and make lots of reckless, impulsive decisions we'll surely regret. But know this—no matter what this world throws at us, I will *never* regret binding myself to you."

I dropped to my knees in front of him.

"Liam Riley, will you take me as your wife?"

Chapter Twenty-Eight

LIAM

I RUBBED AT THE tightness in my chest as I made my way to Connor's apartment on the upper east side. I'd checked my phone at least twenty times, waiting for confirmation from Renae that Cyrena had returned to the hotel where she was getting ready with Lucy.

If she didn't show up in the next hour, Renae and I agreed to abort the mission and meet at a twenty-four-hour wedding chapel in Queens. Just the two of us. I didn't want anything bad to happen to Cyrena, but part of me was praying she didn't make it back in time.

My stomach knotted into a hard ball as I exited the elevator and walked down the swanky hallway covered in expensive modern art toward the penthouse apartment that I was 100 percent sure my brother and his art dealer husband couldn't afford even on his surgeon's salary.

Patrick opened the door before I had the chance to knock. He kissed both my cheeks before giving me a once-over. His dark eyes went watery as he brought a manicured palm to my face.

"You look good, Lee."

"It's nice to see you too, Patrick," I said as he hooked a muscular arm through mine and dragged me inside. The deep V of his red silk kimono revealed a patch of tight black curls that matched his immaculate trimmed mustache and beard. "Connor says you're determined to give me a makeover."

He scrunched his nose at my jeans and gray UH hoodie. "The hair I can work with, but those dark circles under your eyes and that two-day stubble have to go, honey. Follow me. I think we have some concealer left from Connie's emo phase."

His flowy robe floated behind him as he led me to a spare bedroom that had been converted into a walk-in closet, complete with floor-to-ceiling shoe and clothing racks, and a tufted leather bench in the center of the room. Connor stood barefoot in front of a mirror, tucking a fitted dress shirt into a pair of black tuxedo pants.

"What's that?" I asked, eyeing a giant white box with gold letters sitting on the bench.

"Dior, obviously," Patrick said. "It was hand delivered for you first thing this morning by one of Allen's personal assistants."

I pushed inside his head, reading the memory. My gut tightened at the familiar smirk on the delivery man's face as I watched Patrick sign for the box and hand the clipboard back to the forecaster who'd thrown my body into a pipe organ three nights before.

Fuck. I threw my shield around Connor as he lifted the lid. "Wait. Don't open—"

"It's a four-thousand-dollar tux, Lee. Not a bomb," Connor said as he unfolded the tissue to reveal a black-on-black suit and shirt. "Here, it came with a card."

I popped the red wax seal and read the inscription.

Congratulations, Mr. Riley.

Please accept this gift as a token of our future friendship. I have seen what is to come and I have a proposition I look forward to discussing with you and your beautiful bride after the ceremony.

Sincerely, Allen Rossi

Panic surged through the bond. "I need to call Renae."

The phone rang in my hand as I stalked back to the living room.

"Chica, please tell me you're okay." My heart slammed against my ribs.

"I'm fine... I just... I got a box from Allen Rossi."

"What did the delivery person look like?" I asked as Connor trailed behind me.

"I don't know. It was left at the front desk. They gave it to Cyrena when she got back. He sent me a dress. That's weird, right?"

My hands went clammy as I opened the floor-to-ceiling sliding glass door and stepped out onto the terrace, shutting it behind me. "What did the note say?"

"'Congratulations, my queen.' What do you think it means?"

"He knows we're coming for him, and I think he wants to make a deal. My note says he has a proposition for us."

"Should we call off the mission?"

"Is Cyrena there?"

"She's on speaker. Talk quick. Lucy is still in the shower."

I waved Connor off through the window.

"Liam, you were right about the attack in the compound," Cyrena said. "Surveillance drones picked up hundreds of Kateri camped out in the woods, just out of range of our weapons. They haven't made a move yet. The Corps thinks they might be waiting on a signal from the mole."

"Jason has a high enough clearance to deactivate the compound's security measures," Renae added.

"I want to catch Nella as much as you do, but if he's offering to make a deal," Cyrena continued, "I say we hear him out. If we can convince him to order the Kateri to stand down, it could save us another costly attack."

"I agree," Renae said. "If we have an opportunity to save the others, we should take it."

"This plan was your idea, Liam. What's your call, darling?"

I pulled the phone away from my head and leaned my forearms against the glass railing that provided an unobstructed view of the city coming to life beneath the darkening sky.

The last time I was offered a deal that could have saved everyone—give up my bond to Renae in exchange for clemency for everyone who'd helped me escape the Void—I'd refused.

I still didn't regret that decision, but I'd never forgive myself for what happened to my mother and Monika.

"Liam, are you still with us?" Renae asked as I stood and met my brother's worried blue eyes through the window. There was no doubt in my mind that the Nūkiri would find a creative way to punish Connor too if I fucked up an opportunity to catch Rossi.

"Yeah. Let's see what he has to say."

I felt the tugging sensation in my chest again as we said our goodbyes.

"Everything okay?" Connor asked when I stepped back inside.

"Yeah, just pre-wedding jitters." I hated myself for lying to him. "All the details are a little too much. We wanted to keep it simple. The venue and the suit. It's all a little overwhelming."

"That's my fault. I should have given Allen a few parameters. He doesn't do anything in half measures. He's extremely thorough and extremely generous with his gifts."

I glanced around the huge apartment. I'd clocked three bedrooms and three full baths in addition to the gourmet kitchen and killer skyline views.

"How generous?" I pushed in and read his thoughts.

Three million.

"It's not what you think."

"Normal people don't send strangers suits worth four grand." I pinched the bridge of my nose. "What do you do for him? Please don't lie to me, Connor. I need to know who I'm getting into bed with in exchange for his *gifts*."

"You won't owe him anything. I've already taken care of that. I make sure he has access to the university's ongoing proprietary research into gene therapy and genetic modification."

"Do you know what he's doing with it?"

"I don't ask. I just send him the data, and he buys a few of Patrick's paintings from the gallery."

"Or buys you a suit, or an apartment?"

"What do you want me to say, Lee?"

"Nothing." I clasped him on the shoulder. He wasn't the only one who'd sold his soul for something he wasn't willing to live without. "Let's just get through tonight. I want everything to be perfect for Renae."

⁊

The restaurant sat at the top of a bougie hotel. I scratched at my neck where the dress shirt irritated the bite marks the Nūkiri had given me as a souvenir.

A man in a black chef's uniform greeted us in the hall next to a closed-for-private-event sign.

"Welcome to Eden, Mr. Riley. My name is Louis. I'll be your officiant. It's an honor to be a part of your special day."

"Has our host arrived yet?" Connor asked.

"I'm afraid he's been detained by a rather urgent matter and has asked that you begin without him. I'm the only staff here this evening. If you need anything at all, don't hesitate to ask. The restaurant is all yours." He pointed an open palm toward a pair of etched glass doors depicting a coiled snake about to strike.

"If I'd known you could pull strings like this with your donors, babe, I would have insisted on an entirely different wedding." Patrick started snapping photos of the room with his phone.

Connor gave a subtle shake of his head as my eyes found his. Patrick didn't know about his deal with Rossi.

Greenery and hundreds of glass bubbles holding flickering candles covered the ceiling. All but a few tables and chairs had been removed to make room for the domed vine arbor covered in white flowers that looked remarkably like the altar I'd built for Renae on our first night together in the Void when I'd accepted the bond.

An intimate detail only she and I would know.

Someone must have read the memory from one of our heads. Jason couldn't read minds, and it wasn't something Renae would have shared with him. Which meant there was more than one mole.

My entire body prickled with awareness as the near constant tightness that had been tugging at my chest since I'd left Renae at the hotel eased.

"She's here," I said, swallowing the sudden lump in my throat.

Patrick cued up a playlist of soft music on his phone. A minute later, Cyrena came through the doors, clad in a green silk gown. She gave the restaurant an approving glance as she beckoned me over.

"Did you get it?" I asked.

She pulled a little blue box from her bag and handed it to me.

I shoved it in my pocket. "Rossi's not here yet."

"That's probably best. You're a nervous wreck." She pulled out a white flower and pinned it to my lapel.

I fidgeted with the collar of my shirt. "I'm fine. How's Renae?" I asked, even though I could feel her nervous energy through the bond.

"Hungry."

My lip twitched as Cyrena brushed the nonexistent lint from my shoulders. "I'll be honest, darling, I never thought I'd see you in a tux.

It's been a strange road, but I'm glad you found your way here with her. Whatever happens tonight, I'm just happy I could see you like this."

"And how's that?"

"Happy. Or as close to it as you've ever been." She projected the next words into my head. "The pin in your boutonniere contains a concentrated dose of the Corps' tranquilizer drug. If you need to use it, pop the cap off the end and jam it into a large muscle."

"A wedding gift. How thoughtful."

"How else would you know I care? I know my methods haven't always been gentle, but everything I've ever done has been to protect you. Are you ready?"

I took a deep breath and nodded, checking my pocket one last time before taking my place under the altar next to my brother.

Chapter Twenty-Nine

RENAE

My pulse was steady as I stood in front of the etched glass doors. I ran my fingers over the row of real pearl buttons along the fitted cuff of my sleeve. The last time I dreamed about what my wedding gown might look like, I was sixteen. I'd ripped a picture of an eerily similar dress out of one of my mother's Paris fashion magazines the day before I died in 1944.

When I pledged my loyalty to the Corps, I knew I'd never have another human life or any of the things that came with it. I hadn't thought about the ivory silk gown since. Not until I opened the box Allen Rossi had sent me.

How he knew, I couldn't guess. It was a memory I'd never shared with anyone, and Jason didn't have the ability to read me like Liam.

"Do you remember the magazine photos I tacked all over the wall in our room in Oradour?" I asked Lucy as we waited for Cyrena in the lobby outside the restaurant.

She pursed her lips as she shook her head. "All the childhood memories from my past lives bleed together now. I was only six. I have a vivid recollection of that final day and the fire, but not very much of what came before. Why?"

Cyrena slipped through the double glass doors into the hall.

"Just feeling nostalgic. Thank you for being here with me. I know this was all very last minute."

Lucy reached up and squeezed my hand. "If all my lives have taught me anything, it's that memories are fickle and become eroded by time. That's why it's important to be present in each moment and to cherish every ounce of joy we're given."

"If you keep strangling that bouquet, you'll break the stems," Cyrena said, dropping her eyes to the small bunch of baby's breath we'd picked up on the way. It was the only part of this wedding I'd chosen for myself.

"Is Rossi inside?"

Cyrena shook her head. "He didn't want to intrude on your ceremony. He'll join us after. We can begin when you're ready."

I exhaled and gave a little tug on the bond. My chest fluttered as Liam tugged back, pulling me toward him.

Lucy was right. We both knew all too well that tomorrow wasn't guaranteed. That everything you loved could be ripped away in an instant. This wedding was impulsive and dangerous, like everything else in our relationship, and I didn't want to forget a single moment. I unlocked the tomb at my core where I kept my demons buried. If it could preserve the worst parts of my life, it could preserve the best ones too.

"I'm ready," I said.

Soft music floated into the hall as Cyrena opened the doors and motioned Lucy in first. All I could see from where I stood was a ceiling covered in vines and a table with a towering croquembouche—the traditional French wedding cake made of cream puffs and caramel I would have chosen if I'd planned everything myself.

My stomach twisted with the knowledge that Jason had provided Rossi with such detailed dossiers on me, including my past life in France and obsession with pastries.

Cyrena followed the direction of my scowl as she read my thoughts. "I'm sure it's a coincidence. Eden is a French restaurant," she said as she motioned me through the door.

The anxiety ballooning inside me evaporated as my eyes landed on Liam and that cocky smile that made my insides go molten. The way his hair was pulled back away from his face accentuated his scar. My fingers itched to touch every beautiful and broken part of him that lined up with mine.

He projected his voice into my head as I walked down the aisle. "You're stunning."

You look sexy in a tuxedo. I can't wait to take it off you.

"I can't wait to call you my wife."

The officiant's instructions got lost in the intense surge of emotion flowing between Liam and me. At that moment, nothing else mattered. Not our secret plot to capture Rossi or the Kateri's mark on Liam's neck, where they'd claimed his power. Just the two of us and the irrevocable bond neither of us had asked for and now couldn't live without.

Lucy tugged on my dress, breaking the spell as she reached for my bouquet.

"I understand you'd like to exchange your own vows."

"Yes," Liam said, his deep voice wavering. He cleared his throat as he took my hands. "Renae, you didn't give up on me or turn away when I showed you the worst parts of myself. You... you came for me when I was lost and saved me when I wasn't strong enough to save myself."

He turned and took something from Connor. My breath caught as he held a delicate ring to the tip of my finger. Its double bands, one gold and one silver, were connected by a center knot.

"Liam." My eyes watered as he slid it onto my finger.

"Wherever tonight leads us, from this day forward, I promise to take care of my body and my mind and my soul so I can be the man you deserve and give you everything you've given me. And I promise I will never make you eat salmon and rice ever again."

I choked on a laugh as he snaked his arm around my waist and pulled me close to whisper in my ear. "I promise to fulfill every desire you have and to let you devour every part of me." He brushed a strand of hair away from my face as he stared down at me. "Most of all, I promise to apologize when I act like an overprotective ass and to *never* let you go through a single day without feeling how much I fucking love you."

Liam brushed his lips against mine and teased my mouth open.

We're supposed to wait until the end to make out.

He made a noise that sounded like a growl as he deepened the kiss and projected his voice into my head. "No one tells me when I can kiss my wife."

We're not married yet. Not until I say my vows.

Liam released me and clasped my hands.

"You asked me once why I liked skydiving, and I told you it was because it reminded me that I was alive. Falling feels like a rush of fear and excitement all at once, and I imagine falling in love feels like that for most people, too." I took a breath as I swiped at my cheek. "Liam, falling in love with you didn't feel like falling at all. It was more like opening a door and realizing that after a lifetime of running away, I was finally home."

Lucy handed me my bouquet, and I unraveled the leather cord holding it together. Liam's hands glowed white hot when he wielded his gift. He'd never be able to wear a ring again.

I ran my fingers over the charm I'd made. I'd twisted the wire and plastic ring he'd given me on the plane into the shape of an anchor.

"It's nontraditional, but we've never had a conventional relationship. This leather cord is a symbol of the cord that connects our souls, the anchor a reminder that no matter where we are, as long as we're together, we're home."

Tears silvered the corners of his eyes as he leaned forward and let me slip the necklace over his head. "It's perfect."

I brought my hands to his cheeks. "I will fight for you and for us and for the future we deserve. If you have to carry the weight of the world on your shoulders, I'll stand next to you and share the burden. You will never have to face another challenge alone. This is my vow as your wife." *As your Gi'dari, I choose to bind myself to you in this life and all the ones that follow.*

Liam wrapped his arms around my waist as he read my mind. "Is it appropriate to ravish you yet?"

"Almost. Just one more formality to get through," the officiant said. "Do you, Liam, take Renae to be your lawfully wedded wife?"

"I do," Liam said without taking his eyes off mine.

"Renae, do you take Liam to be your lawfully wedded husband?"

"I do."

"By the power invested in me by the State of New York, I declare you husband and wife. You may finally kiss your bride."

Liam bent forward and brushed his lips along my jaw and the column of my throat, sending a flicker of heat through my core as he projected his voice into my head. "Hello, wife."

Hello, husband. I threaded my fingers through his hair and brought his mouth to mine.

Liam grabbed my backside as he kissed me slow and deep. I unfurled my syphons and coiled them around his body. The flavor of his milky sweet heat had never been so intense. It was like rich bourbon vanilla cream.

My stomach growled loud enough for everyone else to hear.

Liam smiled against my lips. "I love it when you're ravenous for me."

Warmth crept up my cheeks as I pulled away. "Sorry, I haven't eaten all day."

"I told you she was hungry," Cyrena said. "Get the girl some cake before she passes out."

"By all means, my friends, come dig into this delicious confection."

My eyes darted to the man with silver-streaked hair. I watched as he plucked a sticky cream puff from the croquembouche and shoved it into his mouth.

"It's nice of you to join us, Mr. Rossi," Liam said as he angled his body in front of me. "I'm sorry you missed the ceremony."

"On the contrary, I had an excellent view," he said, gesturing around the empty room. "We have pinhole cameras all over the restaurant." His gaze landed on Cyrena. "All over the building, in fact. I'm a bit obsessive about security. When you've lived as long as I have, you learn to take precautions. One can't be too careful when they have powerful enemies."

"Well," Connor said as Rossi approached, "we're fortunate to call you a friend. You outdid yourself, Allen. The restaurant looks beautiful. Allow me to introduce you to my brother, Liam, and his wife, Renae."

Rossi grasped Liam's hand, holding it hostage with both of his. "I believe we have a few mutual acquaintances." The man's eyes dropped to the bite marks on Liam's neck. "The Nūkiri sisters offered you a job. I'd like to offer you a better one."

"What's this about?" Lucy asked, extending her shield over me.

Before any of us could answer, Cyrena yanked my sister's body against hers as it twitched. I didn't notice the taser she held to her chest until Lucy's body slumped to the floor.

I lunged forward to help my sister, pulling her into my lap and checking her pulse. She was still breathing.

Lightning wreathed Liam's hands as he raised them against the woman who we'd both trusted with our lives. "How long have you been working for Rossi?" he asked through clenched teeth.

The way Cyrena's body went rigid told me Liam had her under his shield. A vine from the arbor slithered across the floor and snaked up her leg. It coiled around her like a rope holding her captive. "Since the end of the All Souls War, when the Nūkiri fed my child into the Void with all the other Anzillu children."

My hand stilled where it stroked Lucy's hair. Cyrena had told me that story once–when I asked her why she was willing to help me rescue Liam.

"Lee, what's happening right now?" Connor backed toward the exit with Patrick, unable to take his eyes off Liam's glowing hands.

"Allen Rossi was our father's research partner, and I was their failed experiment to create a human with the powers of a living god." The air crackled with static as Liam drew in a charge.

"You were created to be a vessel, not an immortal deity. The powers we hid inside you belong to someone else. They were supposed to remain dormant until the god of tides returned to claim them."

"You're too late," Liam said, tugging down his collar. "The Nūkiri already claimed my power. As soon as I deliver your head to them on a stick, Renae and I will be free."

The glass doors blew open as the immortal male with yellow eyes stormed into the restaurant wearing combat gear. He stood at least a head taller than Liam's six feet.

"Sleep." Connor and Patrick collapsed at his command. "What's taking so long, Issor? My patience is growing thin."

Allen Rossi dropped to knees in reverence to the huge male.

"Who the fuck are you?" Liam asked.

"He's the god of tides, darling," Cyrena said as the vines holding her hostage unraveled. "And it would seem his shield is bigger than yours." She grabbed my arm and yanked me up off the floor.

"My name is Brex zurNaga, and you have something that belongs to me."

"Do I?" Liam asked, standing preternaturally still under the immortal male's compulsion.

"You're holding my mate hostage, and you're going to help me get her back. We attack within the hour. If you help me retrieve all five prisoners without any Kateri casualties, I'll offer you my eternal protection and remove your powers, unbinding you from the Nūkiri for good."

"And if I refuse?"

"Then I'll take what I need from you right now."

I released my syphons as the immortal took another step toward Liam.

Cyrena dug her fingers into my bicep and projected her voice into my mind. "Easy, *reaper*. The immortal has no intention of hurting Liam."

You expect me to trust you after you and Jason betrayed us?

Her voice sounded in my head again. "Jason is in love with you. He'd sooner die than betray you. I knew Liam didn't trust him, so I made Marcella disguise herself as the old man to protect our cover when she met with Rossi on my behalf."

You lied. Marcella was never watching over Monika's family. She was helping you spy on the Corps.

"My mission is to watch over Liam and the power he carries inside him. The god of tides can't take Liam's power without his consent. Read the immortal for yourself if you don't believe me."

I pierced his spectrum with one of my syphons and recognized the intoxicating sweet spice immediately. His energy had the same bold strokes of emotion as Liam's, and he was just as easy to read. The saccharine sweet film on the surface told me he was lying.

"He's bluffing," I said aloud. "If it was that simple to take back his power, he would have done it already. You have to give over your power willingly."

Brex cut his golden eyes to mine. "You're a clever little human." His gaze slid to Cyrena. "Or perhaps Issor's spy has been whispering in your ear and wishes to decline my continued protection from the Nūkiri."

"If you attack the compound, the Corps will kill the hostages before you breech their security," I said.

"Vaza is immortal. She cannot be killed."

"No, but she could lose all the little aliens she's carrying in her womb," Liam said. "But you knew that already. That's why you haven't attacked. You can't get her out safely without us."

Brex's massive hand shot out and wrapped around Liam's throat. "Name your terms, human."

"I won't relinquish my powers, but I'll help you save your pregnant Gi'dari and the others. Tell your alien army to stand down. Renae, Cyrena, and I will return to the compound to free the prisoners with you disguised as Lucy. When it's done, you'll offer your eternal protection to every soul in this room from the Nūkiri's wrath."

"We have a deal, human."

Chapter Thirty

Zwara leaned against the unbreakable glass wall separating our prison cell from the hall. "Brex fell into a blood frenzy that lasted three days when he found out we'd left you behind. Hazi and two other shields had to restrain him to keep him from storming an impenetrable fortress without a plan."

"The news that you'd spawned was the only thing that brought him out of it," the prince said from his seat on the floor next to Inanna. "He sobbed when Issor told him. You have no idea how long he's waited for you, for this. Brex is coming for you, my queen. We need to be ready."

Emotion prickled the inside of my nose as I studied them one by one. Zwara with her stiff posture and flame-red hair. Kor's ebony hide and intelligent eyes. Hazi and Inanna, with their casual grins and matching topknots. It didn't matter that they wore different skin than they had in Eden. I would recognize them in any form. We were all in this together, and for better or worse, they were my family, like Tesk and Brex, and I would do anything to protect them.

"No, not just me," I said. "The god of tides is coming for all of us."

"I understand his interest in you now," Zwara said, dropping her eyes to my belly. It seemed to swell by the hour. "You're carrying the future of our species in your clutch. You'll be the first queen to give birth to gods."

My palm pressed to my stomach instinctively as my heart skipped a beat in my chest. "You think our offspring will be immortal?"

"It's a very distinct possibility," Zwara said.

I ambled off the cot and paced the cell. "Did Brex know there was a chance? That together we could breed gods?" I couldn't breathe.

Inanna stood and grasped my shoulders and spoke aloud. "He didn't tell you the whole story. The Nūkiri enslaved him because they wanted to spawn a race of immortals to rule over. No matter how many times they drugged him and forced him to service them during the rite, it never took. When the high priestess declared him infertile, the goddesses threw him into the pool with their gorzin."

"There was nothing wrong with him. Brex used the only gift he had left to compel his body into temporary sterility. He refused to give that part of himself to anyone other than his Gi'dari. For him, it's only ever been you. He waited for you for two millennia, never giving up hope he would find you.

"He hoped that as his mate, you would one day share his vision and his desire to build a better future for the Kateri and our human cousins. A world free of the Nūkiri and their toxic influence."

I wanted all of those things and more. For myself and for Brex. For the souls in my clutch and for Tesk. I'd been a prisoner of my own life for so long it was hard to imagine anything else. Especially when I was still locked in a cell.

"The human healer keeps examining me every few hours, measuring my stomach and violating my body with his image-capturing tools. He's taken samples of my blood and the fluid inside my womb. It's almost time. I can only hold my eggs another day or two at most. I think he's preparing to take them. If Brex doesn't come soon, I'll have to sacrifice my clutch."

"He'll be here," Hazi said with more confidence than I could let myself believe.

"You don't understand." My chest flared with panic. "They've abused and tortured us. They put collars on our necks, and when we didn't give them what they wanted, they resorted to unimaginable cruelty. I'll consume my entire spawn before I allow the humans to steal them from me."

"You're under a lot of pressure, my queen," Hazi said as he shoved up to his feet. "Surely you don't mean to imply that you would cannibalize your own offspring."

"She may not have a choice," Zwara said. "The Humans can't be trusted with thousands of potentially immortal Kateri under their control. Issor zurNella told me about the godlike children the Nūkiri created to defeat him in the All Souls War. When their experiments were no longer of use as weapons, the goddesses fed them to the Void the same way they tried to feed Brex to their snakes."

"The humans clearly have no compunction about using younglings to do their dirty work," Kor said, nodding to the hall outside our cell where the blue-eyed male stalked toward us with a human child and another female with dark hair.

My heart raced as Hazi, Inanna, and Kor made a protective wall around me. The healer wasn't with them, but something was off. The incessant pull at my ribs eased the way it did when Brex and I were in the same room. He was close. I could feel it in my bones.

I pushed forward between Hazi's and Inanna's shoulders as the lights flashed and the world went pitch black. The cell door clicked open, and a pair of familiar golden eyes stared back at me in the dark.

"Brex?" My hands trembled as I reached for him, unsure if he was real.

"Vaza." He exhaled my name on a raw and ragged breath.

The tight control I'd held over my emotions shattered as he folded his arms around me. I sank into his salt and sun-warmed stone scent. Fear and rage and relief streamed down my cheeks as he kissed me with excruciating gentleness.

"I'm sorry I wasn't here." He dropped to his knees and pressed his forehead to my stomach. "You've given me everything, and I failed to protect you when it mattered most. I'll spend eternity attempting to make it up to you, and still it will not be long enough."

I ran my fingers through his hair as my eyes adjusted to the lack of light. "You're here now. That's all that matters."

The human female cleared her throat and spoke in flawless Kateri to Brex. "Renae killed all the cameras, but we don't have much time before the power comes back on. You need to break their collars before that happens."

"Only a lightning mage can destroy them," I said.

A buzzing sensation kissed my skin as Brex stood, keeping a protective hand on me. "Liam already explained. I'm going to block his gift from burning you while he destroys the collar." Brex nodded to the blue-eyed male.

His hands glowed as he stepped behind me and grabbed the suppression device. An acrid scent stung the inside of my nose as white smoke rose from my neck. The collar gave a defeated hiss as it cracked apart and fell to the floor.

Brex pressed a quick kiss to my forehead before he and Liam repeated the process on the others.

"Who are you?" Zwara asked the human female.

Her mouth curved in a half smile, and she spoke in perfect Kateri. "My name is Cyrena, but we've already met, darling." Her appearance changed into the elderly male version of the healer.

"You're Issor zurNella's spy."

"And you're the High Priestess of Eden. Your prophet assures me we'll be good friends." She shifted back to her slender female form as her vivid green eyes traveled over Zwara. "I look forward to getting to know you better."

The floor lurched beneath my feet, turning my stomach upside down as I stumbled. I pressed a hand to my abdomen to quell the nausea as I straightened.

"What was that?" Hazi asked.

"An earthquake," Brex said. "The Order has amassed in the hills outside the prison with one of Issor zurNella's inventions. A bioweapon that makes the ground shake. They're creating a distraction while we escape."

"Tesk and I are waiting on the opposite side of the property with a vehicle," Kor's female form said.

"Cyrena's a mind mage. She'll create a projection to ensure we're not recognized while Liam leads us out of the compound," Brex said. "If anyone stops us, let him and Cyrena do the talking. We'll meet up with his Gi'dari outside. She's clearing the guards away from the exit."

Inanna gave Issor's spy an approving nod as our appearances changed to mimic the humans and their white bodysuits.

The ground shook again, and Brex wrapped his arms around me from behind, cradling my swollen belly with his palm as the others filed out of the room. "If you see any of the ones who hurt you, tell me, and I'll rip their heads from their shoulders."

"Don't threaten me with a good time, *zealot*."

Brex kissed his mark on my neck and released me. "I missed you too, *wraith*."

We wound through a dizzying maze of passageways and stairs to a cavern full of small vehicles. The other humans rushing about didn't give us a second glance as our group split in two. Kor, Brex, and I went with Liam in one cart while Cyrena trailed behind with Zwara, Hazi, and Inanna.

My stomach churned as we zoomed around and around a spiral shaft leading to the surface. I took slow, steady breaths and tried to focus on the patch of night sky visible high above us. Brex tucked me against his side and traced an idle circle on my palm. The nausea vanished under his compulsion. I closed my eyes and leaned against him, too exhausted to do anything else. I'd forgotten how draining it was to carry a full clutch, especially on the last day as my body prepared to spawn.

Crisp air bit my cheeks, forcing me out of the groggy haze.

"We're almost there," Brex whispered as he squeezed my hand. "We need to go the rest of the way on foot. Tesk and Kor are on the other side of that hill with a vehicle that will fly us to one of Issor's ships. He has a spawning pool and incubation tanks ready and waiting for you," he said as he kissed my temple.

Liam glanced around as we slid to a stop in front of a building with a partially shattered glass dome. "Where's Renae? She should have been here already."

Cyrena pointed to the trees, where a female in a white dress darted into the woods.

Brex gripped my elbow as the ground lurched again and the remaining glass caved in. The door swung open, and the healer stepped out, carrying one of the humans' shock weapons.

"Nice suit," he said, giving our little group an assessing glance. "Would you like to explain why Renae is running away from you on your wedding night?"

I felt a gentle brush at the back of my mind as Inanna translated their conversation and projected it into my head.

"We had a disagreement about who gets to be on top when we fuck for the first time as man and wife." Liam unpinned the odd flower from his jacket. "Nothing for you to worry yourself about."

"See, that's where you're wrong. Because, to me, it looks like you're trying to escape with my prisoners and the mole."

An alarm sounded, and Liam lunged for the healer as the complex lit up like the midday sun.

"Kor, take Vaza to the helicopter. Now," Brex bellowed in Kateri.

Kor's female form bolted toward me, hugging me against their chest. My stomach rolled as they leapt into the sky.

I glanced back and watched Hazi haul Liam's limp body off the ground and onto his shoulder before taking off in a dead run for the trees with Brex and the others. The healer didn't get up to follow. The smile that crept across my face was short-lived as the nausea returned with a vengeance.

Something snapped like a twig as we landed with a hard thud that knocked the air from my chest. Kor screamed and tried to crawl into the woods in the direction we'd just come from, but their leg was bent at an unnatural angle. I rolled over and vomited on the ground.

"Vaza, go. She has Tesk."

"Who?"

"The reaper who took part of my soul."

I pulled myself up and pressed a hand to my cramping belly as I ran through the trees. Sharp thorns clawed at my bare legs. My damaged lungs strained against my ribs. Each breath in and out felt like fire in my chest as I stumbled into a clearing where Tesk and Kor's remaining male form slumped to the ground in front of Liam's Gi'dari.

The air shimmered between them as she sucked out their souls.

A growl tore from my throat as I threw myself at her and knocked her on her ass. "Give them back," I wheezed as I wrapped my hand around her neck. Little bubbles of blood pooled where the tips of my claws punctured her pale flesh.

"Vaza, let her go," Brex said as he skidded to a stop behind me. "She's Liam's Gi'dari, and she's under my protection for helping us escape."

"She ate my sister's soul."

He crouched next to Tesk, checking for a pulse as the others arrived. "Fuck."

The human's pale gold eyes widened as my chest flared with a blood frenzy. I took a deep breath and inhaled her energy the same way she'd inhaled Tesk and Kor. She gripped my arm and bucked against me as I gulped her in.

My skin buzzed as Brex clamped his shield down around me and pulled me off her. "That's enough. We need to go."

Cyrena fell to her knees next to the pale female. "She's still alive."

"Bring her," Brex said.

"No." I groaned and bent forward, clutching my stomach and flashing my fangs as a contraction ripped through my abdomen. "That gluttonous bitch devoured my sister. I don't want her anywhere near our hatchlings. The deal is off."

Brex scooped me up in his arms and pressed a kiss to my temple. "As you say, my queen."

EPILOGUE

RENAE

I WAS AWARE OF three things when I awoke on the cold, hard ground: the unbearable tightness in my chest preventing me from taking a deep breath, the floating sensation in my skull, and the distraught man shaking my shoulders.

He sagged back on his heels and scrubbed his hands over his face as I sat up and scrambled away from the two dead bodies next to me.

"You're lucky I'm the one who found you. I can fix this, but we need to get our stories straight, and you need to do exactly what I say. If anyone asks, you've been working deep undercover at my instruction to flush out the moles. You discovered it was Liam and Cyrena, and you caught them trying to escape with the alien prisoners when the earthquake knocked out the power. When you chased them into the woods to confront them, they overpowered you. The fact that you were able to kill two of the aliens and recover their husks will help ground the lie in."

"I don't understand what you're saying," I said as I grasped my throat and swallowed the dry, fuzzy sensation coating the inside of my mouth.

"No one knows you betrayed the Corps. I'll protect you, because you're my friend and I care about you, but this secret needs to stay between you and me."

My head swam as I used a tree to pull myself off the ground. I clutched at the bodice of the ruined silk gown where it felt like my heart was seizing.

I'd never seen the man before in my life, and I didn't know why I was wearing a wedding dress in the middle of the woods, but his dark eyes seemed kind, and my gut told me I could trust him.

"I need help."

DARK EDEN BOOKS

Garden of Echoes and Ash
Dark Eden Book One
Scars of Seduction and Sacrifice
Dark Eden Book Two
Tide of Deception and Desire
Dark Eden Book Three | Fall 2024

Sign up for the NO DAMSELS NEWSLETTER and get a smoking hot deleted scene from Garden of Echoes and Ash, plus pre-order and release date notifications.

J. Ember Hintz writes steamy sci-fi and fantasy romance. She loves creating dark contemporary worlds and lush alternate realities ripe with mythology and magic. You'll meet ghosts, gods, and monsters in her stories, but never a damsel in distress. She lives near the ocean with her family and two rescue doodles. Her alter ego works in a botanical garden. Job perks include unlimited inspiration for romantic settings and quirky characters.

For author updates and other shenanigans,
join her Facebook Reader Group.

Follow @jemberhintz on Instagram | TikTok | Facebook

AUTHOR'S NOTE

Dear Reader,

If you enjoyed this book, I would be eternally grateful if you would leave a rating or review. As an independent author and publisher, ratings and reviews help widen my audience and contribute to the success of my writing career.

This book would not have been possible without the love and support of my amazing husband, who puts up with my long and unusual working hours and patiently waits for me on the other side of every novel.

A huge thanks to my editing team. To Lena, for her enthusiastic support and for reminding me that if you give an alien two peens, it's like Chekov's gun—you *must* use them both. To Jen, for understanding my wild vision and helping me get there. And to Beth for her unending patience and flexibility—I'm sorry I'm so bad at commas.

XO,

J. Ember